MAXWELL'S GUIDE TO
HEAVEN AND HELL

Also by Alan Taffel

Heaven, Inc. - A Helluva Novel

Maxwell's Guide to Heaven and Hell

Alan Taffel

Names, characters, places, and incidents are either a product of the author's imagination or used fictitiously and any resemblance to actual persons living or dead, business establishments, events, or locales is entirely coincidental and meant in good, clean fun.

Maxwell's Guide to Heaven and Hell

Copyright © 2015
Alan Taffel

Cover art by Cassie Russell

Published by Blairmont Publishing, LLC
P.O. Box 2413
Boone, North Carolina 28607

ISBN-10: 0-9960386-3-9
ISBN-13: 978-0-9960386-3-8

This book is dedicated to my sister, Bonnie Lynn Taffel. Her life was difficult and ended too soon, but her spirit lives on for anyone who knew her and loved her as I did.

1

H igh noon. The two men stood facing each
other, twenty feet between them. There
were only small pools of shadow beneath
each one, the sun being almost directly above them.

One wore a pair of once-black pants now faded to a nondescript gray, a dark blood-colored shirt, and a scuffed leather vest
that had lost its sheen long ago. His Stetson was pulled far down on
his forehead. An 1865 Army Colt hung low at his side in a well-
worn holster, a rawhide tie knotted around his lower thigh holding
the rig in place, his hand menacingly close to the pistol's polished
wooden handles. A half-smoked cigarette he had rolled himself
dangled between his lips.

The other man was clad in black from head to feet: knee boots,
black trousers, a long duster coat, colonel's tie, and a black wide-
brimmed hat with silver conchos adorning the leather band. He
opened the front of his duster and made sure the coat was clear of
the two holsters that carried a pair of matching nickel-plated
engraved Colt Peacemakers with pearl handles that he wore
crisscrossed and high on his waist. Each handle bore the abstract
image of a steer head and horns. His left hand hovered close to the
gun on the right, his right an inch from the pistol on the left. A pair

of leather bandoleers filled with bullets crisscrossed his chest, their brass cartridges glinting in the sunlight.

A couple of shoppers—women laughing loudly—emerged from a storefront midway between the two grim men facing each other down in the street. The women immediately took notice of the gunfighters and fell silent. Neither of the two adversaries appeared to take notice, concentrating on each other only. There were people on both sides of the street, all quiet, intent on the drama unfolding before them.

A crow cawed in the distance.

Neither man said a word to the other. They each had their own strategy. The man in black watched the hands of the man before him. The other stared only at his opponent's eyes.

They drew their weapons almost simultaneously. Two shots were fired, one a fraction late, going high and wide to the right. The man with the cigarette's aim was true, hitting the man in black in the chest. Blood spread quickly as he fell backwards onto the dusty street.

Cigarette Man walked the twenty feet and looked down at the body. The man's blood was slowly receding, the wound closing. He opened his eyes and smiled.

"Damn fine shot, pardner," he said.

"Thanks. Same time next week?"

"Sure. That's good for me."

A member of the Smile Patrol approached, looked down at the man on the ground then at the other. "Are you two just about done here?"

"I reckon so."

"Great." He seemed pleased, turning now to the onlookers. "Okay, folks. Let's move it along. Nothing more to see here. I'm sure you all have great and wonderful plans for your day."

The small crowd disbursed, going about their business.

Another perfect day in Heaven.

*   *   *

For some, life's a beach. For others, it's a bitch. You live and then you die. No getting around it. But then what?

Marvin Miller sat in his office in Heaven's Central Administration Building and thought about the role he played in the afterlife of so many people. It was his job as a Director of Human Resources to help new arrivals consider their options: whether they would like to reside in Heaven or Hell, the exact location and type of home they would occupy, and the type of gainful employment that would be fulfilling and productive both to the individual and to Heavenly society.

Most people were surprised to find out they weren't assigned to either Heaven or Hell: it was their choice. They were equally surprised to learn that they were expected to work once they died. But that was only one aspect out of a number of surprising things regarding their new existence. Preconceived notions about Heaven were thrown aside once people were made aware of the reality of their fate.

There were no Pearly Gates. There was no Judgment Day. No floating around on clouds. No harps, except in symphony orchestras. The weather was always perfect no matter the conditions required for a particular activity. Transportation was simple: most people walked or rode bikes. Longer trips were possible with shuttles. There were no traffic jams and no pollution.

There was no crime, no violence, no disease, no weight gains, no aging, no reality TV shows. Disabled people were no longer burdened by their afflictions.

Housing, clothing, and other amenities were provided. There were no elections and no politicians. People of a conservative bent were probably all twisted about the socialistic aspects of Heaven, but that's the way things were. They had been that way forever and would remain so. Change was not an easy thing in Heaven.

Once deceased, people really only had two major decisions: whether they wanted to reside in Heaven or Hell and what they wanted to do to keep themselves active, the latter being the most difficult.

Heaven's business was collecting and transferring Essence, the commodity that enabled the creation of new life. Essence was donated by Heaven's citizens voluntarily in convenient donation booths found virtually everywhere. Other than donating, most Heavenly residents were not involved in the corporate aspects of the Afterlife. They just went about their daily existence.

Money was not needed for anything at all. That took some getting used to for most new arrivals. After an Earthbound life of finance there was suddenly no need for bankers, tellers, clerks, sales people, sales managers, district managers, regional managers, national managers, stock brokers, securities traders, hedge fund managers, accountants, marketing consultants, branding experts, mortgage brokers, auditors, account executives, tax consultants, loan processors, telemarketers, and many other such careers.

Priests, rabbis, imams, and other religious leaders also found themselves unemployed when they arrived in Heaven. Being dead, people didn't have to rely on faith any longer. Things were so different in Heaven than what they had been led to believe on Earth. Religions themselves fell by the wayside. People just had so much of it wrong. Yes, God existed. After all, someone had to throw that first switch, light that first fuse, get it all started. There was a Heaven. There was a Hell. But that's about it. People realized quickly that everything else they had learned on Earth had been pure conjecture, guesswork, and even superstition. In other words: religion. The problem was that no one had ever died and come back to let the world in on the real scoop. They weren't aware of the fact that the world, its people, the entire Universe was part of God's Great Experiment and He was just sitting back watching it all just to see what happens.

Marvin was aware of this. The workings of it all were of no consequence to him. He had a very precise and specific job to do: find something for all of Heaven's new arrivals to do. And with so many professions being pretty much useless in Heaven, his job wasn't easy. Fortunately, since everyone needed a place to live, there was a big demand for carpenters.

His thoughts kept wandering to that portal in the hallway. It was locked and guarded as usual. Not that he was tempted to try and escape from Heaven again. No, he was fairly content with his existence now. It just amazed him that a trip back to the world of the living—Earth—was as simple as walking through that forbidden doorway. Most of Heaven's residents would be very surprised at just how easy it was to go back. And they might be tempted because this existence was really different in unimaginable ways.

Marvin lost his life leaving a pizza place in New York, paying more attention to his slice-to-go than to the marble bath tub that was being hauled up to a fourth floor apartment above the restaurant. One minute he was outside of Pepperoni Boys and the next he was squashed dead. He didn't remember too much of his actual death but could easily recall feeling somewhat dazed and confused moments later when he arrived in Heaven's Human Resources Department, the very office he worked in now.

In many ways he was the ideal resident of Heaven until he discovered a secret: donations of Essence were addictive. It was a fact that had not been previously revealed to the residents of Heaven. He also learned that a friend, still living in the Earthly realm, was considering suicide.

That was disturbing. For one thing, Marvin was upset that his friend was so distressed. For another, suicides were frowned upon in Heaven. In fact, people who committed suicide were the only people not permitted to enter Heaven—or even Hell for that matter. And if they were allowed to enter, it was only after a very long series of meetings, hearings, and evaluations. It was a process that could take centuries. Since collecting Essence to create new life was the business of Heaven, anyone who ended their life voluntarily tainted their own Essence. It was rendered useless in God's Great Experiment for the human race and highly frowned upon.

Marvin had used the very portal across the hall from his office to escape back to Earth, saved his friend's life, and then returned to stand before a Heavenly Tribunal. There could have been dire consequences for his actions, but God Himself absolved Marvin, finding that their views on Heaven, Earth, and Mankind jived.

Not a bad position to be in.

Marvin was then offered his current job, keeping him busy but not entirely satisfied. Thankfully, his marriage was fulfilling. He found his soul mate in a woman named Bree Daniels. She was herself a rebel, active in an underground group dedicated to changing Heaven, making it the best it could be for everyone. She was also a witch who had been burned at the stake in Salem, Massachusetts hundreds of years before Marvin was even born. Well, he always did have a thing for older women.

Today Marvin worked in Administration, the very bureaucracy Bree had fought against and she, in turn, headed up the Smile Patrol.

Go figure. Life, or in their case, death, goes on.

Marvin pressed a button on the intercom.

"Sylvia? Please send in Mr. Driscoll."

*   *   *

You can't make a buck in Heaven. At one time that would have bothered Berry Driscoll to no end. Literally. First of all, he was dead. Secondly, there was no monetary system in Heaven. And now he had to figure out what to do for the rest of eternity. Something that didn't involve earning a living and making money. It took him long enough just to figure out how to spend his time alive. Now this.

Born Beryl to an absentee father and a waitress mother, he popped out so red and shiny his mother thought he looked like a cute little raspberry. As an older child, when choked by her for some minor infraction, she thought he looked like a blueberry. She was an alcoholic who had a thing for White Russians. She also had a thing for fruit. So the nickname stuck. Berry.

He stood up and walked to the window. He was on a very high floor of an impossibly tall office building, Heaven's Central Administration Building, higher than the clouds drifting slowly below revealing a beautiful city of parks, rivers, and a sense of order and structure that was both exciting and comforting. A mix of modern and traditional, metropolitan and quaint, it was a city where anyone could feel at home immediately. Off in the distance he could see white-capped mountains and, to his left, a beach where the sun glistened on the waves. All perfect because it was, after all, Heaven.

Not a terrible place to spend forever, Berry thought. The actual dying part had not been so bad at all. He'd spent the evening out with friends for dinner and drinks. Afterwards he went home, poured a glass of wine, turned on the TV, and watched *Bringing Up Baby* with Cary Grant and Katharine Hepburn. It was an old screwball comedy that was a favorite. He liked movies late at night that didn't force him to think. He fell asleep on the couch fully clothed before George, the dog in the movie, buried the "intercostal clavicle" much to Cary's dismay. Berry drifted off to sleep before the movie was over and woke up here, in Heaven. Died in his sleep. No pain. No suffering. Couldn't ask for more. Maybe there *was* a God. He figured he'd find out soon enough, considering the circumstances.

Berry looked over at the receptionist who was sitting at her desk chewing gum and reading a magazine. She was a large woman. There was a small oak sign on the desk that had her name on it.

"So I'm really dead, Sylvia," Berry said more than asked.

"Yup. Bit the big one," Sylvia replied without looking up.

"Get many of us through here?"

"Everyone."

"How long have you been here?"

"Since nine o'clock this morning."

"No, I mean—"

"Oh. August 3rd, 1922. My husband and I had a little shop, a laundry, in the Bronx. But it didn't really help make ends meet, know what I mean? So he had a couple things going. Ran some numbers, hustled here and hustled there. Had a friend, Arnie Reynolds, who had his own connections. Boys who ran stuff down from Canada."

"Booze?"

"Yeah, during Prohibition this was. They had the good stuff. Anyway, Arnie had to stash a bunch of cases for a few days and Lou, my husband, offered to put them up in our place. Except it was way more than just a few cases. We couldn't keep them all there in the shop. Too many people in and out all the time. So we had them up in the apartment upstairs. Boxes everywhere. You couldn't get from one room to another."

"A sizable stash."

"To say the least. So, they're up there for over a week. We're walking over them and around them and guess what? No Arnie. Turns out he got popped in some city commissioner's apartment while he and the commissioner's wife were—"

"Entertaining each other?"

"Yeah. For days, apparently, while the guy was supposed to be in Albany for some political convention. Caught a bug or something and went home early. So Lou and I figure Arnie's gone and we have all this booze, you know?"

"Through no fault of your own."

"Exactly. A regular nest egg, know what I mean?"

"I do."

"Except one day Arnie's pals get wise. Come sniffing around."

"Uninvited."

"At 3 a.m. I hear something, get out of bed, and grab one of the bottles off the dresser."

"Just in case."

"Yeah. Anyway, long story short, he had a snub-nosed .38. Never bring a bottle of scotch to a gun fight."

"Always good advice, Sylvia."

"Mr. Miller's the Human Resources Director. He'll get you straightened away soon. Oh! I almost forgot." She opened a drawer in her desk, took out a small book, and handed it across the desk to Berry.

"What's this?" he asked.

"Everybody gets one."

It was a thin book, somewhat smaller than a paperback, with a hard cover. Beautifully bound in what appeared to be leather, the title was embossed with gold letters and read *Maxwell's Guide to Heaven and Hell*.

"Looks too small to be a guide to anything."

"Don't let the size fool you. You'll be surprised how much info they pack into those little gems. It will no doubt come in handy."

Berry reached into his pocket to tip her. It was an old habit. He liked tipping. In fact, he liked over-tipping. She was flattered but explained that tipping was not necessary here. Ever. In fact, no money was ever exchanged for anything at any time. That was something he'd have to get used to. He'd also have to figure out what to do with himself...forever.

Most of what he thought about Heaven was what he had seen in movies, TV shows, and cartoons or had heard about in church. In reality, Heaven looked nothing like the way he had imagined it to be. People in business suits scurried about the offices. Phones rang. Printers clamored. Computers flickered. It looked more like an insurance company.

He decided that looking over the book might help keep him focused while he waited for his meeting. He had so many questions. Berry thought it was unusual that he was given an actual book rather than a laptop or electronic reader. He guessed they were kind of old school here. But helpful. And everyone seemed nice. Sylvia certainly was.

He opened the book to page one.

Welcome! Today is the first day of the rest of your afterlife!
This guide serves to help you transition to your new existence.
It is a compilation of hundreds of thousands of submissions from people just like you who have died. We hope you find it useful, entertaining, and informative.
Within these pages you will discover places to go, things to do, and answers to many of the questions you likely have about your new life in Heaven or Hell.

You are currently at Heaven's Human Resources Department. This experience is usually easy and pleasant, but should you experience any confusion or anxiety, please do not hesitate to inform the receptionist working with you. He or she will immediately direct you to a nearby Transition Center where you will receive treatment to help ease those feelings.

Do not be ashamed. These emotions are common. Above all, do not panic. Symptoms of post-traumatic stress disorder are extremely common in your situation.

You have, after all, just died.

So this was it. Death. The Big D. So be it. What now? What to do for time on end? For eternity? Berry was rarely at a loss for ideas, but this death thing was different. *Well*, he thought, *maybe it didn't have to be.*

*　　*　　*　　*　　*

"Hit me."

Nana dealt him a six. Luke checked his hole card. A five. The seven-year-old realized he was sitting with an eleven. A face card would put him at twenty-one.

"Can I double down?" he asked.

"Are you sure you want to?" Nana asked.

"Yup."

"Okay, then," she said.

"Hit me," Luke repeated.

Luke's little brother Noah smacked him in the shoulder just as their mother scurried into the dining room.

"Don't hit your brother," Laureen Dawber said.

"He *told* me to hit him!"

"He did not. And, Mom, what are you doing? I asked you to read them Bible stories, not teach them to gamble. First it was gin, then poker, now blackjack?"

"I might as well teach them something useful," Nana said.

"Yeah, look at all this I won!" Luke pointed to the large pile of colorfully wrapped chocolate candies on the table in front of him.

"Don't even think about eating all that at one time," Laureen warned him.

"Naw, I'll save some for later."

"You wish," she said as she grabbed a candy off the table and popped it into her mouth.

"Hey!" Luke squealed.

"Don't you have to leave soon? The ride to Miami will probably take you an hour or so," Nana warned.

The ride from Fort Lauderdale to Miami normally took about thirty minutes, but with South Florida traffic it could take anywhere from a half hour to two hours depending on traffic, construction road closures, or torrential rains.

"I'm trying to get out of here, Mom. Where's my cell phone?" Laureen rushed into the bedroom to check her purse.

Noah sat down and Nana dealt him a card.

"Noah, hit or stay?" Nana asked immediately.

14

"Stay."

Nana revealed her two cards.

"Blackjack, babies!"

She checked the kids' hands. A twelve and an eighteen.

"Losers," she teased as she grabbed a few chocolates from each of them, stood up, and walked into the bedroom finding her daughter at the computer.

"What are you doing? You need to get out of here, Laureen."

"I'm just sending a quick e-mail."

"Now? I don't think it'll do you any good to keep the IRS waiting."

"I'm asking everyone to pray for me," Laureen told her.

"I don't think you have to let the whole world in on your problems," Nana said.

"Look, Mom, I can't afford to pay this tax bill."

"You never should have quit the waitress job you had at the diner. If you let them fire you, you could be collecting unemployment."

"I had to quit. I got tired of being groped every time I went into the kitchen to pick up orders," Laureen said defensively. "So, no unemployment, a huge tax bill from last year, and not a penny in child support."

"Well, who asked you to marry that idiot? Imagine, leaving you and the kids to run off to Alaska to become a hunting guide…and then getting eaten by a bear!"

"Just my luck," Laureen said as she hit send.

"Did you ask everyone to pray for you to find a new man, too?"

"Well, Mom, never underestimate the power of prayer. Things happen for a reason, you know."

"No, they don't. Things just happen. Sometimes they work out, sometimes they don't."

Laureen grabbed her purse, rushed into the dining room, kissed her boys goodbye, and started out the door.

"See you later. I'll be back to make supper for the kids. Don't let them spoil their appetites with all that chocolate. I just pray I find a parking spot downtown near the IRS office."

"Okay, you pray for parking, Laureen. I think the Lord is just a little too busy to be your parking attendant," Nana shouted as her daughter slammed the car door.

*   *   *

Excerpt from *Maxwell's Guide to Heaven and Hell*, page 37:

Crime is not a concern in Heaven.

Without a monetary system, there is no incentive for criminal acts such as theft, fraud, or embezzlement.

Goods and services are provided free of charge. Providers are glad to help out as productive members of society. It gives them a sense of purpose and belonging. You will find this to be true in your case as well. You'll be pleased to help others without financial reward as your motivation.

Personal conflicts in Heaven are fairly and justly arbitrated. In these matters, Administration's decisions are final and binding. You will have an opportunity to plead your case, but keep in mind that officials here always know the truth and will rule accordingly.

Because of this, there is no need for police departments or a court system. As a result, lawyers have been determined to be superfluous. That fact is a source of great satisfaction with the populace.

We're sure you'll agree.

It was a perfectly beautiful morning in Heaven...as usual. The temperature was in the mid-seventies and the sky was a gorgeous blue with just a few picturesque clouds to keep the view from getting boring.

Despite the time of day, it was dark inside the windowless warehouse. The small group of men had no trouble getting inside. It wasn't even locked. Typical. They didn't even have to worry about tripping an alarm because there wasn't one. No alarms in Heaven. Somebody flipped a switch and the lights came on, revealing boxes and boxes stacked up on pallets. There were vidscreens, communications devices, computers, and more. A huge cache of electronics.

Joey Falconetti was a large man. Back in South Philly, he was known as Joey Mirrors because of the mirrored aviator sunglasses he often wore. He was also known as Joey the Falcon and Fat Joey but if you called him that to his face he'd probably kill you.

Joey was loyal and dedicated to his boss, Big Sonny Martinelli, overseeing many of Big Sonny's operations including gambling, drugs, collections, and moving merchandise that fell off the back of trucks. He and his wife had a good life. They had a Caddy for each of them, a big house with pillars in front, and got comped in Atlantic City casinos for an occasional weekend. It was a life Joey enjoyed. It was also a life his wife Jeanie worried about constantly. She had seen the pictures in the newspapers of guys getting whacked in small Italian restaurants while they enjoyed their linguine with clam sauce. She began insisting that they eat more Chinese and Thai.

Things were fine until Big Sonny decided that he should start taking it easier, travel more, play more golf, and spend more time with the grandkids. His kid, Little Sonny, would inherit the family business.

As is the case with many new managers in any business, Little Sonny decided to clean house and move in his own team. He was to discuss this with Joey over dinner at Dino's, a small Italian restaurant. Jeanie, thinking about those pictures in the newspapers, suggested they have dim sum instead, but Joey laughed it off as he kissed her goodbye. Jeanie figured she'd never see her husband again.

And she was right.

Joey sat alone as he waited for his linguine with clam sauce. Little Sonny was late. In fact, he never showed at all. Instead, Carmine Bag of Donuts walked up to the table, drew a pistol, and shot twice, the bullets smashing both lenses of Joey's mirrored sun glasses. Everyone in the restaurant claimed later to the police that they hadn't seen a thing. The picture in the morning paper showed Joey's body lying on the floor with blood and brain tissue splattered all over a mural of the Leaning Tower that covered the entire back wall at Dino's.

This morning, in a warehouse off a side street in Heaven, Joey had that sense of excitement he relished in the old days in Philly. He motioned to one of the men who nodded and opened a large garage door just as a panel truck backed up to the loading dock. Everyone but Joey started to move boxes from the warehouse pallets into the truck. Someone snapped his fingers to attract Joey's attention. Joey glanced up to the lookout stationed by a doorway on the second floor. He mouthed the word "guard" and everyone froze.

"I'll take care of him," one of the men told Joey, who nodded his approval. As the smaller man left, the rest of the thieves went back to work.

Morty, the security guard, entered the building on the opposite side of the loading dock and made his way to the office to clock in for work. He had worked for decades as a security guard during his lifetime and chose the same profession in Heaven. Although Heaven didn't need security of any type, Morty was glad they allowed him to continue in the same line of work after he died. It made him happy and he felt useful. It gave him a reason to get up every day. He enjoyed the sense of authority the job gave him as well as the quiet and solitude.

"What's up, doc?"

Morty was surprised to see anyone there at all. The young man had a loopy grin. Morty didn't recognize him and wasn't used to having to deal with anyone this early in his shift if at all. Certainly not until the usual warehouse crew arrived late in the day.

"Do I know you?" Morty asked.

"Lucratelli's the name," the man replied as he reached inside his jacket.

"I hope that's not a gun you're going for."

"Nope. Wrigley's."

*   *   *

Excerpt from *Maxwell's Guide to Heaven and Hell*, page 2:

It is our pleasure to provide you with the information necessary to make your stay in Heaven as enjoyable as possible. You have a choice of residence in any type of neighborhood and environment. You also have a choice as to how you will spend your time.

You may do whatever you wish as long as no one is harmed physically or mentally, including yourself.

Heaven is filled with possibilities. Take advantage of your opportunities.

The best piece of advice we can provide: forget most of what you knew before. It was probably wrong.

The Devil woke up with a start. He never needed an alarm clock; his internal clock was extremely accurate. He glanced sideways and realized he wasn't alone.

"Hey, baby," she said in a coquettish voice.

"Good morning...you," he replied.

"Amy. My name's Amy."

"Right. Amy. I knew that."

"No, you didn't, but that's okay."

The Devil had gotten a bad rap throughout history. He was generally portrayed as a tempter who led people down the road to sin, depravity, crime, violence, and evil. All wrong. He was never thrown out of Heaven and never sought to buy anyone's soul. He had no horns, no tail, and no hooves. In fact, he's a helluva guy...with some quirks. He likes a good prank, possesses a good sense of humor, prefers to get his own way, is very opinionated, and does have a temper. He has always been comfortable in his own skin, dresses like a combination of a pirate, biker, and rock star, and fights off boredom by pursuing that ever-elusive perfect round of golf.

He has had other interests throughout the course of history. Snakes were originally his idea. He came up with the concept for the elephant. Many have attributed the platypus to him but that was actually God's little joke. The first cave painting was due to Lucifer encouraging a Neanderthal named Moukatouka to market a mastodon barbeque to other local cave dwellers. It was the beginning of advertising as well as the start of Mankind's artistic pursuits. Satan's idea for primitive drumming led the way to music. He helped sports develop from talents that early man displayed in hunting and survival. For a while, magic fascinated him. He followed jousting as avidly as fans today follow the NFL. He gave humans a penchant for games of chance.

But for the past few hundred years it was golf that held his interest. Convinced that it was art, sport, and chance all rolled into one neat little game played with sticks and a little white ball, the Devil was obsessed. The goal: to better his previous score by at least one stroke, failing miserably most of the time. It was that kind of game.

Amy, nestled against his side, eased one leg over his thighs.

"Don't even think about it," he told her. "I have a tee time in an hour."

She had been a political aide involved with a congressman from Tennessee. She traveled with the politician whenever he went on taxpayer-financed junkets. The congressman's wife shot and killed Amy in a jealous rage when she found out what was going on. It made the national news but the story blew over in just a couple days. Nothing unusual there.

Amy came in with a group of recruits the day before. They had chosen Hell rather than spend an eternity in Heaven. In Amy's case, she didn't feel like working anymore. That was the case with many people. No one burned in Hell. No one spent eternity in torment. Boredom, maybe, but not torment.

In Heaven, however, people were expected to work. To be part of an active community. They could choose to do anything, but they had to contribute to society. In Hell, people didn't choose anything at all. They were provided with housing, meals, and clothing. Hell certainly was attractive enough. It featured beaches, mountains, large cities, and small villages. But it was like a ski resort in the summer or a beach resort in January. There was simply nothing to do. At all. Ever.

But to someone like Amy who had never been overly ambitious, lounging on the beach and sipping piña coladas seemed like a great way to spend the rest of her days.

"You don't really have to go so soon, do you?" she asked, a wicked gleam in her eye. She slid her whole body on top of his, straddling him between her legs and rubbing herself against him.

"Come on, baby," she purred. "Take me to Hell and back."

"No problem," the Devil replied.

Golf could wait.

*   *   *

Whoosh!

Zoey, a small calico cat, suddenly appeared on a patch of grass shadowed by the large office building on Southwest First Avenue in Miami. Feeling too exposed she quickly ran to a sparse group of bushes that provided some shade and cover. Cats feel best when they think they are invisible.

Zoey wasn't really fond of Miami. She much preferred the laid-back feel and cozy neighborhoods of Fort Lauderdale. More lizards to chase, too. As common as squirrels in northern cities. But she was here for work in what the Tourism Department people called the Magic City. And work was work. Zoey had been assigned by Heaven's Animal Control to check in with a number of families and individuals still living on Earth, but there was nothing saying she couldn't have a little fun while she was here. She crouched in the bushes eyeing a small lizard. She made a half-hearted lunge at the gecko, spooking it. The lizard scampered away, its tail curled high above its back, just as a Toyota Corolla pulled up.

Laureen locked her car door, a necessity in the city, and walked quickly towards the office building. A construction crew working on the busy street noticed the very attractive blond and traded lewd comments with each other. They shouted, "Hey, baby!" and other cat calls. Laureen wondered if they ever had any success with women using those methods. The jackhammers and generators mostly drowned them out, so she couldn't hear exactly what they were saying. She certainly suspected what they were up to, however, and scowled at them before entering the building.

They immediately pegged her as a bitch or a lesbian.

Leo Cairn was already buzzed on coffee but poured himself another cup anyway. It was going to be another long day and he was already in a bad mood. A married couple had just had their lives shattered by him when they found out that their dispute with the IRS wasn't going their way. They were also going through a foreclosure on their home. Their mortgage was under water, they owed more on the house than it was worth. Their situation was hopeless. He hated to destroy their dream of resurrecting their financial situation but that just wasn't going to happen. It was a part of the job that he hated and all too common.

His mood changed drastically when he returned to his office and found Laureen waiting for him.

"Well, good morning!" He flashed a big smile.

"Good morning," she replied, smiling back when she noticed he wasn't wearing a wedding ring.

"You are…Mrs. Dawber?"

"Yes, Laureen. Miss Dawber now. My husband's deceased. I received this notice from your office," she said handing him a copy of the IRS letter. "I have prayed and prayed that we could clear this up as painlessly as possible. Times are very tough for me lately."

"You are a religious woman?" he asked.

"Yes, I suppose I am. Are you? Well, not a woman, of course. You are obviously a man. And a very attractive one at that." She wondered if she was pouring it on too thick. "Do you believe God looks after us?"

"Yes. I do indeed. In fact, I lead a local prayer group from my church every Tuesday night."

"That's very admirable."

"Maybe you'd like to join us sometime?"

"Well, perhaps. So, do you think we'll be able to work something out about my little problem here?"

"Well, let me go through your paperwork first, but, yes, I'm sure we can," he said as he noticed the way her skirt rode up when she crossed her legs.

*   *   *

Excerpt from *Maxwell's Guide to Heaven and Hell*, page 7:

Forever is a very long time. You have no idea.

What you choose to do with your time in Heaven is completely up to you. We all hope you will find something fulfilling for you as well as productive for society.

Remember, as long as you don't hurt or harm yourself or anyone else, you can do anything you want in Heaven. You can be anything or anyone.

We should mention, however, that there are some exceptions. Ours is a peaceful society. It is also a fruitful business, the business of creating Life.

Disruption of our business model is strongly discouraged.

Joey Mirrors' men were almost finished loading the truck when Lucratelli returned.

"The guard?" Joey asked.

"On ice," Lucratelli replied.

"Good," he said with a nod.

"Let's get outta here," he shouted to his men. They closed up the truck, shut the loading dock's large door, and piled into a large sedan parked beside the panel truck.

Joey and Lucratelli were the only ones left standing outside.

"You and Phil will take care of the truck?" Joey asked.

"Sure," said Lucratelli. "Quite a haul."

"Yeah, I figure it's probably all worth about forty, forty-five grand. Maybe more. Not bad for a day's work. Normally I'd run it out to Jackie DeSilva's place. We'd haggle a little and then I'd off it at a substantial profit. Take the wife out to dinner or something."

"Well, the important thing is that you enjoyed yourself. Did you have fun?"

"Just like the old days. I'm sure the boys got a kick out of it, too," Joey said with a smile.

"Glad I could help. See ya 'round the campfire, Joey."

"Yeah. Thanks, Lucratelli." The large man slid into the car and waved as the sedan pulled away.

Lucratelli climbed into the panel truck's passenger seat.

"Okay, Phil. Let's get this jalopy unloaded. Put all this stuff back."

"Just the two of us?" Phil, the driver, asked, obviously not too pleased with the prospect.

"Naw, don't flip your wig. I'm sure Morty the security guard will help. And the warehouse crew should be here any minute."

"I hope Morty wasn't frightened when you popped up out of nowhere."

"Just until he saw my ID card. Once he knew I was Smile Patrol everything was hunky dory. It'll all get put back. He knows nothing ever gets stolen in Heaven, so no harm, no foul. Morty had a little thrill, and we made Joey and the rest of those guys real happy today."

"Yeah. Smile Patrol," said Phil. "I love this job."

*   *   *

Excerpt from *Maxwell's Guide to Heaven and Hell*, page 31:

We would like to make your existence in Heaven as easy and stress-free as possible. The decisions you make will help determine your level of satisfaction. Any and all assistance will be provided to you.

The first decision you must make is a simple one: would you like to reside in Heaven or Hell?

In Heaven, everyone has an opportunity to be productive and work at something you enjoy. Feel free to follow your dream, whatever it may be. We'll assist you in any way possible.

Residents of Heaven contribute to society. Some people continue the work they pursued while still living. Others choose new directions.

You have the ability to travel freely. Travel is quick and easy. Whether you wish to visit the seashore, mountains, or cities, you will find accommodations to suit your particular tastes. These pages contain listings of every resort, hotel, inn, bed and breakfast, or campground to suit your needs. Each offers its own set of facilities and activities.

Your choice of restaurants featuring the best food you have ever tasted as well as infinite recreational activities is unlimited as well. A complete list is provided herein.

All options are found in this guide. Browse page-by-page or simply think of a place or topic and you will be directed to the correct and appropriate entry.

Remember, Heaven is all about options and opportunities. We are here to assist you in making your stay as comfortable as possible.

Berry was reluctant to turn down the corner of the page to save his place. He hated when people did that. He equated it with a distinct lack of respect for art, or literature, or something. He preferred bookmarks. Sometimes he used a business card or maybe just a torn off piece of paper. Whatever worked. He didn't own any actual bookmarks purchased for that sole purpose of saving one's place, but always found something to suffice. In this case, he just stuck his finger in to hold his place for the moment, thinking about the wondrous book he held in his hands. Remarkable, really. When he opened it again, instead of continuing where he left off, the book had itself chosen another passage.

Excerpt from *Maxwell's Guide to Heaven and Hell*, page 31:

Should you choose to reside in Hell, you will find that residents in Hell have nothing they must do. Absolutely nothing.

Rest assured that despite what you have heard, Hell is not a place where people are punished for their indiscretions. Most people anyway. Yes, a few incorrigibles are kept in a special place the Devil has for them and he has a talent for making each and every one of them miserable, but those instances are extremely

rare. We are sure that you won't be subjected to any such situation.

Understand that Hell is just a place to subsist. To hang out. But don't expect the same opportunities and benefits that you have access to in Heaven.

Hell is the perfect residence for the lazy and unmotivated. Not that there's anything wrong with that.

We are not judgmental here.

Berry was fascinated with the small booklet. It was a truly extraordinary volume. At first he was confused by the fact that there was no table of contents or index of any kind. But, browsing through the book, he soon realized that all he had to do was think of a topic and it would miraculously be there when he turned a page. The book was intuitive that way.

"Do you like it here?" Berry asked Marvin.

"Human Resources?"

"No. Heaven."

"Sure, I guess. There's really no other alternative. It is what it is."

"Like your job?"

"Keeps me busy. And I can contribute my time unselfishly."

"Are you a married man?"

"Yes."

"Were you married back when you were alive?"

"No, we met here. She's a witch."

"A bitch?"

"No, a witch. Killed in Salem. Long time ago."

"A witch, huh? That must be…interesting."

"You have no idea. But let's get back to you. Heaven or Hell?" Marvin asked.

"That's a no-brainer. Heaven," Berry replied as he sipped his coffee. The Human Resources Director seemed personable enough. "I'm too much of a doer to just sit around for the rest of time."

"And what is it you'd like to be doing?"

"That's a very good question."

"Well, let's come back to that then. Do you think you'd prefer living in the city or a nice country place?"

"I'm not really a mow-the-lawn and tend-the-garden kind of guy."

"How about a nice loft here in the city? We've just finished construction. Good size, not too big, not too small. Lots of places you could walk to."

"You sound like a real estate agent."

"No commissions though."

"And I'd have to live there for the rest of my so-called existence?"

"If you'd like to move at any time you can submit a new residence request."

"Okay, then. The loft sounds good."

"Done. So back to the big issue: what are you going to do with your time?"

"That's a tough one."

"Not usually. People normally have an idea. You know, a dream they always wanted to pursue. A goal they'd like to accomplish."

"I feel like I'm back in school talking to a guidance counselor. Do you give those tests that wind up telling you that you should be an airline pilot or teacher or something?"

"Sorry."

"What did you do? I mean back when you were alive?"

"I represented artists. Painters, photographers."

"Were you good at it?"

"Not particularly. I did help a friend sell a few paintings for disgustingly large sums of money."

"He was that good?"

"No. He had no talent at all. It was a fluke."

"What happened to him?"

"He died. Now his stuff sells for ten times more than what he was paid for them. I see you worked in TV."

"Yes, that was part of what I did."

"We have a number of TV stations here. Perhaps that would be to your liking," Marvin suggested.

"I don't think so."

Berry was starting to feel pressured. He thought it impossible to decide here and now what he would do for the rest of eternity. It seemed like such a long time. And there was certainly no shortage of time in Heaven.

As he pondered his future he thought that perhaps the book he still held in his hands could provide a clue. He stuck his thumb into the book and looked down. All he saw was the title page again. *No help there*, he thought. *So one thing the book doesn't do is make decisions for you.*

Berry had hit his stride as a TV producer late in life. He'd had a good run. His forte was creating commercials and infomercials that the public would respond to by picking up their phones and calling in orders for any piece of crap that sold for nineteen dollars and ninety five cents plus shipping and handling. There were Quadruple-Edged Wiper Blades, No-Run Stockings, hair curling devices, choppers, slicers, dicers, mincers, a plethora of kitchen devices and beauty products.

As an added incentive to increase sales, Berry was the innovator who came up with the phrase "But wait...there's more!" Then an anonymous voice-over announcer (or marginally famous on-camera talent) would offer a bonus gift just for ordering. Or they would double the order if the customer paid the extra shipping charges which covered the cost of the product anyway. To customers, it was irresistible. For the company, it was extremely profitable. Business boomed, and with his production fees and points on net sales, Berry did alright for himself.

Work was a whirlwind that never seemed to end. Berry was constantly seeking new clients with products. And the products themselves were becoming more and more surreal. Automated cat litter boxes. Self-cleaning toilets. Indoor Astroturf carpeting. Anything and everything. Berry was pitching clients, writing scripts, directing field and studio shoots, producing audio sessions, supervising editing in post-production, negotiating and buying air time, and tracking sales.

He took to snorting cocaine to keep his energy up. Comic Robin Williams once said coke was God's way of telling you you're making too much money. That was probably true in Berry's case. The money was rolling in but a lot of it was going up his nose.

That was also the case with many of the people with whom Berry worked. It wasn't unusual for him to walk into an edit room and find that ubiquitous white power, a mirror, and a razor blade placed on a countertop available for the editors and producers working a late night production session.

Before the novelty wore off it was a good time. Berry liked the idea that coke was illegal. That he was getting away with something. He felt like an outlaw, a rebel. But that soon wore off. People he worked with and partied with were starting to get irritable. So was he. Tempers were short and flared often. People got crazy. He got crazy.

Soon Berry realized that he had an addictive kind of personality. Drugs, booze, work, relationships. They became obsessions. Once he came to understand that aspect of himself he also understood that he wasn't doing coke to get high any longer, he was doing it to feel normal again. He'd wake up in the morning and do a couple lines just to get rid of the headache he felt. A couple more lines to keep him going later. Food became unimportant. Able to stay awake endlessly, he drank more. He felt antsy all day. Another line or two or three would get him right for a half hour or so. He could function again. But he eventually realized that doing a drug to feel normal was too odd. It was a revelation, so he stopped. Cold turkey. It wasn't even difficult. He just decided that enough was enough and never did another line. The man did have will power.

About this time one of his clients was having some success with phone sex lines, both gay and straight. They turned out to be profitable because there were no products that had to be imported into the country, warehoused, and then shipped out to all parts of the country or the world to fulfill phone orders. People would see enticing, risqué commercials and then make a toll-free call. The long distance charges were free but the callers would wind up spending close to five dollars a minute on the sex line. The clients experimented with psychic call lines as well but they weren't going over as well. That is, until Berry discovered Miss Serena, the Queen of Clairvoyance.

She was hard to miss. Dressed in flowing island garments, gaudy earrings, bracelets galore, and a turban wrapped around her head, she came across as a flamboyant hippie gypsy. When he first met her, she was sitting on a bench outside the office building where he worked. He was returning from lunch. She was smoking a large cigar.

"Why you not eat your veggies?" she called out.

"Don't like them," he admitted.

"Not good for you to skip the good stuff. Doctor told you but you no listen."

It was true. Berry's recent exam and blood tests prompted the doctor to advise him to eat better and exercise more.

"You not even fix dat flat tire on your bike. And dat exercise machine in your bedroom? Just a rack for your clothes."

"How do you know that?" Berry inquired.

"Miss Selena know all, mon."

"Such as?" Berry asked.

"Such as you won't be here long, my friend."

"Well, that's true. I'm just here for a meeting."

"Not *here* here…I mean on dis earthly plane."

"We all die."

"But you? Sooner den you tink, my friend. But, no worries, you'll be back."

Berry was intrigued. He sat down on the bench next to her and tested Miss Serena for over half an hour, asking questions about the people passing by and verifying her allegations with each and every one of them. She knew about a young married couple fighting over an interfering mother-in-law. A young man was addicted to pain pills. A college student had just learned she was pregnant. Berry immediately rushed Miss Selena upstairs to meet his partners and clients. One by one, she revealed their innermost secrets until Berry was convinced she was the real deal.

It was the beginning of an era.

The company dropped all the direct response products and sex lines and concentrated on psychic call-ins. For three years Miss Selena dominated the airwaves. She became the spokesperson and face of the company. She mainly appealed to low-income females who called to find out who their baby's daddy was, when their man would be released from jail, how they will find their fortunes, or which man will be The One. They couldn't afford the five-dollar-a-minute calls, but call they did. Some of them racked up hundreds of dollars in billing at a time. They were sent to collections and once their accounts were all settled, they called again.

Miss Selena became a celebrity. Berry and the company made a fortune. But unlike his partners who wanted more and more, Berry was fulfilled. He felt that they were helping humanity, or some portion of it, by having their questions answered. And, in a sense, they were. Berry had found his calling in life. Helping people became more important to him than making money.

The company, however, felt otherwise and was focused on profits, finding new ways to increase calls and speed up collections from the so-called deadbeats who couldn't or wouldn't pay up.

The sheer number of calls made it impossible for Miss Selena to address every caller. Vast numbers of people were hired all over the country to stand in for her. People were being duped. The so-called free calls advertised were actually only free for the first two minutes, yet the average call lasted thirty. When the Federal Trade Commission stepped in to put an end to the whole charade, the partners were fined millions of dollars and Miss Selena was discredited. Berry was the only partner not affected. He had died and gone to Heaven.

Now, Berry sat across the desk from Heaven's Director of Human Resources trying to figure out what to do with himself. During his lifetime, nothing appealed as much as scoring a great sale, moving tons of product across the country, or generating tens of thousands of minutes to call centers. But there was no place for money in Heaven. And Berry was now more interested in making a difference than making money.

So far, there seemed to be no place for him in Heaven.

"Do I have to decide what I'm going to do right this moment?" Berry asked.

"No," answered Marvin, recalling how overwhelming that moment of decision had been for him. "Why don't you take some time to think about it? Get a feel for things. Get settled in. We can meet again—"

The office door suddenly flew open and the Devil strode into the office followed by Zoey, the small calico cat. Lucifer was dressed in jeans, a white T-shirt, and a black leather motorcycle jacket looking like he had just stepped out of *The Wild One* with Marlon Brando. He plopped into an empty desk chair and the feline jumped onto his lap.

"Hello, Zoey," Marvin said.

The cat answered with a soft meow.

"Tee time's in one hour, Marv. Are you in?" the Devil asked.

"Excuse me. I'm in the middle of a meeting here," Marvin replied.

The Devil looked over at Berry and studied him for a second.

"Do you play?"

"There's golf in Heaven?" Berry asked.

"Wouldn't be Heaven without it," stated the Devil.

"Glad to hear it. Yes, I play."

"What's your handicap?"

"My swing," Berry answered.

The Devil laughed. "I like him, Marv. Bring him along."

He got up and left as abruptly as he had entered with Zoey following right behind him.

"You'll have to forgive him," Marvin told Berry. "He's not great in social situations."

"So there *is* a Devil," Berry wondered aloud.

"Oh, yeah, there's a Devil alright."

"So, if the Devil exists, then God actually exists?"

Marvin smiled and pointed a finger upward.

"Up there? Watching over us?" Berry asked.

"This building. Penthouse suite."

Berry nodded. So, he had a golf game coming up with Marvin and the Devil. That should kill about four hours. Now he just had to figure out what to do for the next million years or so.

He again placed his thumb into the book he still held in his lap. Closing his eyes, he hoped that the book would finally offer a solution, only to open his eyes to the same title page: *Maxwell's Guide to Heaven and Hell.*

Okay, he thought, *I'll get through this one way or another.* He always had. But that was during life. And this…well, this was something completely different.

2

E xcerpt from: *Maxwell's Guide to Heaven and Hell*, page 84:

There are plenty of animals in Heaven. They serve various functions, but most importantly they convey information: their close contact with humans on Earth provides the perfect opportunity to know these people intimately.

And with information comes knowledge.

Dogs are certainly useful, but they are so loyal and protective that they can get too close to the people they are assigned to watch. They are also easily distracted from their task. A squirrel, raccoon, another dog, a meal, a good scent, or even a simple treat can sideline them for endless amounts of time. A bone or a ball? Forget about it.

Birds provide a unique perspective: aerial reconnaissance. But avian information is not highly regarded as accurate even in the best circumstances. It's not that their brains are so small; it's just that they're so busy. Flight takes a lot of concentration and birds are generally too preoccupied with flight control, speed, vectors, wind patterns, and the intricacies of landing and navigation to provide accurate information on a continuing basis.

Information provided by cats is the most reliable animal information available.

Whoosh!

Zoey materialized in an instant and looked around to get her bearings.

Fort Lauderdale.

Out in the open, she quickly ducked under a car parked in the driveway of a quaint looking cottage in an effort to feel safe. She thought back to the time she popped up in the middle of the street on Las Olas Boulevard in this city and was almost flattened by a Mercedes whose owner was late for a nail appointment. Since Zoey was already dead—the result of an unfortunate experience with a pit bull—it wouldn't do to have the locals witness her demise only to see her pop up again a moment later totally unscathed. Best to leave nothing to chance.

Plus, old habits die hard. She never knew when she might be spotted by an overzealous Lab or German shepherd. In Heaven, some of her best friends were dogs, but not here.

People have always suspected that something is up with cats. There have been plenty of myths and folklore surrounding cats throughout history. Ancient Egyptians idolized them. Folks in the Middle Ages regarded them with suspicion, thinking they were in league with the Devil.

If they only knew.

Zoey always liked Lauderdale better than Miami. It was less cosmopolitan, less urban. There were distinct little neighborhoods with vegetation providing shade and cover. It was brutally hot in the summer, yes, but the afternoon rainstorms cooled things down.

And there were at least three people and families she was assigned to in Lauderdale who thought she was their cat. They thought they had adopted her, but it was actually the other way around.

She'd sleep at the home of one of her assignments, then after breakfast she'd trot around town doing regular cat stuff until lunchtime when she'd spend her time with another of her charges until it was time to go. Dinners were spent at yet another house, then she'd be on her way again. Everyone thought she was an outside cat who just liked to roam…doing what cats do.

And she was.

*　　　　　　*　　　　　　*

"Mom! Come in here—quick!"

Nana ran in from the living room and found her daughter clutching a plastic tub of spreadable butter, lightly salted with canola oil.

"What's this?" Laureen asked. Her eyes darted from the container to her mother repeatedly.

Nana stood beside Lauren and looked down at the container.

"Margarine?"

"No, it's butter."

"If I've told you once, I've told you a million times, go with margarine. It's healthier."

"That's not what I mean. What do you see in the butter?"

"Is there a bug in there, Laureen? You should take that right back to Winn-Dixie and get your money back."

43

"Mom, look! It's a face!"

Nana leaned over her daughter and peered again into the plastic tub.

"Well, there're some lines."

"It's a face, Mom. Whose face?"

"How the hell would I know?"

"It's Jesus, Mom!" Laureen said almost breathlessly. Her heart was thumping so hard she could feel it in her ears.

"Now that you mention it, it does look like Him. Now, don't that beat all?"

Laureen put the container down carefully on the kitchen counter then turned back to Nana with a look of resolve on her face.

"It's a sign, Mom."

"It's a tub of butter, Laureen."

"No. It's definitely a sign."

"Of what?"

"I don't know, Mom. Let's pray on it, and God will provide the answers."

"Tell you what. You pray on it and let me know. I have to go watch Dr. Phil. He's got that anorexic girl on again."

Laureen put the margarine down on the counter and put her arm around her mother's shoulders. "Momma, this is a clear sign from up above." She looked up at the ceiling.

"Oh, darlin', you definitely have too much time on your hands," Nana told her, shaking her head.

Laureen sighed and noticed a rustling sound behind her. She turned to find her son Luke rummaging through bags of snacks in the cupboard and Noah, knife in hand, reaching for the butter. Laureen beat him to it, scooping up the plastic container.

"What are you doing?" she frantically asked, wrapping her arms around the tub.

"Nothing."

"Don't touch this! It's sacred."

"Sacred butter?" Noah asked.

"Look, boys," she said as she held out the container and let them peek inside. "What do you see?"

"Lunch fixin's?"

"A face! Why, it's the face of Jesus!" she said in a whisper.

"Cool," Luke said in a low, reverential voice as he peered into the plastic container.

When she was no older than Luke or Noah, Laureen loved to lie down on the soft backyard grass and stare at the sky. As the clouds drifted by she could always pick out at least one in which she could make out the distinctive face of Jesus. The image delighted and comforted her.

As she grew older, that same face appeared to her in the most surprising places: a pile of leaves, in the dirt on the hood of her car, in the mold on the bathroom wall of her double-wide, and now in a tub of butter from her own fridge.

A food sighting just had to mean *something*.

*   *   *   *

Excerpt from *Maxwell's Guide to Heaven and Hell*, page 261:

It is generally believed that golf was invented in Edinburgh, Scotland in 1450. The Devil started playing it then. In fact, due to the game's degree of difficulty and resulting frustration, it is believed that the Devil had a hand in its inception, but if you ask him, he'll tell you he had nothing to do with it and that the Scots were and are an inherently miserable people who invented a game that suited and reflected their general outlook on life.

There are numerous beautiful courses catering to various skill levels throughout Heaven. You'll find a complete listing in this guide with pictures, videos, course maps, and yardages. Feel free to contact your local Smile Patrol office to arrange transportation, book a tee time, reserve clubs, and order the appropriate weather for your game.

There is, however, only one course in Hell. It is the Devil's own course and play is strictly limited to invitation-only participants. Should you qualify, please keep in mind that the Devil does NOT like to lose.

Golf is a very Zen game.

You can play every day: it's just you out there. Same course, same clubs, maybe even the same ball, but the game will be totally different every single time. That's one of the reasons the Devil loves it. Another reason is, like millions of other duffers, it gets him away from the office and work.

The product of Heaven is and always has been The Essence of Life. Obtained by donations from individuals residing in Heaven or Hell, this Essence is amassed and utilized to create new life. Some cultures were close to figuring the product out when they came up with the idea of reincarnation. Close, but no cigar. It wasn't a soul for a soul. You didn't "come back" as someone or something else, rather mass amounts of Essence are accumulated and doled out in small quantities to create all sorts of living things. One person's Essence might be added to the mix to create another person, a giraffe, a humpback whale, or a rhododendron. Virtually any living thing. A giant storehouse of possibilities.

Originally, donating Essence was voluntary until it was discovered that upper management concealed vital information from donors. For one thing, donations were addictive. The more someone donated, the more they wanted to donate again and again.

Additionally, it was learned that the more Essence you donated, the less of "you" there was, causing frequent donors to eventually become translucent. That's where the living came up with the idea of ghosts: they were actually seeing people who had returned to the world of the living for one reason or another yet had donated so much of their Essence that they were essentially transparent.

And if a transparent donor continued to donate Essence, they would literally cease to be. Nothing left of them anywhere. In the beginning it was something that happened by mistake. Oops, they're gone. No more Grandma. But eventually people realized that it could be a way out. A way to finally end it all. Some people just grew tired of eternity.

However, most residents of Heaven, and even Hell, made a few donations just to keep the wheels turning. To contribute to God's Great Plan.

Customer service reps dealt with the people who made donations. Production staffs operated the donation centers. Public relations people promoted the idea to the populace. Warehousing and logistics people handled the product. And they were all supervised by a vast management staff.

The Devil was pretty high up there. No, he had not fallen from grace. In fact, his position kept him ridiculously busy. So any time he could get away, he did.

Berry and Marvin had just come off the driving range when they saw the Devil approaching. Impeccably dressed in traditional golf attire of knickers, a sweater vest, shirt and tie, over-the-calf Argyle socks, and a St. Andrews cap, he sported a different image on the golf course than the one he projected in the board room.

"He looks like something out of a Three Stooges movie," Berry marveled. "Or, better yet, Ralph Kramden. Remember that episode? When Ralph and Norton were trying to learn golf from a book? Addressing the ball? 'Hello, ball!'"

"Do yourself a favor and keep that to yourself," Marvin quietly suggested.

No one ever felt close to the Devil; he was the epitome of a loner. But Marvin and Lucifer had a history. Back when the donations scandal broke, Marvin, his wife Bree, and the Devil, were instrumental in exposing just how addictive donating Essence could be. During that same time, an apparent terrorist was sabotaging donation efforts by blowing up donation facilities. Marvin and Bree solved that mystery and were rewarded for their efforts: Marvin was promoted to his current position in Human Resources. Bree, who had been the head of an activist organization called H.U.H.H., an acronym for Help Us Help Heaven, was named the new head of the Smile Patrol.

Lucifer drew closer and Berry noticed another person walking beside him. The two were talking and laughing together as old friends do.

As he watched the duo approach, Berry confided to Marvin, "I can't believe that on my first day in Heaven I'm going to play golf—with the Devil, no less!"

"And with Isaac Newton," added Marvin.

*   *   *

Excerpt from *Maxwell's Guide to Heaven and Hell*, page 6:

Our goal is to help make your existence in Heaven as pleasant and fulfilling as possible.

Activities are unlimited and varied: you may do whatever you want, whenever you want.

Transportation is free and practically instant. Our convenient shuttles and transport portals are available anytime day or night, seven days a week, and all year long.

For reservations, information, or special requests such as equipment needs or weather preferences, please feel free to contact your local Smile Patrol office. Whether you are new to Heaven or a longtime resident, you will find that Smile Patrol personnel are experts in fulfilling your dreams and wishes.

Their knowledge and expertise is invaluable.

Lucratelli entered the office and headed for his desk. As a member of the Smile Patrol, it was his job to cut through red tape, present options, and help plan and execute the activities that enabled the residents of Heaven to live their dreams.

The logo on the office wall read, "Rules Broken Daily." Breaking rules was something Lucratelli always had done very well. Originally from Brooklyn, no one seemed to know or remember his first name. It seemed like he didn't either.

He died on patrol while serving in the Army during World War Two. Only twenty when he died, he still spoke the lingo and favored the fashions of his time, the 1940s. During the Battle of the Bulge in Belgium, stuck behind enemy lines one night, his squad of 82nd Airborne paratroopers had to make their way across a bridge to get to safety. It was freezing and they were wet, cold, and tired. The problem was that a German division was making its way across the same bridge. Since Lucratelli and his buddies were vastly outnumbered, a firefight was out of the question, so they hid from sight alongside the roadway. Lucratelli came up with the idea that his squad should wait until the enemy was almost finished crossing the bridge and then they could fall in behind them, unnoticed in the dark.

"Are you crazy?" he was asked.

"Maybe. You have a better idea?"

With their baggy, pocketed jackets, pants, and jump boots, the paratroopers' uniforms looked more like those the Germans wore than other U.S. soldiers. Plus, it was dark and raining. It was a ballsy move, but maybe the Nazis wouldn't notice the ragtag group falling in behind them. The guys wouldn't engage the enemy; they'd just get to the other side of the river and then leave the road and hightail it back to their own lines.

Lucratelli was a persuasive kind of guy, so his squad decided to try it. Waiting until they spotted a break in the German ranks, they made their way out of the brush and fell in step.

Shuffling along behind the Nazis, the GIs kept as quiet as they could. It almost worked, too, until one of the German soldiers stopped three quarters of the way across the bridge to see if anyone could light the cigarette hanging from his lip. Lucratelli took out the Zippo lighter he always carried, cupped his hands around it, flicked the spinner wheel, and lit the guy's smoke. Inhaling deeply, the German looked at Lucratelli and uttered, "Danke." Lucratelli watched the man's eyes travel from his face down to his uniform and boots. The German shouted, took a step back, and brought his rifle up to Lucratelli's chest.

"That's the thanks I get?" Lucratelli asked.

The next thing he knew, he was in Heaven.

As a teen before the war, he hustled up a buck any way he could and had a reputation and talent for getting things done, legal and sometimes not-so-legal. After his death he worked a number of odd jobs in Heaven, but none of them were satisfying. He'd recently joined the Smile Patrol where Bree Daniels, Marvin Miller's wife, was restructuring the unit. With his unique skills of finding creative ways to make things happen and, when necessary, making problems go away, Lucratelli fit right in.

He had found his calling.

If Heaven had concierges, they would be part of the Smile Patrol. They were the "go to" organization to get anything done. Especially if the requests were unusual.

Lucratelli liked the job—loved it, actually—especially the part that required breaking rules. He was a Smile Patrol superstar assigned to do many out-of-the-ordinary tasks. Easy-going and personable, he felt most of his co-workers were morons who meant well but rarely got things right.

Oh, they usually could handle the small things. Anyone who needed to make reservations, book transportation, or order a particular type of weather for a ski trip or party called the Smile Patrol. When a grouchy old man living alone needed some stimulation, the Smile Patrol sent out groups of mischievous kids to raise a ruckus on his lawn, giving him something to complain about. If a musician dreamed of jamming with Buddy Holly or Jim Morrison, the Smile Patrol could set it up. A wannabe pilot who not only didn't know how to fly but was also afraid of heights had the

Smile Patrol drum up an airplane he could simply taxi around an empty parking lot. If someone wanted tickets to an Elvis or Liberace show, they called the Smile Patrol.

But most of the crew Lucratelli worked with couldn't get even the small things right. Take the series of intercity baseball games that had been played through an entire season and had progressed to the play-offs. Smile Patrol workers started ordering up thunderstorms so the games were rained out. Their reasoning? If the teams couldn't play, and no one lost, no one would be disappointed. That didn't work out so well. Everyone was upset.

Typical Smile Patrol twisted logic.

*   *   *

"It certainly does look like Jesus."

Laureen had invited her neighbors over and they were swarming around the small plastic vat, ogling the tub of butter Laureen had moved from the kitchen to the living room. She had cleared off her coffee table and adjusted the room's pole lamp fixtures to emphasize the importance of the object. But now, with everyone wanting a closer look and with half the small crowd trying to hold it, she was seriously contemplating not leaving it out in the open and instead placing the tub in her china cabinet.

The house was abuzz with activity and Laureen was getting overwhelmed. It seemed that every person there had a question, opinion, and advice to share.

"Where'd you buy it? Winn-Dixie or Publix?"

"Winn-Dixie."

"I didn't realize they were so religious over there."

"You should take photos of it, just in case. That way you have plenty of proof for an insurance adjuster if something happens."

"Are you bringing it to church this weekend?"

"Keep the air conditioning set on frozen so it doesn't melt."

"Did you go through the rest of your refrigerated items? You never know…"

"I hope you don't mind me inviting my prayer group. Where should they all park?"

"Spray some polyurethane on it to harden it up."

"I saw on the news yesterday that someone in France cut open a melon and saw an image of Allah inside. This'll show 'em."

*   *   *

Isaac Newton had been the Devil's caddy for a relatively short time, a couple months. He wasn't particularly athletic but his knowledge of physics allowed Lucifer to experiment with different swings, club face angles, ball characteristics, and more.

Not that it helped his game much.

Shaving a stroke or two off his score was paramount. Over the course of time, those strokes add up. And, in the Devil's case, playing for eternity, there was ample time to work on his game. He had in the past played with a number of former pros—Bobby Jones and Sam Snead were frequent partners for a while—but Lucifer found the professionals to be too competitive. All they wanted was to win and not just by a stroke or two either. The Devil's motive was to certainly beat whoever he played, but he was primarily interested in beating himself. Besting his top scores, if possible, but usually just trying to better his last game.

"Rats."

He didn't cotton to swearing on the golf course if it could be helped. His tee shot on the par-4 third hole strayed right. It was a long, straight hole with a stream running across the fairway at about two hundred fifty yards. Usually a good drive to the center fairway or just a shade to the left would leave him the perfect opportunity for a good approach shot to the green. Going right put a stand of trees in play on his next shot and he'd have to go over them, through them, or around them.

Marvin's tee shot was straight as an arrow but somewhat short. He would be forced to lay up. He didn't think he'd to be able to clear the water on his second shot. Berry's tee shot, however, was long and low. His ball came to rest about ten yards before the water on the left side of the fairway. Perfect.

"That was a masterful shot, my friend," Lucifer said.

"Just luck," Berry replied. "I can't shape my shots. I'm just lucky to get them down there somewhere."

"Modest, too. I like that in a playing partner," Lucifer added.

Berry chuckled to himself. Compliments from the Devil. Who'd have thought it even possible? They all started moving toward their balls. Berry and Marvin walked together.

"If anyone had told me yesterday that I'd be dead and playing golf with the Devil, I'd have thought they were nuts. And he's so personable. Nice fella," he said to Marvin.

"Yeah, he's a piece of work, all right," Marvin replied.

"Not at all like I imagined him to be."

"His reputation precedes him, but he's used to it. Forget what you've heard: he's never bought a soul. He might have his own agenda, but he's not deceitful; he won't lie to you…not knowingly anyway unless he has a good reason. He's certainly rebellious. I don't suggest getting on his bad side. And he's definitely his own person. He's outspoken and very direct as you can tell, but, at the very least, you always know where you stand with him."

"Yet, everyone has this specific image of what he is like," Berry said.

"The living? Superstition. When we're alive, we think we know it all. Amazing how much we got wrong."

"He's a confident player, too," Berry said, "but not obnoxious about it. Reminds me of Kevin Costner in that golf movie. I can't think of the name."

"*Tin Cup?*"

"That's the one," Berry said, turning to Newton. "So, where are we?"

"The third hole," Isaac replied.

"No, I mean where are Heaven and Hell located exactly?"

"They're not anywhere," Newton told him. "Traditionally, people thought of these places as being 'up there' or 'down here', but it doesn't work like that. I'm not sure of the mechanics of it all, but I've spent a very long time trying to figure it out. Challenging. My best guess? It's a dimensional thing. And quite fascinating, too. Think about it: With all the people who have ever lived and died, Heaven is not in the least bit crowded. Geographically, we have mountains, deserts, seashores, oceans, and cities, yet we can take a simple tram or portal doorway and be absolutely anywhere in a matter of minutes or even seconds. We can order our own weather, and people can get different weather in virtually the same place at the same time. We all eat, but not one animal is killed. No one gains a pound. We have no need for bathrooms other than for baths or showers. I could spend my whole life studying all of this and still not come close to figuring it all out."

Marvin was away, so he shot first. He tapped the ball with a pitching wedge and landed a couple yards from the water. Perfect lay-up. Berry took a practice swing, then another, then smacked it across the stream. Landing on the green, his ball rolled just off the back side and settled in the light rough about fifteen yards from the hole.

"Easy up and down from there, my friend," Lucifer said. He hit his eight-iron solidly. The ball soared over the trees on the other side of the water and landed on the green, spinning back towards the hole and coming to rest about four feet from the cup.

"Not a gimme, but it'll do. Chance at a birdie." He smiled, dug in his pocket and pulled out a cigar, lighting it in quick puffs as he strolled across the small bridge fording the stream.

"You can smoke here?" Berry asked.

"Sure. What's it gonna do, kill you? You can do anything you want here as long as you don't hurt someone else," Marvin answered.

"But if we're all dead, how can you be hurt?"

"Emotional hurt. We want everyone to be happy."

"So *is* everyone happy?"

"Somewhat. I guess it depends on what you consider happiness. Or what makes you happy. I don't know. I haven't figured it all out yet. I'm not sure Heaven's figured it all out yet. But we're working on it. I know we're all part of The Plan."

"God's plan…" Berry said. "Have you ever met Him?"

"I have. From what I gathered, we're all part of some on-going experiment. It's like we live our lives on Earth to prepare us for this. Because this is where we really exist forever—or until we find out what's next. Wherever we're headed, we learn the basics on Earth, but get to really be ourselves here. I think the idea is to find your sources of happiness there and enjoy them here. Something like that. I don't know what The Plan is exactly." Marvin nodded toward the Devil. "He probably does."

"Did you two come out here to play or to talk?" the Devil said with a smirk.

Marvin asked for his six-iron, opened his stance, and hit a putting stroke that propelled his ball onto the green. It came to rest less than one inch from the hole.

"A Cuban ball," Berry said with a smile.

"Cuban ball?" Marvin asked.

"Yep. Needed one more revolution."

*   *   **

Excerpt from *Maxwell's Guide to Heaven and Hell*, page 92:

There are no hangovers in Heaven. You can drink all you like and never feel that awful headache the next morning. Alcoholic drinks will not affect you in any way.

We understand that people like the euphoria provided by certain intoxicants, but by eliminating drunk driving, addictions, alcohol poisoning, and irrational behavior, we keep Heaven a safer place to live and work.

The same applies to recreational drugs.

Think of Heaven as a benign Amsterdam.

Mankind and alcohol have shared a long and illustrious history.

And not just humans. Animals have been known to eat rotted fruit that was fermented enough to get them drunk in the wild. Perhaps that's where it all started for people, a race memory left over after tens of thousands of years. Some men do turn into animals after they've had a few.

The oldest recorded recipe is for beer. Archeologists have found beer jugs from the Stone Age. Beer, wine, and other alcoholic beverages have been a part of religious ceremonies since the dawn of civilization.

59

The custom of saying a toast started in ancient Rome when toasted pieces of bread were placed into a drink. Too many and you could get toasted yourself.

In Africa, rum was as valuable as money and was often traded for slaves.

Travelers on the Mayflower put in at Plymouth Rock, not their intended landing site, because they were low on supplies, especially beer.

"The Star Spangled Banner", America's national anthem, was written to the melody of a traditional drinking song.

The phrase "minding your Ps and Qs" was an admonishment not to get too drunk on your pints and quarts.

Since the Middle Ages, beer glasses—ceramic or pewter steins—have had glass bottoms so when someone was "bottoms up" they could still see a potential enemy through the bottom of their drink.

It's been said that people will abide anything except taking away their religion or their alcohol, though people have forsaken their beliefs and then lamented that decision by drowning their sorrows with alcohol.

Lucratelli always enjoyed a good stiff drink himself, and he was pissed that he couldn't get a good buzz on in Heaven. No stranger to bars, as a youngster he made a few bucks—movie and comic book money—by sweeping and cleaning up the tavern his father had owned and operated.

Getting drunk was how Lucratelli got through the war without losing his mind. The part of the war he actually got through before his death, that is. Once his squad liberated and occupied a town, they'd immediately search out the wineries, bars, and restaurants for bottles that hadn't been looted or destroyed. If the search was successful, the soldiers would share until there was no more booze to be had. Then it was on to the next town.

Never one for rules and regulations during his lifetime, Lucratelli was determined to buck the system in Heaven and come up with an alcoholic concoction that did the trick. He was proud of his still, a project he had been passionately working on for quite a while. At the brink of success a number of times, he had, so far, remained unsuccessful and had even hit a few bumps in the road.

After a year of experimentation with different brews and, he thought, close to a breakthrough, his still blew up. Another time it was an overzealous former Alcohol, Tobacco, and Firearms officer who needed a purpose in Heaven, so members of the Smile Patrol had set him on Lucratelli's trail. He harassed Lucratelli for months and then simply vandalized the still.

It made the officer happy and made Lucratelli miserable.

"Where're you at?" Artie Meyers called out.

"Back here, alligator."

Artie walked around the cottage where Lucratelli lived and found him attaching a curled tube to the top of the latest incarnation of the still, a Rube Goldberg-like contraption that gleamed in the sunlight.

"Still at it, huh?"

"Nice pun."

"What?"

"Never mind."

Lucratelli glanced over and noticed the Golden Retriever sitting at Artie's side.

"Who's your pal?"

"I don't know. A stray. He's been following me around all day."

"Someone's checking up on you."

"No reason to. Don't understand it."

"They must have received some kind of complaint," Lucratelli offered.

"Nothin' to complain about. Maybe it's you. What about the still?"

"Nah, I figure there won't be any trouble unless I get lucky. That hasn't exactly been the case. So far, though, I'm cookin' with gas, cuz. Nice pooch, by the way."

They went back a long time. Both were raised in the Bronx and went to school together. Once the war started, Lucratelli went Airborne, Artie became a Ranger. Lucratelli bought it in the war, but Artie made it back. He lasted for another six months until he stopped into his favorite candy store—Julie's—next to the fire station a block over from where he lived on Weeks Avenue. He wanted an egg cream. As he was leaving, a cab driver had a stroke, jumped the curb, and that was that.

Artie looked over the tubes, condenser, and collection pots and realized he had no concept of how this thing worked.

"Where'd you get all this stuff?"

Lucratelli looked up and smiled. "Here and there."

"I'll bet. Fell off the back of a truck, huh?"

"Sort of."

Lucratelli eyed the dog. He had a soft spot for animals.

"You know, I had a dog once."

"I remember. A mutt. What the hell was its name?"

"I called him Watson."

"Right. Like in *Sherlock Holmes*."

"Exactly. That dog and I were inseparable. He went everywhere with me. Got so I thought we could almost read each other's minds. One day I'm taking a leak and the dog pushes the door open and waltzes right in. He stands there and looks up at me like he's saying, 'Hey, I do that, too.' It was a real bonding moment. Then he tried to drink out of the toilet and I realized we had absolutely nothing in common."

Watson died when he was hit by a car on a mountain road up in the Catskills where maybe three cars would pass all day. The driver never stopped. Lucratelli was fourteen.

Lucratelli spent his summers in the Catskills at a bungalow colony near Swan Lake. His mom, his grandmother, and a couple aunts who were his mother's sisters stayed through July and August with the kids and the men of the family would drive up on weekends or whenever they could sneak off for a few days at a time.

The bungalow colonies were cheaper than the hotels and were segregated into Jewish places, Italian, African-American, whatever. They were idyllic summers far from the rough city life to which Lucratelli was accustomed when, during most of the year, he got up, went to school, and after school helped around his dad's bar, the Stumble Inn. It was more likely that patrons would stumble out.

He did his homework on top of liquor cases in the stockroom and learned a lot about human nature in that bar. His dad tried to run a legit business, but it wasn't unusual for young Lucratelli to see numbers being run, card games in the back, shady deals being made, and even drugs being dealt. He learned quickly to keep his mouth shut when he had to and to recognize an opportunity when it arose. It was a rough neighborhood, but he was good with his fists and even faster on his feet when necessary. He grew wise in the ways of the world. He could get things done. He grew older than his years.

Summers in the mountains were a refuge. He spent days picking blueberries with his grandmother who would bake pies with them or put them in a bowl with sour cream. Afternoons were spent playing ball with his cousins or having fun at the pool.

Each bungalow cottage had a kitchen, but many of the women would cook communally in the large hall they called the casino. Large family-style dinners: lasagna, baked ziti, sausage and peppers, steak pizzaiola, eggplant, sometimes all of at once. After dinner, the women would gather around card tables and play cards, usually Canasta, while the men drank and played poker. The young people would chase fireflies or listen to ballgames or music on the radio.

Sometimes they'd go on raids of local farms, carrying off fruits and vegetables with an irate farmer yelling at them as they ran off laughing like loons. Lucratelli was the one who always showed up with a stolen pack of smokes or a bottle they would share while sneaking off to watch the sky for falling stars and make out by the squash and handball courts, abandoned at night.

Lucratelli had a crush on one of his cousins, Samantha. Pretty, blond, and six months older than he was, most of the boys were attracted to her. She developed early, but despite the boys bragging about how far they'd gone with her, she wasn't easy. She knew what they said about her but took it in stride, knowing the boys at the colony said those things just to build themselves up with each other. Lucratelli was tempted to come on to her himself but held off since she was a cousin.

A third cousin, but a cousin just the same.

But they were close and most of what Lucratelli learned about girls he learned from Samantha and her friends. Not sexually. More of how they thought. What they talked about. He liked girls for who they were. And they liked him.

Sometimes on weekends, the two of them would get a ride in to Liberty, the nearest town. It was a treat to get away for a few hours. They'd stop by the bakery and pick up the best brownies they ever had and sneak them into the movie theatre and watch a double feature.

Good times. Until the day Watson was struck down on that country road that never had any traffic, that is. That dog followed

Lucratelli around unleashed everywhere he went. His shadow. His best friend in the world. When he was hit, Lucratelli picked him up, the dog heavy, panting in pain and staring at him. He carried him back to the bungalow colony but not before he died in his arms.

Lucratelli never went back to the mountains. He spent every summer after that in the city and never left until he enlisted. He was the guy in his squad who could get anything, anytime—for the right price. He knew all the quartermasters and all the hustlers. He made people happy. It was the same with the Smile Patrol after his death, fulfilling other people's dreams and never wondering what it was that would make him feel content. He knew something was missing and, though he couldn't identify what it was, it left a gnawing feeling inside him that he didn't even like thinking about.

When he did, he worked on the still.

Lucratelli stepped around to the front of the still, grabbed a metal cup, and loosened a spigot. A clear liquid filled the cup. He held it out for Artie.

"Here. Try this."

Artie took a whiff, raised his eyebrows skeptically, took a deep breath, and sipped cautiously.

"Not bad."

"Tastes okay, but no kick yet. I do think I'm getting closer…"

"Yeah. Ever think that no matter what you come up with, it won't work 'cause we're…you know…dead?"

"Thanks a lot."

"Maybe you ought to consult a chemist or something," Artie suggested.

"Maybe you ought to take a walk with your furry friend over there."

*　　　　　　*　　　　　　*

Whoosh!

Zoey materialized outside the Falafel Stop. She much preferred being somewhere other than New York City. Sure, there were plenty of mice and rats to chase, dogs to torment, and other cats to hang with, but the city was way too busy for her tastes. Still, she had a job to do.

Chelsea could see the dancers from her living room window overlooking Washington Square. The flash mob moved in unison and drew a crowd, just as Chelsea had anticipated. Some people would do anything for a free T-shirt or gift certificate. Others were willing just for the fun of it. Their reason didn't matter much to Chelsea as long as they showed up and, in this case, wore brightly colored shirts with the ScreenPix logo. Her client would love her for this.

As she watched the antics in the park, she absentmindedly fingered the small gold locket she wore on a thin chain around her neck. It contained a picture of her mother and father, taken while they were young, years before Chelsea was born. The habit was comforting to her and she often did it without realizing it. As she gazed out the window, she wished that she could be out there dancing, too. But that was not possible. Not in this lifetime, anyway.

She had started her public relations company a couple years earlier after looking for something that would incorporate her love of social networking and allow her to work from home. Why just text and e-mail friends when she could actually make a living doing something she totally enjoyed?

Someone once said that if you relish what you do, you'll never work a day in your life. Well, it certainly was work, but she loved it and lately her business had really taken off. With the addition of more clients she had branched out from writing press releases for local businesses to promoting products and services for major corporations regionally and nationally. She set up and designed websites, planned events, wrote brochures, set up and updated networking accounts, booked interviews—anything and everything.

Maneuvering her wheelchair away from the bay window, she went back to her desk. Years ago she'd had a medulloblastoma, a cancerous brain tumor. The doctors operated and she had recovered just fine. Then they discovered they hadn't gotten it all. Chelsea thought that's why they called it practicing medicine—they still didn't quite have it down. There was chemo and radiation. Not a fun time.

She went back in for a second operation that appeared to have gone well until she went into a coma that lasted a few days. When she finally woke up, there were residual effects: she had lost some motor skills on the left side of her body—hence the wheelchair—

and she had a partial loss of short-term memory. She compensated by posting small notes all over the wall beside her desk and above the nightstand by her bed.

Technology, medicine, and knowledge had progressed since her surgeries. Had she had the operation even a couple years later, she would have been fine. But, it was what it was. She accepted her situation and managed it in very creative ways. She abhorred pity. Her parents wanted her to remain in their care, but Chelsea insisted on living on her own. It concerned her parents, but over time they grew to respect and admire her. When they both passed away, Chelsea inherited the apartment she grew up in just off the park. Not bad for a twenty-two-year-old.

Chelsea was at her desk viewing a video she'd made of the flash mob dancers. It looked like fun. She missed dancing. She missed a lot of things, but dancing was one of them. Ever since she was a little girl, she'd dreamed of dancing with her father at her wedding. Nothing about that dream was a possibility now and as she thought about that, tears welled up. She fought them off and looked over to the window to distract herself.

Sitting on the sill outside was a small calico cat. Chelsea rolled across the room to open one of the smaller windows to the side of the larger window. The cat turned its head and let out a quiet mewl.

"You're a cutie, aren't you?" Chelsea cooed.

Another soft meow from the cat and it jumped into her living room, walking around and getting the lay of the land.

"Are you hungry? I don't have any cat food, but I can give you some milk."

Chelsea went into the kitchen and filled a small bowl. She put it down next to the fridge and the cat made its way over. It looked up at Chelsea and started lapping at the milk.

"You don't have a collar. Do you belong to someone? I can put some posters up in the neighborhood and post some notices online, but you can stay here for a while. And while you do, I think I'll call you Zoey."

Chelsea never expected to adopt a cat but, truth be told, it was actually the other way around.

*   *   *

Excerpt from *Maxwell's Guide to Heaven and Hell*, page 17:

The Bible is just a book.

It was a beautiful day in Hell. The sun was low. The clouds were magnificent. The drinks were refreshing.

"This is Hell? It's not quite what I expected," Berry admitted.

"Not what anyone expects," Lucifer replied.

Berry, the Devil, Marvin, and Isaac Newton sat on the clubhouse terrace reflecting on their game. Lucifer had won, but that was no surprise.

"Why would anyone want to leave this place?" Berry asked.

"Boredom," Marvin answered. "There's not much to do here."

"Well, I wouldn't say that. I have plenty to do," Lucifer said.

"Deal with sinners you mean?" Berry inquired.

"Sinners? I prefer to think of them as…well, people who've made bad choices. I personally don't believe that evil exists."

"That's kind of funny coming from the Devil himself," Berry noted.

Marvin shot him a look as if to say he'd gone too far, but Satan seemed to take it in stride.

"Everyone has the potential to do evil. There's no question about that. But what's the root cause? Hate? Frustration? Intolerance? Fear? They all manifest themselves one way or another. But by the same token, within every one of us there is the potential for forgiveness, understanding, mercy, and love.

"People are complex beings. No one is forced to stay in Hell," said Satan. "That's an individual choice. Heaven or Hell. You made it, everyone does. Want to move? Totally possible, unless you're an incorrigible. We won't stand for people harming one another in any way."

"So those are the people you torment?"

The Devil laughed. "I've never tormented anyone. Well, there may be a couple of women I've known who might disagree," he said, laughing again at his own joke. "Seriously, people do atone and change their ways. We're actually very forgiving here, unless harm is intended. If a person can't reform, we'll help them, but if they won't reform, that's a different story. We'll deal with them differently. We'll take their Essence and be done with them. They just won't *be* anymore."

"But the Bible—"

"Forget the Bible. It has nothing to do with us. Conceived by man, written by man."

"Some believe it's the word of God."

"And some people believed the Earth was flat. Others thought if you played a Beatles album backwards there would be secret messages. Well, Paul's not dead...yet, and the Earth is round. Religion? It doesn't really exist here. Oh, there are some holdovers, but people certainly don't need a church, synagogue, mosque, or other structure. The closest things you'll find here are meeting halls. Social places. Rites and ceremonies are unnecessary and as far as the Bible goes, you're likely to get more out of that book you received when you got here."

Berry reached into his back pocket and pulled out *Maxwell's Guide to Heaven and Hell* and placed it on the table in front of him.

"So why are we here?" Berry asked.

"To have a drink after our game," Lucifer answered.

"No. Why do we exist?"

"Part of the experiment," Marvin said.

"Experiment?"

"To see what becomes of the species. What you are capable of," Lucifer explained.

"Don't you know?"

"Hell, no. Look, I've been around since way before the first of you crawled out of the ooze and set foot on dry land. And let me tell you, it's been interesting to observe."

"That's all you do? Observe?"

"When God created life on Earth, He wanted to see what would happen."

Berry was amazed. "You mean to say He can't control what happens?"

"Can't? No. *Won't*. Consider this: there are twenty-one billion sneezes every day. People say 'God bless you'. If God blessed every one of them, would there be time for anything else? He has His priorities."

"So we have free will? We can do what we want?"

"Haven't you always? Oh, we've provided some guidelines—"

"The Ten Commandments?"

Lucifer laughed again. "Let's just say guidelines, okay? The rest is up to you. Sure, we've given you a little prod once in a while."

"Such as?"

"Coffee."

"Coffee?"

"A simple bean, really, that changed your world."

"Really?"

"Really."

"How so?"

"It was originally appreciated in the Middle East. You've heard it called java, right? Thanks to the British East India Company, its popularity spread to Europe. All of a sudden people in Italy, France, and England are sitting down and enjoying their cup of joe.

"Now, here's the good part. What do people get from a cup or two of coffee? A buzz. They are stimulated and they talk and talk some more. Coffee houses sprang up where people sat around and talked about everything under the sun. In some places, people discussed politics. In others, daily events or science. It could have been anything. But the point is they talked. If you didn't make it to the coffee shop that day, you missed out on the daily opinions of the talkers. Op-eds, really. So attendees began writing summaries of what everyone was talking about. Eventually these separate recaps were compiled and evolved into newspapers. So now you can read the news, check out the latest sales, find a used car, and read an obit. All because we nudged the human race into cultivating, roasting, and brewing little beans.

"And that's just the tip of the iceberg. Look at what you've been through: ice ages, drought, floods, wars, disease. But your kind has survived."

"With a little nudge here and there?"

"If necessary. But the important thing was to see where you guys would take it. Amazing, really. You learned to clothe yourselves, build shelters. You learned to farm instead of forage. You took the hint with fire and the wheel. As I said, little pushes and prods here and there. Like technology. We have vidscreens and devices far more advanced than your TVs, computers, and smartphones. And we've had them for a very, very long time. You're just catching up. We can travel instantly; you've just recently learned to fly.

"But you've also gone off in your own direction. You've invented war and a multitude of weapons and ways to do each other in. There's crime. And selfishness. It's amazing how many ways you people have devised to be mean to each other."

Berry sat for a moment taking it all in. "What about love? And charity? And compassion?"

Lucifer smiled. "All noble. See? There's hope for you yet. Look at your own personal history, Berry. You marketed stuff to the masses. Sometimes useful items, sometimes just junk. There are those who might say you exploited them for your own personal profit. My impression of someone like that? A cold-hearted, carnival-barker kind of guy. A snake oil salesman. But you're not like that. It's not who you are. You've evolved. You seem like a nice man. You may have started out just wanting to make a living. After a while, you did what you did not just to make another buck but to try and make people happy. Hopefully, you'll use that sentiment here.

"Life on Earth, before people pass away, is kind of a training ground. If you find the keys to your own happiness there, you'll thrive here. Unhappy in life, you'll be unhappy here. Your own happiness and fulfillment is not determined *for* you but *by* you."

Berry stared at the small book on the table in front of him. "People should know this stuff."

Lucifer smiled. "They do...here."

"No, I mean *before* they get here. Imagine what the world—the living world—would be like if they had this knowledge. If they read it all right here," Berry tapped on the book's cover.

"Yeah? How would they do that?"

"What if we made it available?" Berry asked.

"Impossible," Marvin piped up.

"I thought nothing was impossible here," Berry stated.

Marvin was quick to answer.

"Too many roadblocks. Figuratively and literally. There are feasibility studies, manpower computations, travel permits, cause and effect reports. It could take a very, very long time. If you get permission at all."

"It would shake things up some, wouldn't it?" Lucifer grinned slyly.

3

Another lawyer in Fort Lauderdale was arrested for operating a Ponzi scheme. There were two drive-by shootings in Miami. Three Broward County Commissioners were indicted on bribery charges. A rapper in Dade County was running for public office. A water main in Southwest Miami broke and held up traffic throughout rush hour. In Lighthouse Point, Animal Control officers were trying to capture an alligator that ate a small dog and was currently lounging in a backyard pool.

It was a slow news day in South Florida.

Laureen and Nana hit on the idea of charging admission fees to see the face of Jesus in Laureen's tub of whipped butter and business was even better than expected. People lined up outside the doublewide for hours while parked cars filled the narrow lanes of the Sleepy Lagoon Trailer Park and spilled out onto the surrounding streets causing major traffic snarls. Remote trucks from every local TV station were on the scene. Helicopters flew overhead. Audio and video cables ran everywhere.

Reporters were either questioning the folks waiting on line to see the tub of butter or talking on their cell phones with their assignment editors or producers. All of them were trying to interview Laureen.

"To what do you attribute this appearance?"

Maxwell's Guide to Heaven and Hell

Laureen tried to take hold of the microphone, but the savvy reporter knew better.

"Who can say what God intends?" Laureen answered. "I certainly wouldn't even pretend to know. Even though He talks to me on a regular basis."

"How regular?"

"Every day. God is riding shotgun."

"In your car?"

"Everywhere in my life."

"Like 'God is My Co-Pilot'?"

"No. Don't be ridiculous. I can't fly a plane. He rides shotgun. He's got my back."

To the Dawbers, the afternoon was a blur of activity. Excitement was at a fever pitch. Nana was busy collecting and counting money. The kids were running rampant without supervision. And Laureen was doing her best to answer the onslaught of questions.

"You've apparently benefited financially from all of this. Was that your motivation?"

"My motivations are not important," Laureen admitted. "The Lord wanted us to experience this. Open your heart to Jesus and you will be shown the way."

The onlookers roared their approval.

"Have you been shown the way?"

"Every day is a journey."

"What will you do with the money?"

"Why are you so fixated on the money?" Laureen asked. "Look, as an American, I have rights. The right to proudly display whatever I want. The right to make a living. The right to be left alone to follow the Lord's path. He didn't create us to be stifled by the media or anyone else."

More applause and a number of "amens" from her audience.

"I hardly think you are being stifled," the reporter said cautiously.

"We didn't fight the Revolutionary War to give up our freedoms, you know. Slavery is over."

"Aren't you thinking of the Civil War?"

*   *   *

Excerpt from *Maxwell's Guide to Heaven and Hell*, page 4:

Consider Heaven your own private playground.

You can go anywhere and do anything. The only limitation is your own imagination. If you can dream it, you can do it.

This is a lesson you should have learned during your lifetime on Earth, but no worries: you have eternity to adapt.

Lucratelli was nervous. Not because Bree, the head of the Smile Patrol, called and asked him to stop into the office for a meeting, though she didn't say why. Usually left to his devices, Lucratelli occasionally attended staff meetings, but he didn't much like them. This was different though. It was a one-on-one meeting with his boss. He told her he would be there right after the event he was holding for the Fourth Street Flyers.

No, it wasn't his boss that gave him anxiety. It was the Flyers that made him nervous. The group of skydiving enthusiasts got together and approached the Smile Patrol about an event they wanted to put on. There were twenty-eight of them and they all wanted to jump. Even as a former paratrooper, Lucratelli couldn't relate. He had only jumped out of airplanes because he was ordered to do so. But this was different. The Flyers jumped for the thrill of it.

Lucratelli had enlisted during World War Two and after basic training he trained as a searchlight operator. When he learned that he could not only receive combat pay but additional jump pay, he volunteered for jump school at Fort Benning, Georgia.

Besides jumping out of perfectly functioning C-47 transport planes, jump school was fine. The parachute ride at Coney Island had always been his favorite amusement park ride anyway.

There was also the camaraderie with the guys in his outfit. Paratroopers considered themselves the elite. They wore different uniforms than regular Army, and they wore jump boots. But it was more than the attire. They had an attitude, a swagger.

And, in Georgia, off the base, they thought they were untouchable. When one of the guys in the squad was arrested on leave one night for being drunk and disorderly, Lucratelli took offense. It wasn't as if an Airborne M.P. busted him. This was a street cop. Unheard of.

So, that night Lucratelli stole a Jeep from the motor pool and headed to town with a couple buddies. The police station was a small stone building with a decorative fountain in front. Lucratelli tossed a purloined grenade into the fountain, blowing out the wall of his buddy's cell, and they all escaped back to their barracks. Fortunately, no one was injured. The guys should have spent years in the stockade but, as luck would have it, they were shipped overseas early the next morning before anyone came around to investigate what had happened.

Combat jumps were frightening. Often, Lucratelli's unit made their jumps under cover of darkness the night before an invasion. With luck, they would hit the ground without being discovered. Other times they were not so fortunate. Not only was there the jumping out of an airplane part—frightening enough—but there were also people shooting at you. Shrapnel and bullets flew everywhere. The first time Lucratelli was wounded, it was because the U.S. Navy hadn't been informed of the airborne jump. When the naval ships heard the planes overhead racing to the jump zone, they opened fire with everything they had. Still, Lucratelli had a job to do and stood up, hooked to the static line, and stepped out of the plane's doorway. Feeling the familiar jolt, he looked up to confirm that his chute had deployed correctly, then he grabbed the risers to steer his canopy. He only had a couple hundred feet to the ground; combat jumps were low. He felt a sudden sting in his left hand, but it wasn't until he hit the ground and prepared to bury his chute that he realized a bullet had passed directly through his hand.

Lucratelli jumped because he had to. It was war—and a few extra bucks. But these Fourth Street Flyers were different. They jumped for the hell of it. Adrenaline junkies.

They had approached the Smile Patrol and asked for help arranging their outing. Lucratelli filled out the appropriate permits for land usage, air space, and weather and found some planes and pilots that were available. He met and had coffee with the group early in the morning before they took off. He stayed on the ground just waiting for the planes to reach the proper altitude before the Flyers leaped into the air.

It didn't take long. The lead pilot gave the Flyers the green light and, one by one, out they went. Lucratelli had been talking to the pilot by phone and knew the jumpers were already free-falling. He could hear the drone of the planes. He looked up and squinted, unable to see anything yet.

Then he could just make out tiny dots in the sky. They seemed to just float there but Lucratelli realized they were getting larger. He started making out shapes, arms, and legs and they grew larger and larger until—

Woomph!

Woomph!

Woomph!

With no parachutes to slow their descent, bodies slammed into the ground all around Lucratelli at an enormous speed. One after another. It was raining skydivers. Twenty-eight of them tumbled out of the sky and landed all over the field. Lucratelli ran in different directions to avoid being pummeled by falling bodies. He stopped short just as one of them hit the dirt right in front of him. The skydiver stayed there on the ground for a second or two then popped right up and smiled. Lucratelli smiled back. Among the living, you didn't need a parachute at all to skydive once; you only needed a parachute to skydive twice. Here in Heaven, they weren't needed at all.

"How was it?" Lucratelli asked.

"Awesome, dude!"

"It didn't hurt?"

"Naw. Just for a second."

Lucratelli knew this was Heaven and they were already dead, so hitting terra firma was no big deal. Just another day on the Smile Patrol.

But he still thought they were a bunch of crazy fuckers.

*   *   *

"You've got to see this."

Robert Maggert ran ANN, America's News Now, a television news organization with a definite right-wing conservative bias. He insisted his producers and anchors take a stand on each and every story that went out on their air. He was on a mission to help take back the country from what he perceived to be a leftist, socialist agenda propagated by the party in power.

His assistant leaned over Maggert's desk and put a tablet device down so the boss could see a news feature sent in by the network's affiliate station in South Florida. It was Laureen Dawber sharing her views on everything from evolution to climate change.

"Good-looking woman," Maggert stated.

"And everything she says sounds like it comes directly from your playbook," the assistant noted. "We've had more phone calls and letters about her than anything else in the last couple days. People either love her or hate her, but a vast majority of our viewers adore her."

"What's her story?" Maggert asked.

"Single mom, widow, two kids. Lauderdale. Lives with her mother. Claims she has a tub of butter with the face of Jesus. Causing quite a ruckus down there. We have all the interviews."

"People seem to like her, huh?"

"To say the least. She definitely appeals to our demographic."

"Any affiliations we know of? Politically active?"

"No. Just trying to get by."

"Okay, let's start grooming her. Make her an offer. Maybe start her out on a 'Street Talk' segment and see how it goes. If we get some kind of ratings numbers, we'll bring her in as a commentator."

"Remember, she's a virgin."

"I thought she had kids?"

"I mean a TV virgin. This feature was her first time on-air."

"Well, let's try her out. Don't make any promises and keep it cheap. Who knows? She may be good for us. She might also just be a whackadoo."

*   *   *

When it came to business, Berry always did his homework. He'd research every conceivable aspect of a product and its marketing potential before he would even attempt to foist it on the television public. So it was appropriate that he applied the same principle to his transition to the afterlife.

He never actually told anyone what he was planning. He went about the usual step of choosing Heaven over Hell, was assigned a residence, and let it be known that his job choice would be some kind of creative marketing. He could possibly promote events or theatre performances, maybe concerts. But no one really bought it. It was obvious at the golf game that Berry's passion was focused on *Maxwell's Guide to Heaven and Hell.*

From Berry's point of view, it was a chance to radically change the world of the living. Just like each and every product he hawked throughout his career, he really believed his own hype. He thought every item he sold would sell like gangbusters and positively affect people's lives. He looked at *The Guide* in a similar manner but thought that this offer would be too good for anyone to refuse. It would have real impact. It would provide people with hope, a reason to live, and verification that there was an afterlife and a God.

Of course, everyone else thought differently. Satan, generally restless and bored, thought it might provide some entertainment value. Marvin worried about the repercussions and discussed the situation with his wife Bree who, as head of the Smile Patrol, thought it was a real can of worms. To Lucratelli, however, it was just another job, especially since Bree intentionally neglected to fill Lucratelli in on Berry's intentions. Sometimes it was difficult enough just to get him to stay on task.

Berry had requested to meet a number of people residing in Heaven. He was seeking some advice and guidance. Lucratelli thought it would be just another boring assignment and expressed his feelings to his boss.

"So now I'm a secretary? Setting up appointments for this yahoo?" he whined.

"You'll also escort him to his meetings and report back to me," Bree told him.

"Sounds like a lot of wasted time and energy to me. Why don't you give this assignment to one of them?" He gestured to the other Smile Patrol workers in the office.

"This one is…delicate. It needs your special skills."

"You think flattery's gonna work?"

"How about bribery?" she asked.

"Bribery?"

"I hear you've got a special project you're working on."

"Oh?" Lucratelli played innocent. He wasn't stupid. It could be any one of a number of things and he didn't want to give anything up to the boss.

"That contraption behind your place?"

"Oh, that. Just a hobby."

"I'll bet. It'll never work you know."

"Maybe, maybe not. I think it will."

"I could have it shut down…"

Lucratelli knew that was a possibility. Bree was very powerful without being obnoxious about it. Over the years he had learned to respect her abilities and he'd grown to like her as a person. He also knew she'd been a witch who'd been burned at the stake during the Salem witch trials. As an activist, she had really helped buck the system in Heaven and that was one of the reasons she was put in charge of the Smile Patrol to begin with. Breaking rules? One of her favorite things to do. And his, too.

"But you won't," Lucratelli smiled roguishly.

"No, I probably won't. Just do it for me. As a favor."

"Okay, as a favor." As he got up to leave, Lucratelli turned back to Bree. "By the way, how'd you know the still was there?"

"A little birdie told me."

"I doubt it. Birds are…well, birds. It was probably that Golden Retriever that Artie brought around to my place."

And it was.

*　　　　　*　　　　　*

Excerpt from *Maxwell's Guide to Heaven and Hell*, page 41:

Religions were invented by humans on Earth to deal with things people didn't know or didn't understand. Here in Heaven you are free to worship any way you like, anywhere you feel comfortable. Organized religions are not prevalent or necessary here.

Cosequently, you will not find any churches, mosques, or synagogues. You will, however, find a multitude of social halls and open spaces. Please consult your local Smile Patrol office for information on reserving these facilities.

With our excellent communications network, you can consult with anyone at any time. You can send direct messages to God as well.

Please understand the Lord is very busy and responds to those that contact Him on a first come, first served basis. It will be determined whether or not your inquiry is valid.

There are no guarantees you will receive a response.

Ever.

The church was more than huge; it was a megachurch. Spread out over acres, it offered a preschool, elementary school, teen activity centers, meeting rooms, bar-b-que and park settings, outdoor prayer areas, and its own multi-story parking garage. The chapel itself was the size of an arena. Services were broadcast throughout the facility and every weekend live shows crewed by the church's own production team streamed over the internet and appeared on television stations all over the country.

Dress code was casual. It didn't matter what you wore, just that you showed up. But on this day, an extraordinary number of parishioners were wearing white tee shirts emblazoned with the words "God Is Riding Shotgun." The shirts were available for nineteen ninety-five at Laureen Dawber's home, online at

ReligiousMiraclesRus.com, and also at the church's gift shop. Laureen donated ten percent of all proceeds to the church.

The pastor, Dr. James McKinnon, delivered a fire and brimstone sermon on the deterioration of the country that centered on gay rights and gay marriage, things he considered an abomination.

To Laureen, it didn't really matter what the sermon was actually about. She found solace just in the act of showing up. Not that she didn't participate. She did, enthusiastically. But it was being there and sharing the experience with the congregation that made a difference to her. Among her social circle of friends, relatives, and coworkers there were some people who understood very clearly why she attended this particular church. There were others who thought she was a complete loon. Over time, to her relief, the detractors drew farther and farther away. She was tired of always having to defend her position. And here, at church, there were literally thousands of like-minded people who didn't need convincing.

As glad as she was to be there, she was having a very difficult time staying awake. The constant parade of visitors to her home was helping financially, but it was also wearing on her and her family. She was exhausted. So was Nana who, on this Sunday morning, was alternating between reprimanding the kids when they misbehaved and poking her daughter every time Laureen started to doze off. With the large crowd in the chapel and her fatigue washing over her, Laureen took no notice at all of the two men in suits and ties sitting a couple of rows behind her. They were paying no attention at all to Dr. McKinnon.

"She's a looker, isn't she?"

"Not bad at all. First time I've seen a church with its own professional lighting grid," said the blond, looking up at the rows and rows of video lights hanging from the ceiling.

"I meant Dawber."

"Oh, right," replied the blond man. "All hi-def cameras, too. And jibs. They must have some hefty production budget."

"You're a gearhead, you know that?"

"And proud of it, my friend."

After a few minutes the sermon was over and a Christian rock band called Johnny's Angels serenaded the thousands of attendees as they started leaving the immense chapel to break up into smaller groups. While some left for their cars, others escorted their children to classrooms or made their way to the gift store, the three restaurants, the snack bar, basketball courts, baseball field, the small amusement theme park next door known as Apostleland, or the many picnic and bar-b-que areas that were all on-site.

Laureen and her family shared a pavilion in the picnic area with another family. While they were firing up the grill, the other family's oldest male had no qualms about sharing some of his opinions with anyone within earshot.

"My opinions are my opinions and I'm constantly offended by the lack of respect we are all shown by those who don't particularly share our points of view. These people don't know shit from

Shinola and if they want to believe what they want to believe, they should just move somewhere else. To some country that will put up with their kind. I hope they do. That'll leave this great country of ours to the people who deserve it."

As she unpacked hamburger and hot dog rolls, his wife tried to calm him down.

"Now, Franklin, don't go getting yourself all riled up again. You're going to ruin everybody's afternoon."

She nodded at the two men in suits who were sitting on a nearby picnic table.

"Don't fret it, ma'am," one of them said. "There's a man who obviously loves his country."

Franklin looked their way, squinting as he sized them up, and smiled. "I sure do. I'm a real American, not like those people that moved in across the street from us. They don't even look American. They're brown or something. And their food smells funny."

"Well, Franklin," Laureen chimed in, "it would certainly make your life easier if everyone agreed with you. Maybe after a time, they will. That would be nice."

"That would be nice," one of the suits agreed as he sidled up next to Laureen. "Can I help you with anything?"

"No," she replied. "I've got this covered. Would you like a cool drink?"

"No, thank you, Ms. Dawber."

"Do we know each other?" asked Laureen.

"I'm sorry. Please let us introduce ourselves. I'm Mark Plagget and this is my associate Phillip Flynn." He handed Laureen a business card stating that he was a talent coordinator for America's News Now.

Laureen looked up at him and smiled. "So you're here to talk to Franklin about America?"

"No, Ms. Dawber," he said with a smile. "We're actually here to talk to you."

*   *   *

Excerpt from *Maxwell's Guide to Heaven and Hell*, page 103:

You will find many types of people in Heaven and Hell from all areas of the globe and all eras in time.

Communication will be possible regardless of one's own language.

Please be aware that there are many cultural differences between peoples. We ask that you respect these differences.

As many people from the past have gained some sort of fame or notoriety, you are also requested to respect their privacy. Rather than approach them yourself, you'll want to arrange for a "Meet and Greet" which may be set up through Smile Patrol representatives.

Oscar Wilde was a twerp. Berry thought he was just so full of himself and seemed more interested in being "on" all the time instead of giving any useful advice or direction. Rather than being entertaining or droll, it was just annoying.

Berry was looking for answers. Thinking he could use the Smile Patrol's resources to hook him up with some of the finest minds in history to set him on the right path, the trip was turning out to be less than what he expected.

It all started when Lucratelli pulled up in front of Berry's place in an empty shuttle.

"Are you Beryl?"

"They call me Berry."

"They call me Lucratelli. Hop in," he'd said with a smile.

"Where'd you get this?" Berry asked.

"I called in a favor at Transportation. The guy owed me big time."

"Should I ask why?"

"Believe me, you don't want to know."

The trip started well but after hours of traveling and interviews Berry was no closer to a plan than he was when he started. At least he and Lucratelli were getting along well considering the only things they had in common were that they were both from New York and they were both dead.

The fact that answers to Berry's dilemma weren't forthcoming just seemed to reinforce his resolve: to let the living people on Earth know that there was more to their existence than they would have thought possible.

Berry gazed out the window and watched the scenery roll by. Heaven amazed him. Small towns, cities, countryside. On one particular street he was amazed to see people sunbathing on lounge chairs in their yard while, another house away, children built a snowman. It rained on one side of the street while the sun shone on the other. Businesspeople in suits walked briskly with briefcases in hand. Cowboys rode their horses and tipped their hats to the women they met along the way. Aborigines held a bar-b-que. Indian tribes danced. Murals were being painted on the sides of skyscrapers. People drank in sidewalk cafes as Grand Prix cars raced down the street. Knights in armor walked alongside geishas. Yachts moved gracefully down a river as Eskimos paddled kayaks nearby. Ninjas played tennis. Vikings mowed the lawn. It was an amazing display of history and cultures that seemed to be common to every street and thoroughfare. Lucratelli was unfazed; Berry was fascinated. Less fascinating, however, were the conversations with the famous and infamous people he had set out to see.

A little while into their visit with Thomas Edison, the inventor reiterated that "the value of an idea lies in the using of it." Berry liked Edison immensely and took that to heart. He knew distributing the book was The Great Idea of his life—well, his death. He just needed to put all his ducks in a row.

The common thread between all the products Berry ever marketed on TV was the fact that he actually believed that people needed those fairly worthless things. To him, Crazy Hair Curls, Microwave Magic, Supreme Spatula, and Pet Gloves were more than a way of making a living. He sincerely thought he was bettering the lives of the people who bought them.

He was thrilled about the prospect of introducing the world to *Maxwell's Guide to Heaven and Hell*, but he didn't want to go off half-cocked. No, this would definitely take some real knowledge of how things worked in Heaven. He was also a very honest person. He knew that although he held a copy of the most significant and important product he'd ever sold or would ever sell, he didn't legally have the rights to the book. He would have to acquire them somehow. What better way to bring hope, optimism, and understanding to the public than to release this amazing tome on Earth?

He would also have to ensure that he could somehow return to the living world once he acquired the rights so he could do a bang-up job of promoting and marketing the book. That's why he sought out a variety of personalities, all with different areas of expertise.

Not wanting to reveal his plan, Berry told them he was producing a documentary on notable residents of Heaven. No one pressed him for details, but no one provided too much information either.

It started with Solomon. Berry was seeking wisdom, but their encounter reminded Berry of trying to get an answer from a rabbi. Every question was answered with a story or parable.

"It reminds me of the…"

Never mind.

Philosophers were grating on Berry's nerves, too. Plato, Socrates, Nietzsche, Camus all looked at the realm of possibilities but had no distinct answers.

Berry then moved on to marketing legends, great salespeople, and even writers for ideas about marketing books. Hemingway was no help. He was a drunk who was frustrated that he couldn't have a "real" drink. Lucratelli told him he'd have to get back to him on that. A nice enough host, Hemingway nonetheless had nothing useful to offer Berry other than a rundown of his favorite baits and fishing haunts.

Berry learned more about the physics of Heaven from Isaac Newton on the golf course than he did from Albert Einstein who constantly mooned over Marilyn Monroe and insisted on playing the violin...endlessly.

P.T. Barnum had some useful marketing tips, but he had no respect for the people he cheated and duped. That went against the grain for Berry.

Meeting with many of the luminaries from the past was proving to be a fairly worthless and frustrating experience.

"I thought Heaven was supposed to make a person happy," Berry lamented.

"Doesn't work like that, doc," Lucratelli told him. "Happiness comes from within. It's all up to you."

They were resting on a couple of beach loungers next to Lucratelli's still. Lucratelli offered Berry a glass of his finest hooch. Berry had his on the rocks. Lucratelli preferred it neat.

"Not really too bad, I have to say," Berry offered.

"Thanks. I think within a batch or two I should really be cookin' with gas. Real killer-diller. Know what I mean? Oh, and thanks for taking the time to let me talk to some of those chemists."

"Hopefully it was instructive."

"I think so. We'll see. So, pardon me for getting personal, but what the hell were we doing? What exactly were you looking to find?"

"You didn't buy the documentary story?" Berry asked.

"Well, doc, you don't exactly strike me as the Cecil B. DeMille type. No offense."

"Thanks. None taken."

They sat and sipped.

"So what's this caper all about?" Lucratelli asked.

Berry thought for a moment then reached into his pocket and pulled out his copy of *Maxwell's Guide to Heaven and Hell*.

"It's all about this."

"What about it?"

"I want to take it back."

"Back?"

"Back."

"Back where?"

"To Earth. The world. To the living."

Lucratelli thought about that for a moment then broke out into a fit of laughter.

"It's possible, right?" Berry asked. "People have gone back, right?"

"You're serious?"

"Absolutely."

"Yeah, doc, people have gone back. With a sanction and without. Heck, you met Marvin Miller? He went back."

"Marvin did? How? What for?"

"I can't really divulge any specifics. Smile Patrol ethics, you know?" Lucratelli looked around. He knew they were alone, but you couldn't be too careful. There might be a stray critter around. "He did it to help a friend out. To save his life. Got into a lot of trouble for it, too."

"It doesn't appear to have hurt him any," Berry mentioned. "Didn't they tell you why we've been seeing all these people?"

"Nah. Just another assignment to me. But now you've got me interested."

Berry pressed him. "How interested?"

"Maybe interested enough to help you out."

"Why would you do that? I wouldn't want to get you in any hot water."

"Fat chance of that. I'm on the Smile Patrol. They give us a lot of leeway. But, besides that, I can get things done when I want to. Let's just say things are getting a little routine around here. I could stand a change of pace, a little adventure."

"So, if we were going to do this, we'd need a way to get back to Earth."

"That's easily done...for me, anyway."

"Somehow I don't doubt that." Berry motioned with the book. "Who's in charge of this thing? Who owns the rights? Who puts it together? Who can I pitch this idea to?"

"Well, doc, we'd have to go to Maxwell," Lucratelli told him.

"Maxwell? Would that be a person or a place?"

"That would be both."

4

Nana rounded the corner to find Cindy Jenkins blow drying Laureen's hair.

"You look totally different," she said with amazement.

Laureen could see that her mother's lips were moving but couldn't make out a thing she said over the high-pitched whine of the dryer. She motioned to Cindy to switch it off.

"What?"

"You look so different," Nana repeated.

"So do you!" The two of them started giggling like two school girls getting away with something naughty.

"I can't believe one of my clients is going to be on the TV," Cindy was googly-eyed, beside herself with pride and admiration.

"I know," Nana said. "Ain't it a hoot?" And they all three started laughing again. Luke and Noah, forced to suffer the embarrassing fate of waiting for their mother and grandmother in the salon, had been immersed in their handheld video games. They rolled their eyes at each other and went back to MetroBlaster.

Laureen was scheduled for her first appearance on America's News Now. Its nightly opinion show *Get Real with Ric Arno* interviewed people from all over the country for their take on the day's news. On any given night the show's guests were a mix of the usual network commentators, a politician or two, an expert in one field or another, and selected people from the general public who were supposed to represent the viewing audience's opinions. In actuality, they were all selected to further the network's right-wing agenda. Laureen was one of the latter. Her segment would be shot and fed to the network in New York from their Miami affiliate station.

In order to look her best, Laureen decided to make an appointment at the Makeover Manor ("You'll Leave Here A Totally Different Person!") where they cut, restyled, and colored her hair, applied her makeup, and helped her choose an outfit to wear. Since the network was footing the bill and things were good financially due to increasing sales of admission tickets, T-shirts, and replicas of Miracle Butter, Laureen decided to treat her mom as well.

"I would never have the courage to go on TV," Cindy confessed, busying herself with Laureen's hair.

"I didn't think I would either," Laureen admitted. "But I prayed on it and prayed on it and chose to go wherever the Lord led me."

"Amen to that," commented Cindy.

"Yeah," Nana chimed in laughing again, "and that big fat talent fee they're paying had absolutely nothing to do with it at all."

With that, they all started laughing again, causing Noah and Luke to turn up the volume on their gaming devices.

*   *   *

Bree waved Lucratelli into her office. He sauntered in, sat down, and promptly stretched his legs out on top of her desk. He looked very relaxed. It was, he thought, an effective ploy.

Bree looked up and nodded her head in the general direction of his ankles. Lucratelli immediately dropped his feet and sat upright.

"So what's going on?" Bree asked.

"Nothin' much, boss."

Bree stared at him, unconvinced.

"We spent some time traveling around. He wanted the lowdown from a bunch of geezers."

"And?" she asked.

"And…that's it. They weren't much help, I guess. Seemed like a big waste of time to me, but who am I to say?"

"What was he looking to find out?"

"No idea."

"So are you done?"

"Above my pay grade, boss. That's up to you. I think he does want to see some more people."

Lucratelli decided to keep Berry's request to find the creator of *Maxwell's Guide to Heaven and Hell* well under Bree's radar. He felt a bead of sweat run down his back but kept his smile plastered on. He didn't like lying to her or anyone else for that matter. For one thing, he respected her. For another, she was no slouch. Through her activism, Bree had changed the way things were done in Heaven. Her reward was this position as head of the Smile Patrol and though she didn't especially relish her position as an administrator, she was a real rebel, and Smile Patrol people knew how to not just bend the rules but break them when necessary. And she, like Lucratelli, had a way of getting things done.

And finding things out.

*   *   *

There is nothing like a live show to get the adrenaline going. The crew in ANN's New York Control Room Two, studio, and remote locations across the country were pros. They did the show every night, but there was always a heightened awareness just before showtime that THIS IS IT. That no matter what happened, it was live. There was no fixing it in post-production.

It was rare that everything came off without a hitch. It might be a misspelled graphic, a roll-in that had no audio, talent that didn't hear a cue through their earpiece, anything. The sign of a really good crew, an experienced one, was finding the problem and fixing it. Fast.

The day was spent preparing. Packages were edited, scripts were written, name titles and other graphics were composed and saved, teases and stingers were prerecorded, and the "money reel" of commercials was compiled. The tasks seemed almost endless.

Satellite feeds were coming through, tapes and digital playback machines were cued, and the control room monitors—dozens of them—were the brightest things in the dimly lit control room. Almost everyone wore headsets and at seven fifty-nine and fifty seconds they could hear the countdown to air.

"Ready to roll and track A," said Peter, the show's director. He watched his on-air monitor as the promo ran for ANN's nightly line up. Master Control let him know that he would be hot in just a second. Peter checked to make sure his technical director had the board in black so that the transition to this control room would be seamless. He glanced at the clock.

"Have a good show, everybody. Have fun. Don't fuck up. And three...two...roll A. Take and track A," Peter snapped.

The show open began with an extravaganza of music, 3-D graphics, and video that started *Get Real with Ric Arno* every Monday through Friday at 8:00 pm. The package was put together by a team of freelancers who created what they thought was the perfect blend of action, sound, and color that created a sense of excitement and immediacy. For this, they were paid an exorbitant sum of money. But amortized over the number of times it had been used, the network was able to justify the expense.

Peter had directed this show for the past two years. The crew felt comfortable with him and vice versa. He wasn't a screamer. He stayed even-keeled no matter what, believing that a calm director meant a calm crew. No sense in a tirade that would get someone flustered. No one needed to be unfocused on a live show. One weak link could blow the whole thing.

"Ten seconds to the tease," an assistant director chimed in.

The show's open was a doughnut. There was a thirty second hole twenty seconds in that highlighted what the viewers could expect on this particular episode. The tease had taken hours to prepare and was cued up and ready to roll.

"Thanks…standby D…and roll and track D. Effect to D."

The technical director had preset a digital effect to transition from the open to the tease. As the tease ran, he hit a button that would reverse the effect to return to the remainder of the open.

"Five left to the tease," the A.D. chimed in again.

"Okay, standby A. And…effect to A." With five seconds left in the open, a full screen show title trailed out longer than necessary, just in case pad was needed for any reason.

"Standby camera one…ready to cue Ric. And…mike, and cue Ric. Effect to camera one. And one, give me a slow push in to Ric."

The camera person did just that.

"Very nice, one. Font him."

The graphics operator already had Ric Arno's name displayed on a preview monitor. The technical director effected a slide so that the name appeared to coast in from the left side of the screen and settle superimposed over the lower third of the screen. It sat there as Peter read it to himself twice, just to make sure the viewers had time to register who they were watching.

"And…lose the font."

The name title slid off the screen.

"So far so good," Peter remarked to no one in particular.

Laureen Dawber wasn't privy to any of this. She was over a thousand miles away from Control Room Two in a studio in Miami where a hair and make-up person applied powder to the shiny spots on her face. A microphone was clipped to her blouse, the cord running under her shirt and out at the waist of her pants. She had twenty minutes before her segment came up but her heart was already pounding. Her own adrenaline levels were up, like she was all hopped up on three cups of coffee which, in fact, she was.

*   *   *

"Okay. What is it?" Marvin asked.

"What's what?"

"Whatever's bothering you."

"What makes you think anything's bothering me?" Bree feigned calmness.

"I don't know. It could be the way you're stabbing the pizza instead of slicing it?"

Bree stopped lacerating the homemade pie, took a deep breath, and then sliced it into eight even triangles. The salad was already tossed with her Italian dressing. It was Marvin's favorite. She placed a slice on each of their plates.

"So, how was your day?" she inquired.

"Not bad. Well, boring really. I was thinking—"

"They're up to something," she blurted out.

"I'm fine. How are you?" Marvin already knew it was a lost cause.

"They think they can put one over on me? Well, they're certainly mistaken. I wouldn't—"

"Who are we talking about?" Marvin asked as he chewed.

106

"Lucratelli," she told him.

"I'm hardly surprised," Marvin said between bites.

"And that Berry Driscoll. The one you played golf with."

"Oh, yeah. Nice guy actually. He's—"

"Documentary, my foot. It's the book, I know it."

"The book?"

"*The Guide*. Maxwell's. I know that's it."

"And how would you know that? Spies?" Marvin was more interested in the salad.

"Cats."

"Oh! The A-Team." It would be cats. Marvin knew about witches and their familiars. Cats played a major role in witchcraft history. And Bree certainly wouldn't be opposed to utilizing every trick in her bag if need be. Marvin opened the pizza box and helped himself to another slice. "And what would he—they—be doing with *The Guide*?"

"Taking it back! To Earth."

That got Marvin's full attention.

"Oh, come on. Going back? He just got here."

"That didn't stop you."

Always to the point, Bree. "I had a life to save. You know that. Besides, I was too stupid to know better. Well, not to worry. He has no visa."

"Neither did you. He's going to get back one way or another. And he's going to take the book with him."

"So, what? Everybody has one."

"Here, not there."

"So, stop him," he suggested.

"I don't know. What if that's the one thing that really makes him happy? I mean, that's our whole purpose on the Smile Patrol, isn't it? To fulfill dreams?"

"Then I'll stop him. You don't really know what he's up to. There's a difference between dreams and schemes, you know."

"Is there? Really?" she asked. "Look, I don't want you to get involved. And don't tell anyone else. This is between you and me. I mean, on the one hand, I have a responsibility to the Organization, don't I? I'm an administrator after all."

"Yeah, a grown up," Marvin said, teasingly.

"Stop it. Be serious. On the other hand, I've dedicated my whole being to making sure people can fulfill themselves here in Heaven. I don't know what to do." She took to absentmindedly stabbing the pizza again.

"I can see that," Marvin told her. "So, what do you think he'd do if he did manage to go back? How does the book figure in to it?"

"I don't know yet."

"You don't know? What's the matter? The cats are slacking off?"

She shot him a look. *At times she has no sense of humor*, Marvin thought.

*　　　　　　*　　　　　　*

Excerpt from *Maxwell's Guide to Heaven and Hell*, page 3:

One of the decisions you must make relates to housing. Dwellings are available for individuals, couples, and families. These are provided free of charge, naturally.

Where you live may be determined by personal preference. It is suggested that you live close to your place of work so as not to tax our transport systems.

Rural, urban, suburban, wilderness; whatever you choose will be made available for you. A representative from the Department of Housing will assist you with all arrangements.

Many communities are based on common interests or family ties. There are artist's colonies, musician enclaves, etc. There are also communities based upon vocation or avocation.

In some cases, people choose to live in entire communities made up of relatives or ancestors from all periods of time. To some people, this is most desirable. To others it is like the ultimate holiday dinner gone wrong.

Lucratelli was on the case.

He stared at the vidscreen that sat on the desk in an alcove in his house intent on learning anything he could about Maxwell that might help Berry. Cab Calloway's "Jumpin' Jive" played in the background. As he sat scanning information, his feet had a life of their own and danced the Lindy along with the music.

He had tried *The Guide*, but when he thought of Maxwell and opened the book it only referred him to sections that warned him about acquiring information surreptitiously. Great. Reprimanded by a book.

The vidscreen helped, giving him some background on the town of Maxwell and its heritage of *The Guide* being compiled there. Contributors from all over Heaven had submitted facts, articles, and suggestions.

Funny, Lucratelli thought. *Copy from one person and it's plagiarism. Borrow from many and it's research.*

Submissions for the book apparently had been evaluated for accuracy, interest level, and usefulness and those that made the grade were incorporated into the book by members of the Maxwell family. Although the handbook was generally considered to have been published by Heaven's Communications Department, it was actually the Maxwell clan. Generations of them.

For the Maxwell clan in the town of the same name, it was a labor of love. Everyone who lived there was a relative and they all knew each other. Sort of like Kentucky. And, boy, was it hell for the postal workers sorting mail when everyone had the same last name.

Almost all of the Maxwells were involved with the book in one way or another: writing, editing, production, distribution, and even translations. It was a service the family had willfully performed for as long as anyone could remember.

Cyrus Maxwell was the editor-in-chief. Originally from England, he had immigrated to the United States and, until his death, worked as a professor at New York University. He wasn't the oldest or most experienced Maxwell to assume the editor's position, but for some reason his relatives thought he was ideally suited for it.

The song "St. James Infirmary" filled the room while Lucratelli searched for anything personal about this Cyrus Maxwell person: likes or dislikes, character flaws, conflicts with neighbors, relatives, friends, or coworkers both here in Heaven and on Earth. But, nothing. No skeletons in the closet.

He found connections related to Maxwell's teaching career at NYU, but Lucratelli waved them off. Other links offered him a glimpse into papers and essays written during Maxwell's tenure at the university, but he rejected those as well.

Lucratelli was about to move on when he caught a thumbnail that grabbed his attention. He enlarged it and found it to be a publicity shot of Cyrus Maxwell's daughter Chelsea who owned and operated a public relations company based in New York.

There was far more information on her than on her father. Lucratelli buzzed through company pages, read her blogs, cruised social networking sites, picture postings, whatever he could find. And he was pretty resourceful.

Lucratelli had thought twice about being in cahoots with Berry. Sure, fun was fun, but was it worth losing everything? He was beginning to see the huge risk it would be messing with *The Guide* in any way, but staring at Chelsea Maxwell's picture, he felt a sense of growing resolve.

Lucratelli had some experience with women. Girls, really. Mainly bobbysoxers he knew from school and the neighborhood. And though he'd had some experience, he certainly didn't consider himself a real wolf.

He'd lost his virginity at fourteen to a woman who lived across the street. She was a divorcée who'd get undressed in front of her open window. Lucratelli spent many evenings staring out his bedroom window hoping for a glimpse. It occasionally paid off and when he delivered a bottle she'd ordered from his father's bar, he was invited in. She was already half in the bag and empty bottles and full ashtrays littered her apartment. Up close, she was frowzier than he'd imagined, but that just added to the forbidden aspect of being with an older woman.

During the war, Lucratelli dallied with a few of the locals, but, fun as they were, he found them too countrified or something. Lonely? Desperate? They were victims of the war who just craved some connection, some solace. His time with them made him feel guilty and uneasy.

He tended to like city girls. Dames who were smart and cracked wise. They were certainly few and far between. It wasn't often he felt himself get all doll crazy, but this one, this Chelsea Maxwell? She was a double doll and right up his alley.

Sure, he'd help Berry out.

For purely unselfish reasons, of course.

*   *   *

Laureen Dawber was never very political. The opinions she had regarding social issues were pretty much determined for her by the church and reinforced by the news media she actually paid attention to...mainly America's News Now and the right-wing radio talk shows. She was against abortion under any circumstances, believed the government was too intrusive in the lives of its citizens, thought we were all taxed unnecessarily, considered marriage to be a sacred union between one man and one woman, and supported deregulation for banks and corporations.

The producers at Ric Arno's show were fully aware of her political bent, of course. They had their own agenda and she fit nicely into it. Laureen was invited on the show specifically to comment on her church's recent move to eliminate all mention of evolution in the textbooks used at its schools and, by extension, the county's public schools as well.

"I'm not related to any monkey. If evolution was true, wouldn't we see those changes happening? Wouldn't apes be driving cars? Or using computers? Or hosting TV shows, Mr. Arno?" She was getting miffed, not used to being put on the spot.

"You know what you people do?" Laureen asked. "You start off a newscast or show by saying 'Good evening' and then you proceed to tell us why it isn't so good after all. We're getting tired of it. The media needs to start telling people about what *really* matters. Like God and country and family values. The things people care about."

Mark Plagget and Phil Flynn who had recruited Laureen watched the live feed with Robert Maggert and laughed their asses off. "Pretty feisty, isn't she?" Maggert asked. Flynn was busily checking tweets on his laptop. They knew from the instant feedback that they had a winner on their hands. Laureen was attractive, outspoken, and not easily intimidated. She would make a nice addition to the ANN family. Back in Miami, Arno was pressing the issue.

"Scientists tell us, Ms. Dawber, that changes and mutations happen over millions of years and that they are not evident through casual observation."

"Impossible," Laureen stated. "According to the Bible, the Lord created the world only about four thousand years ago."

"That's contrary to scientists who tell us that radiocarbon dating evidence puts the Earth's age at about four and a half billion years," Arno told her. Personally, he agreed with what she was saying but went along with his network's mandate to try to appear balanced and fair. Anyone watching, however, knew it wasn't.

Laureen thought for a second. "Then God gave the Earth the impression of age. He made things look older and seem older than they really are. But they're not."

"So you have no problem with your children's school teaching Creationism exclusively?"

"Not at all; evolution's just a theory," Laureen said.

"And that's your belief?"

"It's in the Bible. I believe in God and His word. Simple. If it's in the Bible, I believe it."

And she did, too.

*   *   *

The picture on the wall was skewed slightly to the left. Walking down the hallway to his study, Cyrus Maxwell stopped to adjust it. He tilted it to the right, then left, then right again, uttered a soft, "Oh dear," and repeated the whole process until he felt comfortable with the photograph's positioning. He stopped once more in the hallway to pick up a small clump of dog hair on the floor. Chloe was a good dog and he loved her dearly, but she did shed an awful lot. He sometimes jokingly thought that he might make a pillow out of all the hair he picked up. The stray clump was deposited in the wastepaper basket next to Cyrus's desk.

The room was paneled in dark wood. It contained a very old roll top desk with an expansive work surface which, despite its size, was cluttered with a workstation, books, legal pads, notes, and various Post-Its and reminders. The room also held a leather loveseat, two comfy chairs, a marble globe of the Earth, bookshelves filled with leather bound volumes on every subject that could hold the interest of a middle-aged man, and a number of paintings and photographs, mainly of family members.

Cyrus spent exactly seven hours a day in this room—by choice—compiling material for *Maxwell's Guide to Heaven and Hell*. It was an on-going process as information constantly streamed in electronically, by mail, and even by word of mouth. The editing was something Cyrus had done since arriving in Heaven a few years ago and while he found the work daunting, it was also immensely satisfying, all things considered. As a collaborative Maxwell clan effort, he would never feel the sense of accomplishment he might have felt completing a book of his own. Perhaps someday, but not with this project. It was ongoing and would literally never be done.

Living in a town in Heaven populated only by his relatives was a good thing to Cyrus. He led a very comfortable life with his family while he lived on Earth and outside of now living alone little had changed since his death. Other than actually dying, of course.

His life after death was filled with familiar habits. He found comfort in routine. He loved his house and enjoyed puttering around on Saturdays and gardening each Sunday. He worked on *The Guide* Monday through Friday and visited or hosted family whenever possible. He was happy. Content. Satisfied.

He did miss his wife, however. She had become caught up in the practice of donating Essence before it was discovered that it was addictive. She got carried away. Each time she went to a Donation Center she came back a little less whole and a little more transparent. Towards the end it was like living with a ghost; Cyrus could actually see right through her. Eventually she, like others before her, donated herself right out of existence.

Cyrus found solace in the close proximity of the family members that populated the town of Maxwell. With the exception of his daughter Chelsea who was still alive, Cyrus was near the people he cared about the most and he worked at a job that completely satisfied him. Life—rather, the afterlife—was good.

He woke every morning at precisely six thirty, walked Chloe the dog, and then sat on the redwood deck attached to the rear of his house enjoying a coffee—cream, no sugar—and read the newspapers. Heaven was so vast and populous that it took a while to keep up on things. At precisely eight in the morning, he'd pour himself a second cup, wash out the coffeemaker, and make his way into the study where he would spend the next seven hours of his day. He rarely finished his second cup of coffee. After work, he'd take Chloe for her afternoon walk and then garden or do repairs around the house. Perhaps he'd work in the woodshop in the garage. Lately he was partial to birdhouses. He ate dinner at exactly seven, did the dishes, and returned to the deck to smoke his one cigar of the day, a ritual he adored. He'd then read or watch TV or a movie until it was time to walk Chloe again. Bedtime was ten thirty every weeknight, eleven on weekends. This was his routine every day, week, and month since he had passed on and begun his afterlife in Heaven. He was an unassuming, gentle man who enjoyed a peaceful existence with a minimal amount of stress.

Until the knock at his door.

5

The band was named 99% Total Devastation. They weren't signed to a major record label, opting instead to go independent and release their first CD, *Bunker Buster*, on their own. They sold an impressive one hundred thousand units in two weeks.

Chelsea met them when they all attended college together and remained friendly with the boys in the band over the years. She was thrilled when they asked her to help promote their upcoming second release, *Cruise Missile Babes*.

The album's debut was at a release party in a Greenwich Village nightclub. Chelsea had arranged for radio and magazine interviews prior to the show. Thanks to her talent for social and guerrilla marketing, ticket sales were brisk and the club was packed.

And the cookies were a hit.

One of Chelsea's ideas was to offer the crowd Misfortune Cookies. Just like Chinese fortune cookies, these were cellophane-wrapped folds, each containing a small slip of paper. Instead of inspiring and positive messages, however, these cookies played up the album's theme with negative missives.

They were fun to write and Chelsea and the band were getting a kick out of the way the crowd of club kids and media types reacted to the messages. A young woman with purple and orange hair opened a cookie that read, "You're doomed." The band's bass player grabbed one that warned, "Duck for cover." A Goth couple drew, "All is lost" and was thrilled by it. A record executive courting the band received, "There is no silver lining." His assistant got, "Sometimes all that glitters is just glitter." "The sky IS falling" went to one of the bartenders. A group of students from a nearby university tore open a couple cookies that said, "Love is NOT all you need" and "The best things in life are NOT free." Fraternity brothers drew, "Your personality is no asset," "Your future plans are worthless," and "Looks ARE everything—a fact that doesn't look promising for you." The lead singer's parents were there and his mother broke open a cookie to find, "You shouldn't breed." She laughed and to no one in particular said, "Too late."

Despite the general tenor of the band, album names, and the Misfortune Cookie messages, the lads in the band were good-natured and fun to be around. Chelsea always enjoyed the time she spent with them and this night was no different.

"Nice treads," the drummer told her, looking at her sneakers. "How do you keep them so clean?"

"I don't walk much," she replied with a smile from her wheelchair.

"Oh, sorry. Wasn't thinking."

"It's okay. Not your fault. The chair, I mean."

"We're on soon. Gotta go."

"Okay. Um…break a leg!" Chelsea called after him. He stopped and turned to reply with a "You, too," but thought better of it. "My chair would have to have pin striping and flames painted on the side," he told her instead.

"Fuzzy dice?" she asked.

"And mag wheels!"

*　　　　　　　*　　　　　　　*

Driving into the town of Maxwell, Berry and Lucratelli passed the Maxwell Hotel, Hotel Maxwell, the Maxwell Inn, Maxwell Suites, and Motel Maxwell. There was a Maxwell's Restaurant, Mama Maxwell's, Maxwell's Bar-B-Que, Maxwell Steakhouse, and MaxBurgers. They saw the Maxwell Movie Palace, Maxwell MegaPlex, Cinema Maxwell, and a Maxwell Art Theatre. The town also boasted a Maxwell Sporting Goods, Maxwell Mall, and a Maxwell Pharmacy. Being Heaven, there was no need for medicine at the drugstore but it was a great place to buy razors, soap, and sit at the lunch counter and order a Maxwell Malt made by Maude Maxwell.

There was also a Tavern 28. That name baffled Berry and Lucratelli until they learned it was owned by twenty-eight generations of Maxwells. The current proprietor, Edward Maxwell, provided them with directions to the house of his third cousin, Cyrus Maxwell. Berry and Lucratelli headed down Maxwell Avenue, took a right at Maxwell Street, a left on Maxwell Court, and finally arrived at their destination: 2122 Maxwell Lane.

Hearing a knock at his door, Cyrus Maxwell opened it to see two men he didn't recognize. One was older than the other, in his

120

fifties, balding, and dressed in a comfortable-looking pullover, sports coat, and jeans. The younger man appeared to be in his twenties and wore a white T-shirt visible under an open, loose-fitting Hawaiian shirt and billowy pleated trousers.

"Cyrus Maxwell?" Berry inquired.

"This is highly unusual," replied Cyrus, a comment more to himself than for the two men addressing him, both of whom detected an English accent.

"Unusual to have visitors?" Lucratelli asked, puffing on a cigar.

"Visitors I don't know. Especially at this time of night."

"It's only seven thirty," Lucratelli remarked, looking at his Timex.

"May we come in?" asked Berry.

"I hardly think so."

Lucratelli took another couple puffs, blowing the smoke nonchalantly in Cyrus's direction.

"Cuban?" Cyrus asked.

"No, I'm Italian."

"Your cigar...is it Cuban?"

"Yes." Lucratelli took out the other three he had stashed in his shirt pocket. "I have them rolled for me by an old friend, Raul Montoya. He was one of the best in Havana."

"I was just about to enjoy a smoke of my own on the back deck," Cyrus mumbled, obviously conflicted.

"Well, we won't disturb you then. We'll drop by another time. Always nice to meet a man who can appreciate a good cigar."

Lucratelli and Berry turned to leave. Cyrus didn't close the door.

"What did you want to see me about?" Cyrus asked, softening and curious.

Both Berry and Lucratelli took a deep breath, grinned to each other, and turned back towards Cyrus.

"*Maxwell's Guide*," Berry told him, very grateful that Lucratelli had remembered to bring the cigars.

"Well, you should have inquired at Communications or Public Relations or somewhere. Oh dear. I might be able to help, of course. Perhaps—"

"Perhaps over a smoke?" Lucratelli offered.

"Oh, I wouldn't want to presume…"

"Nonsense," Berry said. "No trouble at all. Our pleasure."

Berry turned to Lucratelli, smiling.

*   *   *

The rooms were filled with unpacked boxes. The visitation fees, shirt sales, and TV appearances were changing their lives and Laureen was finally able to move from her trailer into a house she was renting for the four of them.

It was on a quiet street in Fort Lauderdale, not far from the city's upscale shopping and dining mecca, Las Olas Boulevard. It was a good-sized cottage with a nice backyard dominated by a huge mango tree. The fruit fell all over the yard and the boys were busy every afternoon picking the mangos up before they rotted and mice got to them. Laureen and Nana made mango salsa, mango chutney, and all sorts of delicacies, but there was still more of the fruit than they knew what to do with and they usually left a plastic bin on the street with a "Free Mangos" sign so neighbors and passersby could help themselves.

There was a small swimming pool in the back yard and a basketball net in the driveway. Between those and mango patrol, Laureen's boys had plenty to keep themselves occupied.

The area was called Victoria Park. Close to downtown and just a bike ride to the beach, it was a lovely neighborhood that had changed a lot over the years. Once made up of small, modest houses, there was now an abundance of renovated places. Houses that had sold for twenty or thirty thousand were now listed in the three to four hundred thousand dollar range. And, although Sailboat Bend, Rio Vista, and other areas of the city were up-and-coming, Victoria Park remained a desirable location. Mini-mansions sprang up on just about every block. Despite its gentrification, residents still saw the occasional male hooker plying his trade in the street and homeless people roaming the alleys between the main streets but less frequently now than years before. And there were plenty of families on the street with kids for the boys to play with.

"What are you two doing?" Laureen asked.

"Nothin'," Luke and Noah answered simultaneously.

"Why aren't you outside?"

"We're playing."

"How many times have I told you that you are not to play that video game?"

"Why not?"

"Shut that down. Now."

"But, Mom…"

"Don't 'Mom' me. Superheroes. False idols. That's not what I taught you. Why don't you do something useful? Like clean your rooms?"

The two boys just stared blankly at her.

"Okay, then go out back and pick up mangos before any critters get to them."

The boys perked up at the thought of wild animals in their own backyard and scrambled outside. Laureen sat down at the computer.

"Where do you want the linens?" Nana yelled from another room. "Bedroom closet or hallway closet?"

"The hall. That's the linen closet," Laureen answered sarcastically.

Nana walked in the room. "Sorry, it didn't have a sign on it. What are you up to?"

"Nothing much."

Nana peered over her daughter's shoulder. "You have got to be kidding me."

Laureen was logged on to Heavenly Hub, a Christian dating site.

"Can I have a little privacy?" Laureen asked.

"This is the way you think you'll find a man? Just put on a short skirt and go have a drink somewhere. You're a good-looking woman. Some stud'll pop up, believe me. You could use a little fun," Nana said with a bawdy laugh.

"Don't be crude, Ma. The Hub is worth a try. At least I'll know it's a man God intends me to meet."

"Sure. Know what? If I agreed with you, we'd both be wrong. And if a match from The Hub doesn't work out, then what? God was mistaken?"

"You have such little faith, Ma."

"And you, dear daughter, have such little sense."

       *   *   *

The three men sat on comfortable lawn furniture sipping brandy, albeit without the warm glow one would usually get from fine spirits, fine cigars, and perfect weather. Balmy breezes stirred the leaves on the trees in the yard. The conversation ranged from favorite cars and sports to movies and the men were relishing their time together. Cyrus had just told them about a trip to Kenya he had taken with his wife before their daughter was born.

"I only went hunting once," Berry admitted.

"Oh, I didn't do any hunting," Cyrus said. "At least not with a gun. I used my Pentax. I had a telephoto lens that let me get some amazing photographs."

"What did you hunt?" Lucratelli asked Berry.

"I was a kid, really," Berry began. "Maybe twelve. My dad had a friend who owned a farm and we went out there with a couple of .22's. Mine had a scope. We were looking for varmints. Crows, rabbits. Anything that might be getting to the crops.

"I wasn't a bad shot. I took a safety course and my dad and I would shoot at targets all day sometimes. At least it seemed that way. Got so I could hit records, 45s that my dad would toss in the air. If I missed, I told him the shot must have just passed through the hole in the center of the record.

"Anyway, we were walking along this dirt road and we spotted a rabbit about a hundred yards away. My dad tells me to go for it. I crouched down, took aim through the scope, held my breath, let it out slowly, and squeezed off a round. The rabbit fell over.

"We made our way up the road and when we reached the spot where the rabbit was, I could see it quivering on the ground. I hit it but hadn't killed it. I looked at my dad. He told me I had to finish it off. I could either shoot it or pound it with the stock of my rifle. Either way, I had to put it out of its misery.

"It seemed so cruel to me. It was one thing shooting at it from a distance. But seeing that rabbit there, helpless and suffering, that did me in. I broke down in tears and started apologizing to the animal. My dad finished it off as I walked away. He thought I was a wimp. But he never pressed me when I refused to ever go hunting with him again. He understood I just didn't have it in me."

They were quiet for a moment. Lucratelli broke the silence.

"During the war my squad was situated outside of a farmhouse in Italy. We were told to hold our position. After a while we realized there were only a couple of Germans inside. I guess they were using the place as a forward observation post."

"How did you know there were only a couple of them?" Berry asked.

"We watched them as they went to the outhouse. They'd zig and zag through the yard until they reached it and zigzag their way back. We were so bored we amused ourselves by taking a couple potshots at them as they scampered back and forth. This went on for a couple days. Then, by accident, I hit one of them. He lay there wounded and moaning. The guys in my squad kept telling me to put him out of his misery."

"But you resisted?" Berry asked.

"Not at all. It wasn't like your rabbit. I had no qualms about finishing him off. He wouldn't have even thought about it if the situation was reversed."

"Or so you tell yourself," Cyrus said.

"We once came across a field in Malmedy. Eighty American prisoners of war were massacred there. We found the bodies. These GIs thought the war was over for them. They thought they were going to be loaded into trucks to go to the concentration camps, but when the trucks pulled up, the Nazis lowered the gates revealing machine guns. They cut them down like animals. For no reason. From that time on we had no mercy. War is war. You do what you have to do."

"War wounds everyone," Cyrus said quietly. "Dying, that's another matter. We've all been there, done that. Dying doesn't hurt. Well, maybe just for a second, but for the most part death only hurts those who are left behind. Wives, parents, children, friends, lovers. It leaves psychic wounds that may never heal. Dying for a cause is one thing, but senseless killing or dying for no reason? That's shameful."

"I guess when God decides your time's up there's nothing you can do about it," Berry remarked.

"God has nothing to do with it. Things just happen," Cyrus said.

They puffed away in silence for a few moments.

"Interesting work you do, Cyrus," Berry remarked.

"Yes, yes, indeed. It's very satisfying," Cyrus nodded. "Enjoying the brandy?"

"Very much," Berry said.

"Excellent," Lucratelli admitted. It suddenly occurred to him that he was in the presence of a man who had a vast amount of knowledge and decided to press him on a subject close to his heart. "What is it that prevents us from getting a good drunk on anyway?"

Cyrus chuckled. "Actually, nothing. Of course, you have to take into consideration the fact that we are dead. That does put a damper on some things, you know?"

"You mean because we're not really here?" Lucratelli asked.

"Well, my friend, we are certainly here."

"Then what is it?" Lucratelli pressed on. "Backwards atoms or something?"

"Well, we are here," Cyrus said. "You can't think of things as they were in life. Here in Heaven we can eat, but we never gain weight. We can travel great distances in the blink of an eye.

Regardless of the number of people—astronomical numbers really—it's never crowded. We can control our own weather. I don't think it's really a question of our being here. It's more *how* we're here. A question of cycles or rhythms, if you will. Match those and you might be onto something. You'll find a wealth of material in *The Guide*, if you know what to ask about, of course."

"Yes, *The Guide*," Berry said. "I've been meaning to ask you about that."

*   *   *

The club was loud, hot...sweaty. People were dressed in their finest club gear. There were Goths done up with black hair, clothing, and fingernails. There were a few long mohawks here and there. Psychobilly guys and gals showed off their tats and fifties looks. There were punks, emo kids, and people in business suits. The crowd ran the gamut. Chelsea, with her subdued Bettie Page pin-up look, fit right in.

She wasn't usually much of a drinker, but the music and atmosphere took over and she threw caution to the wind. Everything was going great. The band was received well, the Misfortune Cookies were a hit, and management was pleased with the turnout. Chelsea even got a new gig out of it: the club's owner wanted her to promote the special events they held from time to time. All was right with the world, and the Bay Breezes went down easily.

That was the case with the road manager as well except his drinks of choice were bourbons and beers. He hadn't been operating at full capacity when he and the crew had set things up before the show.

The flash pots, utilized to create a shower of fireworks-type displays, had been placed too close to the stage's decorations of flags from around the world, curtains, and posters. All of them were flammable.

During a highlight of the band's third set, the room was shaken by the sight and sound of the set's four urns spewing colorful pyro. Almost immediately the areas on both sides of the stage began to burn, flames reaching ever farther and higher.

At first, the crowd thought it was part of the show. Slowly, however, they realized that wasn't the case. People started screaming. Then, seemingly everyone started running for the doors.

At the front door, people pushed each other aside in a panic. Patrons fell and were stepped on, crushed downward by others trying to make their way outside. The front door became a choke point as the club filled with noxious smoke and fumes. The first people at the door made it out, others were blocked in the crush of bodies. No one seemed to make progress.

The back door was blocked by cases of beer and other supplies management had either forgotten to move or didn't think about until it was too late. Clubgoers who rushed to the back frantically pushed boxes out of the way, wasting precious time. When they finally were able to reach the rear exit, they found to their dismay that it was locked.

At first, Chelsea sat motionless in her wheelchair. Whether it was the alcohol haze or the sheer shock of the situation, she was rooted in place. She nervously fondled the locket dangling on the chain around her neck. When she did try to move, she couldn't make any headway in the room. Her chair was too bulky, debris was piling up on the floor, and people were blocking her way. Panicked partiers spun her around until she was dizzy and beginning to panic herself.

The band's drummer made his way towards Chelsea, but she never noticed him trying to help; he never made it. A group of people pushed past him, knocking him to the floor, unconscious.

The smoke in the club was thick. It was difficult to see. People crowded around and past Chelsea, yet she remained immobilized. Looking up, she prepared to face the inevitable. If this was the way she was to die, so be it. She thought of her life, how hard it was to cope with her disability, the lack of love she felt, how she missed her parents, how her business was just coming together, and all the things she still wanted to do. She thought that might be the last thought of many of the people surrounding her as they passed on: unfinished business.

Something in her refused to give up, though. Chelsea struggled one more time with her chair then thought it might be best to give up on it. Perhaps she could crawl to safety? The number of bodies on the floor deterred her from that.

There was such an intense din of screams and yelling that Chelsea never heard the faint "meow" near her. As she prepared to surrender to her fate and face her death with dignity, she bowed her head and took as deep a breath as the smoke would allow. Opening her eyes, she saw Zoey, the small calico, on the floor in front of her. Zoey emitted another soft "meow" and jumped into Chelsea's lap. Woozy from the heat, smoke, and fumes, Chelsea swooned and instinctively hugged Zoey close.

Whooosh!

The sounds were different. There were no acrid odors—just a faint wisp of cinnamon—and no heat. Chelsea came to and realized she was sitting in her wheelchair on a sidewalk about a block from the burning club. Firefighters were just arriving. Police cars screeched to a halt outside the club.

She didn't know how she made it out alive, not realizing that it was the small calico cat that saved her life by whooshing her out of the burning club just in time. Chelsea assumed that some human in the club had helped her escape while she was unconscious. She petted the small cat curled up on her lap, grateful that Zoey had made it out alive as well.

Chelsea unhooked the chain she wore around her neck and detached the little gold locket. She fastened it to Zoey's thin leather collar.

"You're a lucky little gal," Chelsea said gently. "Trailing me around the apartment is one thing, but you never should have followed me in to that nightclub, Zoey." Still in shock and woozy, none of the night's events were making much sense to her.

Zoey, on the other hand, was grateful that she could watch over her ward and be there when she was needed.

It was, after all, her job. And she was good at it.

6

Excerpt from *Maxwell's Guide to Heaven and Hell*, page 28:

Many of our Frequently Asked Questions have to do with why bad things happen.

The basic answer is because they do. There is no rhyme or reason. Bad things happen to good people all the time. And good things happen to people who may not be so nice. It's just the way of things. It's not intentional. Some people are lucky that way. They just scoot through life and nothing bad happens to them. But in the end, it's just a numbers game. Playing the odds. There are exceptions, of course, such as when God actually steps in and offers a little help, usually to answer unselfish prayers made on behalf of someone else.

Those instances are like the Lord's little course corrections.

Darkness fell as the three men chatted on the back deck of Maxwell's house. The cigars and brandy put them in a restful mood and the conversation stretched out longer than expected, but there was no rush. The weather was perfect and the company enjoyable.

"I have to commend you on the job you've done with *The Guide*," Berry told Cyrus. "I've found it to be most useful in the short time I've been here in Heaven." Berry was honest in his appraisal.

"Thank you," Cyrus replied. "It's a work in progress that my entire family is very proud of."

"The book is so informative. Almost intuitive. Does it have some form of artificial intelligence?" Berry asked, only semi-joking.

"Actual intelligence," Cyrus answered matter-of-factly.

"How does that work?"

"I couldn't tell you."

"Top secret?"

"No, nothing like that. I just don't know for the life of me how it is accomplished," Cyrus admitted. "I don't do any type of programming or anything. Just writing and editing. The book was operational long before I got involved. Fascinating, though, isn't it?"

"Without a doubt. And all-encompassing."

"Yes, we try."

"It must be nice to have all the answers."

"I don't. But the Lord certainly does."

"You've spent time with him?"

"On occasion."

Lucratelli, who had been staring at the stars thinking about cycles, rhythms, and rum, piped up. "What's his deal?" he asked.

"Deal?"

"Yeah. I haven't met him. I'm curious. Does He hear prayers? Does He answer them? What's on His mind these days?"

"I wouldn't presume to second guess what the Lord is—"

"But if you had to venture a guess?" Lucratelli pressed on. "I've been praying for an answer to this distilling thing for years. But batch after batch, I'm frustrated. You would think He might cut me a break instead of treating me like some galoot, ya know?"

"Try putting your requests through the proper channels like in a memo to a superior or through vidmail or a letter," Cyrus suggested.

"And they might get answered?" Lucratelli asked, thinking he was onto something here.

Cyrus smiled. "Well, probably not. He doesn't like to micromanage, so He doesn't get involved in every minute detail of each person's existence. Look at it from His perspective: Prayers are usually selfish. People pray to make more money or to get a better job or even to get the answer to some question they are certainly capable of figuring out on their own, like your distillery issues. Besides, He's so busy, it can be difficult talking to Him. And He knows He's always right, so there's no arguing with Him," Cyrus laughed. "It's very frustrating sometimes."

"I would imagine. So, the big question is: Why are we here?" Berry asked.

"Indeed, why *are* you two here exactly?" Cyrus asked.

"No, I mean, why did we live? What's the purpose of it all if we're just going to die and wind up here for eternity?"

"Training wheels, I think," Cyrus said.

"Training wheels?" Berry asked.

"So to speak."

"How so?"

"We are put in the world to grow as human beings. And we do grow, literally and figuratively, until we figure out what our place in the Universe might be, what would make us complete and happy. Gentlemen, as long or short as a lifetime may seem, we are all going to spend a very, very long time here in the afterlife, so it behooves us to learn how to exist individually and collectively before we get to Heaven or Hell."

"So, finding the key to one's happiness is crucial," Berry commented pensively.

"Indeed. Finding the answer during your lifetime on Earth will make the afterlife happier and more fulfilling in every way. It's up to us as individuals to learn to know ourselves. Every day is a new opportunity to reinvent ourselves or to find the key to what really makes us happy. It's the chance to change one's destiny.

"Now, not to be rude, but back to my question: Why are you here? The two of you. At my house?"

"The book," Lucratelli blurted out. Berry had intended to take a more indirect route.

"*The Guide?*" Cyrus asked.

"Yes," Berry answered. "I think everyone should have one."

"But everyone does have one," Cyrus said, somewhat confused.

"Yes, everyone in Heaven and Hell. But I mean everyone— including the living."

Cyrus took that in for a moment as he took another pull on his cigar.

"Quite impossible," Cyrus concluded.

"I don't think so," Berry said firmly.

"Oh dear," Cyrus added.

"Got any more brandy?" Lucratelli asked. "I have a feeling this is gonna be a long night."

*   *   *

Engineers had wired the golf course so that Satan could play a round any time he felt the urge, day or night. Days were usually reserved for invited guests, night rounds were for practice.

The Devil was playing what he considered a cheater's round: taking a shot and, if he didn't like it, dropping another ball and trying the shot again. It was something he would never do in a regular round with partners but he found it helped his game. The unlimited mulligans gave him a sense of what was right and wrong with his swing and built muscle memory for the good swings.

The eleventh hole was a dog-leg left. His drive had landed in the center of the fairway, just clearing the trees on the left that could have blocked his approach to the green. He was one hundred fifty-five yards to the hole, usually an easy approach shot for him, but he kept hitting left. On this day, his nine-iron was not his friend. He dropped ball after ball and repeated his mistake time and again. Finally, turning his right hand inward fractionally, he corrected the hook that was making this shot a living hell.

Sitting seven-under-par on his cheater's round and putting the green on eleven, he received the call. After he hung up, he slammed his putter in his bag and doubled back towards the clubhouse. Another round ruined on a perfectly beautiful night in Hell.

$*$ $*$ $*$

Laureen Dawber had a lot of people angry with her.

While browsing through the interest she was receiving on Heavenly Hub, she checked the new blog she had set up recently: *Mothers for Moral Decency*. Her original intention was to create a community of like-minded people who agreed with her religious and political views. Thanks to plugs during her TV appearances, she had accumulated a few thousand followers relatively quickly and the number was growing daily.

Everyday occurrences spurred her mission on.

She had recently taken her boys to a concert to see their favorite group, a trio of brothers who took the pop world by storm. But instead of getting into the festival spirit at the event, Laureen was appalled. The audience was mostly comprised of tween girls accompanied by at least one of their parents and wearing whorish outfits that literally made her blush. And their moms weren't any more conservative than the tweens.

What really got her, though, was the number of pentagrams worn around necks, emblazoned on T-shirts, dangling from earrings, even part of the stage graphics. Laureen could count the number of crosses she saw on one hand, but the signs of the Devil were abundant.

Going to the mall was no different. Little sluts walking around with arms full of shopping bags, overtly flirting with every boy in sight. She felt embarrassed for her sons, but they seemed to take it in stride, enjoying the attention from girls, sharing lewd comments, and giggling to each other. The video game store was chock full of violent games with sexual overtones. The movie theater showed films and trailers that were explicit. Even billboards they saw on the way home were suggestive.

Laureen had never considered herself to be a prude, but she felt enough was enough.

"Hell in a Handbasket" was the title of her first web posting, an essay condemning the lack of morals in today's society. Every day she posted another diatribe, and her following grew and grew.

But along with supporters who echoed Laureen's feelings, there were tons of e-mails from people who disagreed with her. She couldn't relate. Why was society so permissive? How could parents not protect their children from these evil influences? And why were her devout religious views considered so "out there" in this day and age?

Something had to be done. And she was just the person to do it.

*   *   *

Excerpt from *Maxwell's Guide to Heaven and Hell*, page 72:

Transport anywhere is fast, easy, and free. The one exception is transport back to Earth.

140

The ability to freely travel from Heaven to Earth is not impossible but is reserved solely for those with prior permissions and the correct visas.

Should you have the need to put in a travel application, please make an appointment with a representative from Administration.

Expect a waiting period of at least one year.

The Devil strode into Smile Patrol headquarters, bypassed the receptionist who wasn't thrilled about having to work late, and plunked himself down into a chair in front of Bree's desk. He waved his hand and the door slammed closed.

"Rough day? Lose your *Caddyshack* gopher club cover out on the course?" she asked.

"Very funny. I hate meetings. I especially hate after-hours meetings," he told her.

"So I've noticed. Look," Bree said seriously, leaning forward. "I've got a problem."

"I can see that," said Lucifer. "Maybe a stylist or a personal trainer…"

"Ha ha. This is serious. I think we've got a couple jumpers."

"Yeah, I know. Your guy. Luca—whatever his name is."

"Lucratelli."

"And that new arrival, the TV guy. Maybe even Cyrus Maxwell."

"You knew? How?"

"Nothing gets by me. Not for long, anyway. So, what's your problem?"

141

"I don't know what to do about it. On the one hand, I should probably put a stop to it before it goes too far. On the other hand, maybe I should let it go. Who am I to get in their way? It's their dream, you know? I'm here to ensure people's happiness, not crush it. What do you think?"

The Devil pointed to the sign in the office: Rules Broken Daily.

"Good credo," he said. "I live by it myself most of the time. Let me look into it. Maybe they'll give it up on their own, maybe not. If we think they need a little reigning in, we'll do something about it, but at least we'll be on top of it from the beginning. That way you can't take any heat for anything."

"I don't want to put this on you. I'm sure you have more than enough on your plate."

"No problemo. Glad to do it," Lucifer smiled.

"Hey, wait a minute," Bree said, suddenly suspicious of his intent. "You've got some kind of angle on this already, haven't you? You must know what's going on and what's going to happen."

"Aww, Bree. Do you trust me that little? Come on, we've worked together often enough for you to know I always have the best of intentions. Besides, it's too far out to make any sort of prediction."

"Too far out?" she asked.

"Like hurricanes on Earth. A week or more away and everybody's watching those cones for the projected path. They might know it's going to make landfall, but it's still too far away to know where or exactly when. Too many variables. Same with these guys. I'll just keep an eye on the cone for you."

"So, now you're a meteorologist. You are a real piece of work."

"Yes, so I've been told. Let's just say I like to know which way the wind's blowing. We'll leave it at that. Besides, I'm actually curious what those knuckleheads have on their collective minds. It could be a good thing. They might really stir the pot up. We could all use a little change around here. The same old, same old gets boring, know what I mean?"

And Bree certainly did.

*   *   *

"Who owns the rights to *The Guide*, Cyrus? You?" Berry asked.

"No," Cyrus answered. "The book belongs to everyone. Every resident here in the afterlife, that is."

"Would it still work back on Earth?" That was a pertinent question.

"There's no way of telling for sure, but, yes, I do believe it would. The book's functions are integral and not reliant on time or place."

"Good. That settles that. Cut and dried," Berry said.

"No, nothing is settled," Cyrus said, his rising, shaking voice betraying his growing anger. "That's not that. That's not anything. Dear me. It's not cut, and it's not dried. What you are intending is highly irregular. Probably immoral. Possibly illegal. And I won't be a party to it."

"Well, let me ask you a simple question, Cyrus. Why did you start working on the book in the first place?" Berry pressed.

"To help people, I suppose."

"Exactly. I got started in television originally to sell products. To make money. After a while, I made more money than I thought was possible."

"Money has no value here," Cyrus said impatiently.

"True. But, once I made my money my motives changed. I wanted to help people live better, easier lives. That's my motivation now. To make life better for people, *before* they get here. I want to make a difference. To change the world."

"Well, it would certainly change things," Cyrus admitted.

"Of course it would. Wouldn't you want to be a part of that?" Berry asked. "Look, you don't seem to me to be the kind of fellow who would leave all the comforts of home to go off on some frivolous adventure."

"I should say not," Cyrus agreed.

"But this is not a frivolous adventure at all. It's a world-changing opportunity."

Lucratelli had been quiet for a while, just taking it all in as an observer. He wasn't a traditional businessperson, but he did know how to get things done.

"What about your daughter?" he asked.

"What? My daughter? What does she have to do with this?"

"Nothing…yet." Lucratelli's research was finally paying off. "But, there she is, alone in the world, sitting in that wheelchair and wondering what will become of her. Sad, isn't it? You and your wife passed away and left her all alone. She'd probably like to meet someone."

"Like you?" Cyrus asked sarcastically.

"Maybe like me, or anyone. That's not the point. She's alone. Probably lonely. Maybe with no hope at all. Wouldn't you like to know that she could gain hope and a sense of purpose and destiny to her life by reading the book? That she would know that there is a Heaven and despite her hardships everything will work out for her in the afterlife? Don't you think that would give her great happiness and something to live for? Don't you want to provide that security for her?"

"And—by extension—all the people in the world?" Berry interjected. "The living would have a renewed sense of joy and purpose as well. They would know that God exists and that salvation is possible."

Lucratelli thought Berry was starting to sound like one of those tent revival preachers.

"Hallelujah!" he shouted.

Berry shot him a look and then redirected his attention back to Cyrus.

"Why toil away for eternity on a book that's only seen by people who are dead? You have it in your power to change the world! To give hope to the living!"

"And to your daughter," Lucratelli added.

"If you were to do this, how would you accomplish it?" Cyrus asked.

"Leave that to us," Lucratelli said confidently. "I have a certain knack for getting things done."

"I don't doubt that. You do seem the type."

"I'll take that as a compliment."

"I wouldn't if I were you."

"What about the fame? The glory? The notoriety?"

"What do you mean?" asked Cyrus.

"Think of how you'll be viewed by the media, the people," Lucratelli told him. "You'll be a celebrity of the highest order. Instant table at restaurants. Autograph seekers wherever you go. Limos. You'll have to beat the dames off with a stick."

"Listen," said Berry, leaning in towards Cyrus for effect. "You could change the world. Along the order of a Moses or Mohammed. You could be the next prophet. You could change the world. Change religion."

"Are you familiar with Seneca?" Cyrus asked.

"Sure, upstate New York. In the Finger Lakes," Lucratelli said between puffs on his cigar.

"Seneca was a Roman philosopher who once said, 'Religion is regarded by common people as true, by the wise as false, and by rulers as useful.' I have no desire to be the next prophet and no desire to help the two of you with this scheme. I have a very peaceful, fulfilling existence right here and have no intention of following you two fools into what will probably be a disastrous endeavor."

Lucratelli was frustrated, but Berry took the lead.

"Mr. Maxwell—Cyrus—I thank you for your time. I'm sorry we wasted your evening."

Berry stood, and Lucratelli followed his lead. Cyrus saw them to the door and thanked them for the cigars.

"I wish you luck, gentlemen," Cyrus said as he closed the front door behind them.

Berry and Lucratelli walked away from the cottage, their enthusiasm somewhat dampened.

"We need him," Berry said. "Even if it's just to make sure *The Guide* works on Earth."

"Oh, he'll go with us," Lucratelli told him. "He just doesn't know it yet."

7

S ome ladies started showing up hours early, dragging their husbands and kids along. Minivans streamed into the vendor parking area, making it look like a PTA event.

Laureen's Mothers for Moral Decency Rally was being held at a stadium just north of downtown Fort Lauderdale. Originally a home for the Baltimore Orioles' spring training, the stadium had also been home to minor league games, the County Fair, a Blues Festival, and other events over the years.

Food vendors put the final touches on their booths that offered sausage and pepper sandwiches, hot dogs and burgers, arepas, Italian ices, and all the usual foods normally found at a South Florida fair or carnival.

America's News Now was on hand with a satellite truck, its large dish hoisted high on a twenty foot mast over their van. Laureen's appearances on the network had helped boost its ratings and, despite their clear political bias, they were now the number one cable news network in the country. Local TV and radio crews were present or on their way.

Anyone and everyone wanting to market a product or message to the anticipated throngs was there setting up a booth—local newspapers, cable and satellite TV companies, banks, insurance companies, air conditioning companies.

Laureen was already overwhelmed. She had spent weeks filing for permits, signing sponsors, lining up vendors, hiring security, booking guest speakers, renting tents and public address systems, and promoting the event. She didn't do it all by herself, but she was consulted every step of the way.

Since a right-wing, conservative, religious-oriented event was right up their alley, America's News Now helped organize and promote it. The fees they paid Laureen, along with sponsor money, helped fund the event. Some speakers volunteered their services, others required payment for their time. Either way, all of them needed hotel rooms, limos, and air fare. If Laureen was lucky, she would break even on the actual event. Ticket sales would be the icing on the cake, making the endeavor profitable.

But she wasn't doing it for the money. Laureen sincerely believed that she and the people she supported had a message that needed to be presented to the American public. Along with bounce houses and face painting booths for the kids, there were booths set up to provide information and resources for anyone interested in helping to ban abortions, debunk climate change, or even keep gays out of the military. People pushed pretzels and petitions.

"We'd better get things rolling here," Nana suggested. She and Laureen were inside the tent that housed the rally's organizing committee. There were laptops on folding tables, rows of walkie-talkies plugged in and charging, and people on cell phones everywhere.

"It's kind of early, isn't it?" Laureen asked.

"It's ten o'clock. It's go-time."

Laureen looked outside the tent to take in the situation on the stadium grounds.

"I know," she said, noticing Laureen's concern. "There aren't too many people here yet."

"No, there aren't," Laureen replied. "I think there were actually more people at my husband's funeral."

"Yeah, there were," Nana agreed, "and nobody even *liked* him."

*   *   *

"Put some elbow grease into it," Berry suggested.

They were in Lucratelli's kitchen. Lucratelli was at the large double sink scrubbing away at the disassembled components of his still. He had tried everything from seeking advice from former Appalachian moonshiners to having Native American medicine men chant over the contraption. So far, nothing, but he was determined.

"So how do you propose we get there?" Berry asked.

Lucratelli was busy scrubbing.

"Am I talking to myself?"

"What? I can't hear you over the water running. Get where?" Lucratelli asked, preoccupied.

"How do we get there? We certainly can't hop on the closest shuttle bus. Any of the official portals are out of the question. They'll be monitored 24/7, I'm sure."

"We could hitch," Lucratelli suggested.

"Hitch?"

"Hitch a ride with some mutt or something. Animals travel back and forth all the time."

"Is that so? Spying on people, huh?"

"No, nothing sinister. Maybe someone here wants to check on a living relative or friend. Maybe Administration just wants to get an idea of what's up-and-coming. Who knows? None of my business anyway. Ever have a pet yourself?"

"A few." Berry thought about the menagerie of animals he had over the course of his lifetime: fish, hamsters, turtles, parakeets, a stray cat, and three dogs. "I once had a friend who was blind in one eye. He owned a horse that was also blind in one eye—the other eye."

Lucratelli laughed. "So I guess between the two of them they could walk in a straight line? Ever catch one of your pets eying you up, especially when you were doing something out of the ordinary?"

"I had a German Shepard who would watch when I was having sex with anyone."

"Yeah, they like that. Anyway, they report back."

"Back where?" Berry asked. He was already running through his memories of having clandestine trysts with wives of friends or business colleagues. He was always secure in the knowledge that these instances were discreet. Now, not so much.

"Back here."

"That's what I was afraid of."

*　　　　　*　　　　　*

The minister from Laureen's megachurch introduced the first guest speaker, a Southern Baptist minister who railed against the government. He claimed he was under investigation for telling his congregation who to vote for in recent local elections and said the government was looking in to his church's tax exempt status for a violation of separation of church and state. He was under the distinct impression that no government had the right to tell any member of the clergy what they could or couldn't preach from the pulpit.

He got a smattering of applause, not for a lack of enthusiasm for his message but because there was virtually no crowd. All in all, only about thirty-five people showed up for the entire event. With live shots scheduled from the event all afternoon, the America's News Now producers had to really scramble.

Another speaker prompted the "crowd" to contact their local, state, and national representatives to ban all funding for Planned Parenthood claiming the organization was nothing more than abortion factories.

One speaker extolled the work of a group of scientists who claimed that there was no evidence of global warming or climate change. He never identified any of the scientists by name.

There was also a speaker claiming that the U.S. education system was doing nothing but indoctrinating our children with ridiculous notions such as evolution and critical thinking and that home schooling was the solution.

Laureen's own speech leaned heavily on her now familiar message that God was riding shotgun in her life and could do so in everyone else's life if they only gave themselves up to the Lord. She related her own experience of letting go of all her concerns and worries by letting God direct her through each and every decision.

The ANN news crew simply avoided any audience or wide shots. The studio anchors threw to a remote reporter who set up his piece by standing in front of a booth or a sign; the director would cut away to the speaker on stage, and then insert a random pre-taped interview with an attendee or two. Tight shots were required to avoid seeing the empty stadium, but since the segments were only two or three minute updates airing every hour throughout the afternoon, the network was satisfied that all was going well. The general public had the perception that the rally was a huge success. The only thing the news people were disappointed about was that they had hoped to get footage of protesters who claimed the event was exclusive and racist. A little controversy and conflict was always good for ratings, but when the protesters saw the meager size of the crowd, they just went home.

Laureen was distraught that so few people attended her rally, but the network was ecstatic with the coverage that made the event seem larger and more significant than anyone imagined and made Laureen more of an icon with their viewership. It was a win-win for everyone. The magic of television.

*   *   *

Excerpt from *Maxwell's Guide to Heaven and Hell*, page 483:

Some rules are made to be broken.
The trick is to figure out which ones.

Lucratelli's nose started running. He alternately wiped down the still and dabbed at his face with the same towel.

"That's gross," said Berry. "What were you, raised by animals?"

"Martians," Lucratelli answered as he went back to drying the distillation equipment. "I was convinced my father was a Martian," Lucratelli admitted.

"Was he green?" Berry asked.

"No."

"Antennas on his head or anything?"

"Come on. No, I just realized when I was a kid that I never really knew anything about my Dad. I mean, he got up, went to work, came home to eat dinner, and then went back to his bar. Naturally, I wasn't born when my folks met, so I didn't know much about his past. Just whatever my mother told me. I asked about it. She couldn't understand why I wouldn't believe her when she told me he was from Earth just like us. And who knows if she was telling me the truth? For all I knew, he just dropped in from space. Maybe she did too. So I figured they were probably Martians."

"That's absurd. No kid is ever around to see the parents born," Berry told him.

"Exactly. So for all I know, they could have been Martians."

"You've seen too much Buck Rogers."

"So I guess I was just a mook," Lucratelli said.

"Let's hope with age came wisdom." Berry got up to stretch. Glancing over at Lucratelli's vidscreens, he noticed the picture of Maxwell's daughter. "Good looking girl."

Lucratelli jumped up, gazed at Chelsea's picture, and then closed the screen.

"Well, he loves his daughter and may want to help her."

"What, do you have a thing for her?"

Lucratelli was embarrassed. "No. I just want to help too."

"Okay, let's not let anything screw this up. We need to do this thing right. We need to get to New York."

"Why New York?" Lucratelli asked, inwardly thrilled that he might be getting back home.

"Because it's the epicenter of publishing. Where else would you go with a book? I think I've figured out what to do once we get down there, but we'll need to get away without attracting any attention or anyone's wrath. We *are* going to have to come back, you know."

"Bring me back a pastrami sandwich from Katz's on Houston Street," the Devil said. He strode across the room smiling broadly, dropped a bag on Lucratelli's kitchen table, and sat down.

"We had no idea…" Lucratelli stammered.

"I know."

"Look, we're just talking," Berry offered.

Satan kept smiling. "I might just want to help."

"Why would you want to do that?" Lucratelli inquired suspiciously.

"The easy answer might be because I'm bored. It might be fun."

"Fun? Berry asked. "We're not thinking of this as some kind of vacation."

"Good, because what you're planning is very serious."

"We're aware of that," Berry said.

"You should be. Truth is, it's a good idea. Maybe even a great one. And we tend to encourage great ideas."

"Really?" Lucratelli asked, still leery.

"Really. Look, what separates mankind from the animals?"

"A driver's license?" asked Berry.

"Trousers?" chimed in Lucratelli.

"Are you two through? Ideas. Plain and simple. The human race started out as scavengers who took to hunting, then farming. You developed communities. You improved. You learned. You had good ideas, get it? That's the point, isn't it? You were set on course and we wanted to see what you'd come up with. You've had some pretty crazy ideas. Some real lulus, believe me. But every so often, you'd come up with something real. A good idea. Or a truly great idea. This plan of yours might just be one of those good ones."

"Or a great one?" Berry asked, encouraged.

"That remains to be seen, but we'll never know if you don't try. Or don't succeed."

"So you're going to help?" Lucratelli asked.

156

"No. You won't get any overt help from me. I can't get involved."

"But you are involved," Berry added.

"No, I'm not. I was never here." Lucifer smiled broadly again. He was so likeable sometimes, Berry thought.

"What's in the bag?" Lucratelli asked.

"Malt."

"Malt?" Lucratelli was intrigued.

"A little peace offering. In friendship. I heard you were doing some distilling, and I thought this might help."

"Where are they from?" Lucratelli was getting excited.

"From down there. They just might do the trick for you."

"Down there? From Earth? How did you get them?"

"The Smile Patrol isn't the only group that can get things done around here," the Devil said as he stood to leave.

"Hey. Wait a minute," Berry said. "How did you know what we were up to?"

The Devil gave a short whistle. Out of a minute crack between the floor and baseboard in the kitchen crawled a small cockroach. It paused for a second and then scurried across the floor, climbed up the table leg, and settled itself on top of the table next to the bag of malt.

"Oh," Berry said, looking at Lucratelli, "your place was bugged."

*   *   *

157

From across the ballroom, she couldn't hear what they were saying, but they sure were having a good time. The three men weren't loud or rowdy, just relaxed with each other and the situation, unlike Chelsea who always felt out of place at weddings. One of the men kept glancing in her direction. She had noticed him from the beginning, keeping silent tabs on his activities for a while now. Other wedding guests were talking to her and she did her best to keep up her end of the conversations, but she was distracted.

After a short while, with some obvious prodding from his friends, he started walking over to where she was seated. She didn't know why but she felt nervous. Not afraid, just excited and, at the same time, wishing she were somewhere else.

An older woman, the bride's aunt, impeded his way across the room. He politely exchanged a few words with her and took her empty glass. She whispered something in his ear and Chelsea could see him literally turn red, but he smiled graciously, excused himself, and continued to the table where Chelsea sat alone.

"Are you taking drink orders?" she asked him as he approached.

"Do I look like a waiter?"

"Actually you do in that monkey suit," she replied with a laugh.

He smiled a smile so broad and real that she wanted to smile along with him. And she realized she was doing just that.

"I'll be glad to get anything you need," he told her. "What happened to your table companions? Did they abandon you?"

"I guess they're all on the dance floor."

"Can I interest you in a dance?" he asked sweetly.

"Don't you have drinks to deliver?"

"They can wait." He extended his hand. "What do you say?"

She had taken off her shoes earlier but nestled her feet back into them, hoping it wasn't too obvious. She stood up and was relieved to see that even though she was wearing heels he wasn't too short or too tall for her. He was just right.

They walked to the center of the dance floor as the band started playing Santo and Johnny's "Sleepwalk."

"This song always makes me want to dance," he said as he took her in his arms.

"Always?"

"It could come on the car radio and I'd have to stop, get out, and slow dance on the side of the road. It's a favorite."

"That must be annoying in traffic," she said.

He laughed and they danced on, swaying together, sharing a perfect moment until a ringing started drowning out the music.

"Are you expecting a call?" he asked.

She had trouble hearing him over the incessant ringing.

"What?" she asked.

"Pardon me?"

They were having trouble hearing each other, the phone becoming more and more insistent.

"Maybe I should go," she suggested but he shook his head, indicating that he couldn't hear what she was saying.

"It's the phone," he yelled.

"Yes, I know," she told him but he couldn't hear a word she said. "Damn phone!"

She slowly opened her eyes. It was light in the room. Morning. She picked up her phone and looked at the caller I.D.

A client, she realized.

She shifted herself over to the side of the bed and pulled her wheelchair closer.

*   *   *

Lucratelli was spending a lot of time at his vidscreen. He had convinced himself that it was research to move the project along, but that was just a thinly veiled attempt to justify looking in on Chelsea. He didn't think he was stalking her from afar, just checking in to see how she was doing. But the fact was that he was smitten. It was unusual for him. Plus, he had died young. That did tend to put a damper on the love life.

He looked in on Chelsea's website and her social networking posts. He couldn't respond and wouldn't know what to say to her anyway. That he found her attractive? That he was fascinated with her even though he had never met her? He knew he was acting like a lug but he couldn't help it.

A howling outside distracted him. Getting up from the desk he peered out the window but couldn't see what caused the ruckus. He walked outside. Still nothing. Then, turning the corner of the house, he noticed a small calico cat meowing up a storm. At first he thought the cat was fending off an attacker, but that wasn't the case.

He realized what was going on, though, when the cat noticed him and, trying to run away, fell over its own feet, got up, then staggered a few more feet before keeling over again.

The cat was drunk. It apparently had been licking around the still and gotten snockered. Lucratelli walked slowly to where the cat was lying in the grass.

"What's up, doc?" he said to the calico. "You sampling the new batch? Guess it works, huh?"

Lucratelli's heart thumped rapidly in his chest from the excitement that after all this time—and a little help from Lucifer— his brewing attempt was finally successful. More than successful, judging by the cat's response.

He kneeled down and stroked the cat's fur. It opened its eyes, tried to get up, and then decided against it. It lifted one paw almost absent-mindedly, making it easier for Lucratelli to pet its stomach and to notice the gold locket attached to its collar.

Perfect.

He scooped the cat up in his arms. It gave a little mewl and then closed its eyes again. Lucratelli tried to disturb the little fellow as little as possible as he tapped the keys on his wrist unit. He waited a couple seconds while he connected.

"Berry," he said, "you'd better come right over. I think I've found our ride."

8

Ellen Leffert walked briskly up the street, arrived at Laureen Dawber's house, and pounded on the front door until Laureen appeared.

"I want you to look at my son," she said, her voice quivering with adrenalin.

Laureen looked down at the neighbor's son Mark whose right eye sported a shiner the size of a golf ball.

"My goodness," Laureen gasped. "What happened?"

"Your son Luke. That's what happened. He punched Mark in the eye. Didn't he?" she asked, looking down at her boy.

Mark, embarrassed by the whole thing, nodded his head and looked away sheepishly.

"Luke would never do such a thing," Laureen stated, appalled.

"Really? Really? Do you know why Luke hit him? Because Luke said that Mark killed Jesus!! Isn't that right, Mark?"

"I didn't kill him. I didn't even know him," replied the young boy.

"We'll get to the bottom of this," Laureen said. "Noah!" she called in to the house. Noah appeared almost instantly since he was listening in from behind the front door trying to suppress his laughter.

"Where's your brother?" Laureen asked.

"He's out at Publix with Nana."

"Did you see him hit Mark?" Laureen's eyes squinted to let him know she was serious.

"Yes."

"Why did he do that?"

"Luke said Jews killed Jesus and Mark's a Jew."

Laureen looked back down at Mark.

"Is that right?"

"Yup, I'm Jewish."

"No, I mean, is that what happened?"

"Yes, ma'am."

"You see?" said Ellen. "There is no excuse for that type of behavior. Imagine, hitting my son because he doesn't believe in what you believe."

"That's the problem," said Laureen.

"What are you talking about?" Ellen asked.

"You haven't accepted Jesus into your life."

"No, we haven't. We're Jewish."

"That's exactly what I'm talking about. You are entitled to believe whatever you want to believe—"

"Thank you."

"—even if what you believe is wrong."

"I didn't come over here to argue," Ellen said.

"Then what did you come over for?"

"Certainly not to fight."

"No?"

"No, but now it's on my list. Look, when Luke gets home I fully expect you to march him directly to my house to apologize to Mark. And I hope you'll see to it that he gets the proper punishment for what he's done."

"I'll deal with my son the way I see fit."

"Well, maybe I should contact an attorney."

"Really? An attorney? Over a little neighborhood fisticuffs?"

"Bullying…and…and a hate crime! That's what it is, and I won't stand for it," Ellen said in a huff, turning and walking down the driveway with Mark in tow. "You call yourself a Christian?" she called back.

"That's exactly what I call myself," Laureen shouted from her doorway. "You know you *will* fry in hell because you haven't accepted Jesus as your Lord and Savior."

"You stupid bitch. Going to church doesn't make you a Christian any more than standing in this driveway makes me a car!"

"What?"

*   *   *

Excerpt from *Maxwell's Guide to Heaven and Hell*, page 91:

Weather anywhere, anytime you need it.

Your local Smile Patrol office will help you arrange for the perfect weather for any activity. Perfect powder for skiing? A stiff breeze for kite flying? Rain to help the garden grow?

Not a problem.

Don't be a victim of the weather; demand the best weather possible from your local Smile Patrol!

As always, it was another perfect day in Heaven. The sky was as blue as a movie starlet's eyes. There was a faint floral scent in the air. A slight wind stirred the leaves.

Berry stepped off the transport shuttle a block away from Lucratelli's house, drinking in the fresh air as he walked. It was a street of good-sized cottages, some close to the road, some set further back on their lots affording the residents a large front or rear yard. The area was heavily treed which gave the whole neighborhood a rural, spacious feel and though none of the houses sat too closely to each other, it retained a sense of neighborhood.

A bicyclist pedaled by and waved. Berry smiled and waved back. People were so friendly here. Since he'd arrived in Heaven, there was no turmoil that he was aware of. No arguing or discord of any type except for Cyrus refusing to go along with his plan. People got along. They pursued their dreams to attain goals. *Perhaps in dying,* he thought, *people really do find the key to their own happiness.*

He couldn't remember when he'd last felt this good. He stepped onto Lucratelli's front porch and knocked on the front door, humming softly to himself. When no one answered, he knocked again. Still no answer.

Probably working in the back, he figured. Hopping off the porch, he rounded the house, ducking under the red maple by the back corner, and entered the back yard. There he spied Lucratelli under a small dark cloud hovering about four feet above his head. Rain poured down from the cloud all around Lucratelli while the rest of the yard was dry and bathed in sunshine.

"Shower broken?"

"No."

It looked to Berry as if Lucratelli was sobbing.

"Are you crying?"

"No."

"You are."

"No, I'm not. It's the rain." Lucratelli took a swig from a jug he clutched with his right hand.

"There's nothing to be ashamed of," Berry offered.

"It's the rain. Got it?"

"Right. Mind if I have a seat?" he asked as he pulled up a lawn chair and positioned it about a yard from the downpour.

"Suit yourself." Another swig.

They sat like that for a few minutes. As Berry watched puffy white clouds roll by, Lucratelli alternated between convulsive sobbing and taking hits from the jug.

"So, wanna tell me what's wrong?" Berry asked.

"Nothin'."

Another couple minutes passed.

"So, you're one of those melancholy drunks."

"I'm not drunk," Lucratelli told him after another swig.

"And I'm not bald."

"Oh, you're bald alright," Lucratelli said, laughing.

"And you're pretty drunk, amico."

"Yeah, I am!" Lucratelli took another long pull on the jug and laughed. Then he sobbed uncontrollably. "I never had a life. I was never in love. I died too young. No wife, no children, no career, no nothing." His crying increased until Berry couldn't make out his words.

"You went to Europe," Berry tried pointing out the bright side.

"It was World War Two, not a vacation. My walking tour of North Africa, Italy, France, Holland, Belgium. Shit. And I died." Another long drink.

"Well, we all had to go some time." Berry tried to think of other upsides. "You've had cheesecake at Junior's in Brooklyn, right?"

"I have."

"You're not a virgin, right?"

"So?"

"So, there you go. You've had great food, got laid, and seen the world. Not so bad."

"I guess…"

"And you still have all your hair."

"When you put it that way…"

"And you still have your whole life in front of you. Well, you're dead, but you know what I mean. You could still meet someone and fall in love."

"You ever been in love?"

"I have."

"Married?"

167

"Three times."

"Three? What, did they cheat on you or something?"

"No."

"You cheat on them?"

"Not once."

"So?"

"So, I guess with each of them I just fell out of love at some point. I just woke up one morning and felt different, disconnected. Suddenly, we had nothing in common. My own fault entirely. They just didn't do it for me anymore. They knew it and left. It was the right thing for them to do."

"No hard feelings, huh?"

"No, not at all. I still like every one of them immensely. Great gals."

"I think I'm in love," Lucratelli admitted. "But she doesn't even know I exist."

"Isn't that always the case?" Berry asked. "You should feel good about that. And you have a great job. Not everyone gets on the Smile Patrol."

Lucratelli started to brighten up. "You're right." He extended the jug towards Berry.

"Want some?"

"Sure, but turn off the water works, will you?"

Lucratelli punched a couple keys on his wrist device and the rain stopped as quickly as if someone turned off a tap. The little dark cloud fizzled out. Berry took the jug and took a long pull.

"Wow, that's…unique."

"Special blend," said Lucratelli. "Do me a favor and don't tell anybody about this."

"The hooch?"

"Well, that too. But I mean, uh, the waterworks and all."

"You got it. No problem. We all have our moments," Berry said.

Lucratelli eagerly changed the subject. "I thought about jerry-rigging a transport booth. That would be easy enough, but that would just get us around Heaven. You know, out to the beach or up to the mountains, but not back to Earth like we need."

"So what do you suggest? You mentioned something about finding our ride?"

Lucratelli smiled broadly and gestured wildly. "We can hitch a ride with that cat."

"What cat?" Berry asked.

"The one that's been keeping an eye on Cyrus's daughter Chelsea. I recognized the locket the cat wears from Chelsea's pictures."

"Why would the cat come here?"

"Beats me, but it's here. Passed out over there." Lucratelli turned to point Zoey out to Berry.

"Where?" Berry asked. The small calico was nowhere to be seen.

*　　　　　　　　*　　　　　　　　*

Laureen couldn't get used to the headphones. They messed up her hair and made her ears ache. She didn't feel comfortable until her producer and engineer, who she nicknamed Dr. Audio, substituted the standard set of cans for a set of small, light ear buds.

Her notoriety as a community activist and a sometime pundit on America's News Now paved the way for her new radio show. Laureen purchased a block of time from a local Fort Lauderdale AM station that used to have a Top 40 format but found that advertisers paid more on right-wing talk radio. It wasn't difficult for Laureen to find local sponsors. Many were members of her congregation promoting their businesses. She covered the air time cost with a trade/barter deal: she gave the station back a couple minutes here and there for promos and some of their own sponsorships. She made enough money to earn a decent living working only a few hours a day. Her show ran from 11 a.m. to 2 p.m. Monday through Friday and afforded her the opportunity to get the kids to school in the morning before the show and pick them up afterwards. Life was good.

"I'm not ashamed to say that I'm a Christian," she said adamantly.

"Neither am I, but that's a private matter. My beliefs have nothing to do with my job," replied Bob Mustin, city manager of one of Broward County's smaller municipalities.

"It has everything to do with your job when you are preventing the Ten Commandments from adorning your precious City Hall."

Laureen was on the attack, and it was easier since her guest was a call-in and not sitting in the studio with her.

"We have to respect the complaints lodged by some of our citizens," Mustin told her.

"Sure, citizens who have no love of God, our country, or the Bible."

"We have constitutional and public policy issues. We can't allow the city to be perceived as endorsing any one particular religious belief or viewpoint."

"But we live in a Christian country."

"Actually, we don't. Our country is mainly made up of Christians, yes, but we also are home to Jews, Muslims, and Buddhists—people of every faith."

"Or no faith. Atheists. I'm so sick of people trying to tell us what we can or can't do."

"Well, we do have laws. And the Constitution," he offered.

"Then maybe they should be changed. Let's see what our callers have to say about that. Jack in Boca, are you there?"

*　　　　　*　　　　　*

Lucratelli walked into the Smile Patrol office a little hung over. Well, more than a little. He wasn't really looking for another assignment, just trying to kill some time. With Bree and Satan keeping tabs on them, neither Berry nor Lucratelli knew how they were going to make the jump back to Earth. The standard portals, such as the one at the Administration building, usually were watched as a matter of protocol, but would certainly be watched more closely with the two under suspicion. Chelsea's cat seemed their most advantageous option but now even that seemed unlikely because they couldn't find the little calico anywhere. So, for the time being, it was back to work.

Lucratelli logged on to his vidscreen and checked the assignment boards. Someone needed to set up an Elvis impersonator contest with Elvis and Colonel Tom Parker judging. A group of former-life politicians were holding an election, not for any particular office, just to see who would win the most votes. It was an ego thing. The New York Yankees All-Time All-Star game needed to be coordinated. A consortium of artists and scientists wanted to dye the rivers different colors: the scientists wanted to track patterns while the artists wanted to observe how the different hues would interact. Pretty normal stuff for the Smile Patrol and nothing that piqued Lucratelli's interest.

"What's the boss up to?" he asked the receptionist, noticing that the door to Bree's office was closed.

"Meeting. She wanted to see you if you came in today. Are you gonna stick around, hot shot?"

"Fat chance, beautiful," Lucratelli said as he sat himself down on the corner of her desk. He noticed the short skirt riding up her legs and, when he looked up again, saw that she had noticed him looking. And she smiled.

*   *   *

On the other side of Bree's office door Zoey sat quietly nursing a headache as the head of the Smile Patrol went on and on.

"I'm so disappointed in you. I sent you out there to bring back pertinent information. And what do you do? You get drunk. Very nice. I should have sent a dog. I would have had access to much more reliable information."

Zoey doubted that. Dogs were so easily distracted. Wave a stick, mention a biscuit, or send an interesting scent their way and they go way off track. Zoey knew that many people thought they were adorable, but she didn't.

Bree had had plenty of experience with cats in her earthly life as a witch in Salem, Massachusetts during the Salem Witch Trials. For the longest time she'd had one that did her bidding, aided her, and provided loyalty and affection. She knew the powers cats held. She also knew they go their own way, affectionate when they feel like it and attentive when they want to be. She could tell that Zoey, tired and hung over, was only half-interested in what she had to say.

Zoey didn't feel like a spy or informant; she considered herself a facilitator. As she saw it, her loyalty rested with the wards that she visited, adopted, and let into her heart. Through her observations, she provided useful information that helped the people she was keeping an eye on. In Chelsea Maxwell's case, Zoey felt genuine affection as well as some concern. Zoey sensed sadness in her, a sadness that had nothing to do with her disability because Chelsea handled her condition very well on her own. It was more about Chelsea never having been loved or in love. There are some people who don't need or want that in their lives, while there are others who need a real connection with another person. Some are obsessed with the idea, in fact. Zoey knew instinctively that Chelsea's life would be enhanced and elevated to a new level by love.

Zoey had been with Lucratelli, albeit somewhat hazy due to the moonshine, when he ordered up his personal rainstorm and sobbed his way through most of their afternoon together. She witnessed him pouring out his emotions when Berry arrived. She knew he, too, wanted to feel true love and that he was attracted on many levels to Chelsea. And she was determined to help make something happen for them both.

She licked her paws, cleaning them diligently while Bree droned on, half-paying attention in that way cats have of appearing disinterested while knowing full well what's going on around them.

"Okay. That's it," Bree told her. "Get back out there on your rounds. Keep a special eye on those two jokers. Fill me in on anything—anything—they're up to. And no more drinking. You look pitiful, by the way." Bree stepped over to the door and opened it. "Now get back out there. I'm done with you."

Zoey hopped off the chair and made her way through the lobby. Lucratelli noticed the cat with the locket, darted over to scoop Zoey up in his arms, and bolted for the door.

"Hey! Don't you want to see the boss?" the receptionist asked.

"Later, Toots. Much later. Gotta go. I'll send her a postcard."

And he was gone.

9

E xcerpt for *Maxwell's Guide to Heaven and Hell*, page 678:
Some people need to know how a clock works; some just want to know what time it is.

"Oh dear."

It was the second time the two men knocked on Cyrus Maxwell's door unexpectedly.

"We've come to ask you to reconsider."

"Well, you have apparently made an unnecessary trip, gentlemen. But as long as you're here you might as well come in for some tea."

Maxwell opened the door wider to allow Berry and Lucratelli inside. When his dog Chloe noticed the small calico cat cradled in Lucratelli's arms, she craned her head up. Zoey jumped down to the floor and the two animals circled each other, sniffed around private parts, and then settled on the rug by the couch almost lying against each other.

"We have to move this along," Berry said.

"Bon voyage," replied Cyrus.

"Look, we need you to come with us. We have to make sure the book will work on Earth and you are the one person who is most familiar with it."

"I told you I don't know how it works. It just does."

"Will it work back there?"

"There's no way to tell."

"Well, we'll find out when we get there."

"There is no 'we'. I am not going. Plain and simple. In fact, you can consider yourselves very lucky that I haven't reported you to the authorities."

"You wouldn't..."

"I haven't, but I just might if you keep badgering me. A man's home, especially in Heaven, is his sanctuary, and you, gentlemen, are invading my privacy. I had a nice calm existence here until you showed up. Now my stress levels are elevated: I'm nervous, I'm anxious, and I demand you leave me out of this whole business. I expect you will honor my request in this matter."

"I'll tell you what I expect," Berry told him, "I expect some company. And very soon."

*   *   *

Bree wasn't stupid. She knew what Berry and Lucratelli were up to, but she didn't know when or how they would actually accomplish the jump back to Earth. She decided to be proactive and deploy a number of Smile Patrol Tactical Units.

There are no police in Heaven or Hell, not in the traditional sense at least. Instead, there are special units of the Smile Patrol. Usually employed for crowd control at events and other routine assignments, there is also an elite division of Special Ops squads who, on occasion, are deployed on very special missions. Consisting mainly of former police officers and military personnel, their regimental motto is "Keeping You Happy—Whether You Like It Or Not."

The first squad arrived at Berry's place but found no one and nothing of interest. His home was neat and nondescript as if no one had ever stayed there at all. In fact, he was rarely sleeping these days. He spent his evenings out at cafes, movies—anywhere to avoid spending his nights wide awake in an empty house. Although it was probably due to nerves, he was convinced he had simply forgotten how to fall asleep.

At the same time operatives were searching Berry's place, a second squad raided Lucratelli's house. They carefully made their way from room to room until they were satisfied that the house was clear while two Smile Patrol agents examined the strange apparatus Lucratelli had in the back yard.

"What do you make of it?"

"Looks like a still of some sort," said one, lighting up a cigarette.

"Better be careful with that butt," warned the other.

"Yeah, you're right." He took one last puff then dropped it to the ground which was soaked with Lucratelli's latest concoction.

Before the agent could stamp it out, the ground below him caught fire, spreading rapidly. The flames made a beeline for the main part of the still where they seemed to smolder and fizzle out.

"That's fortunate," remarked the other agent, relieved.

Suddenly there was an immense explosion, blowing the wiring, cisterns, containers, and other components sky high. The two agents were knocked over but recovered quickly enough to run for cover from the debris raining down around them as a huge cloud of dark smoke billowed upward triggering a sensor Lucratelli had installed on his back porch.

*   *   *

"It's time," Lucratelli told Berry and Cyrus. His wrist device had been buzzing incessantly until he tapped the faceplate. "They've been to my place."

Standing on the front porch the three of them exchanged anxious glances, then, in unison, looked to see what was creating the rumbling at the end of Cyrus's long driveway. It was an ominous-looking Smile Patrol Tactical Vehicle painted matte black and filled with Smile Patrol operatives, a few of whom had burned and charred uniforms from the explosion at Lucratelli's house. They were determined, and they were very pissed.

"That's it, Cyrus," Berry said. "You have no choice any longer. You need to come with us…*now*."

"I hardly think so…"

"Look, you have two choices: come with us or take your chances with them."

"I have nothing to worry about from them. I'll explain that I have no involvement in any of this. Simple."

"Not simple. We have the book. We're taking it with us. They'll think you were complicit and by denying it, you'll make matters worse for yourself. You're in it now, whether you like it or not. And I don't think the guys in that squad car are going to be too gentle or understanding."

Lucratelli scooped Zoey up into his arms.

"Oh dear," Cyrus mumbled, wringing his hands.

"Let's move it!" Lucratelli urged.

"Oh dear, let me throw a couple things together," Cyrus ran inside and quickly shuttled between the rooms of his house stuffing a shaving kit and items of clothing into an overnight case.

"Cyrus, now! And don't forget the book," Berry suggested.

"Oh dear, yes." Cyrus ran to his desk, took a couple copies of *The Guide*, and placed them in his overnight case as well. He hurried back to the porch but only got as far as the doorway. "I should take a vidscreen. The interface might help make it possible to copy the book so that it works properly on...well, where we're going."

"Good thought," said Berry.

"Oh! Let me send a text to my cousin so that he comes over to feed Chloe." He tapped on his wrist device frantically. "Oh dear," he mumbled.

"Can you stop saying that?" Lucratelli asked.

179

"Saying what?"

"That 'Oh dear.' "

"Yes, certainly. Oh dear. Oh, I'm sorry."

Lucratelli looked at Berry with an 'I told you so' expression on his face.

Cyrus was darting around stopping to consider items he should bring and deciding nothing. His mind was racing but not really working at all.

"An umbrella!" he shouted to himself and ran back inside again. He pulled a green and white golf umbrella from an umbrella stand. "No, no. That won't do." He stuck it back inside the stand and chose instead his standard black umbrella.

"Just the ticket, I'd say."

"Expecting rain?" Lucratelli asked.

"I do believe that a gentleman should always be prepared for any event, my good man. To tell you the truth, I don't know what to expect."

Standing on the front porch they didn't quite know what to do. Zoey was nestled in Lucratelli's arms so Berry and Cyrus each linked one of their arms around one of his. Zoey let out a small mewl.

"Okay, here we go," Berry said enthusiastically.

They waited for a moment, but nothing happened.

"Oh dear me," Cyrus uttered. Lucratelli rolled his eyes. They all stared at the small calico.

With a squeal of brakes and the sound of crunching gravel, the mobile unit came to a sudden rest twenty yards from where the three men were standing holding a cat. A half-dozen agents bolted from their vehicles and raced to the front porch. When they arrived, there was no one there. Just a faint wisp of cinnamon.

10

Whooosh!

New Yorkers made their way down the sidewalk near Washington Square unaware that the three men and a cat impeding their travel were dead fugitives from Heaven. The jump back to the world of the living was breathtaking and somewhat scary. First, there was a vibration that didn't emanate from Zoey as much as emanate around her. Then, there was a sense of speed and of the body being propelled through an instant of overwhelming acceleration. An abrupt end to the sensations came with a faint odor of cinnamon.

"Are we there yet?" asked Lucratelli.

"What are you, like, six years old?" Berry asked. "Yes, we're apparently there."

"You two can let go now," Lucratelli said.

Berry and Cyrus released the hold they had on Lucratelli's arms.

Zoey leaped down from Lucratelli's arms and scampered away, unconcerned with the three men who'd hitched a ride.

"Stop that cat!" Cyrus demanded.

"Good luck with that," Lucratelli said.

There were people all over. Construction sounds filled the air. A crane, positioned at the top of a nearby building, towered over the street. Taxi horns honked. Traffic was backed up. The air smelled different than the fragrant wisps of Heavenly breezes.

"I have to seriously protest," Cyrus stated. "This is outrageous. Abducting me is not acceptable. I demand to be returned this instant!"

"Yeah, that's not gonna happen."

"It smells funny," Cyrus noticed.

"Pollution. I guess there wasn't much of it when you were still living here," Berry told him.

"I feel like a sandwich," Lucratelli said out of the blue. "I know a great place just a couple blocks from here."

"Brilliant," Berry remarked. "First of all, we're not here for lunch. This is no vacation. We have things to do. Besides, what would you use for money?"

"Not a problem." Lucratelli approached a man walking towards them.

"Excuse me, buddy. Could you spare some change for a bite to eat?"

The man kept walking, paying no attention whatsoever to Lucratelli. It was the same with the person after him, and the next, and another.

"Typical New Yorkers," Berry remarked.

"Perhaps they can't see us or hear us," Cyrus offered. "Maybe we're like spirits or ghosts. It's possible they can't perceive our presence here on this worldly plane." He wandered back and forth on the sidewalk as he spoke.

A teenager texting on a cell phone looked up just in time to avoid walking into Cyrus.

"Watch it, you old fart," he warned Cyrus.

"Does that answer your question?" Berry asked.

*   *   *

Excerpt from *Maxwell's Guide to Heaven and Hell*, page 492

In Heaven you have the opportunity to catch up on old times with members of your family who have passed away years, decades, or even centuries before you.

For some people, that is bliss. And, we understand, for some people it is not.

Heaven's Genealogy Department will be glad to assist you in arranging visits or preventing them.

Whatever makes you happy.

Be careful what you ask for.

Chelsea had ordered a medium pizza with peppers and onions from Pepperoni Boys. While she waited for it to be delivered she rolled around the apartment tidying things up. She wondered about Zoey. She hadn't seen the small feline for a few days and, although that was quite normal for cats in general and Zoey in particular, Chelsea was still somewhat concerned.

She never expected to have her own pet of any kind. Most people don't. But for thousands of years, mankind and animals have had a mutually beneficial relationship. People with pets are more likely to live longer, healthier, happier lives.

Growing up, Chelsea's family had always had a dog. There was a small terrier named Skippy who yapped a lot. They also had a goofy, knuckleheaded Golden Retriever named Murphy who liked to eat shoes. She'd never really considered having a pet as an adult, though. It was costly and she'd be responsible for something other than herself. Walking a dog in her wheelchair might be difficult as well. She hadn't been sure she was prepared for all of that. But, now, here she was with a cat. A cat that's gone missing at that.

Business was good lately and her company was growing. She hadn't been able to hire any help yet, but the projects were coming in more frequently and some of them were really fun.

She was currently working on a project called A Day at the (Drag) Races, a charity event where teams of up to six drag queens raced homemade "vehicles" that looked like anything from a giant high-heeled shoe to a four poster bed by pushing them down the street. All proceeds went to AIDS research and testing. Last year's event had raised a significant amount of money and Chelsea was hoping that the races this year would fare even better.

She was just about to log on to her computer to answer e-mails when there was a knock at the front door. Expecting it to be the delivery guy with her pizza, she rolled her chair over and reached for the doorknob. When she opened the door, the first thing she saw was Zoey looking back at her. *Alive and finally home*, Chelsea thought. She then looked up and saw the good-looking young man holding the small cat. He smiled. Chelsea instinctively smiled back. Next to the young man stood an older, balding man. Neither Lucratelli nor Berry said a word as they stepped aside and an even older man came into view. Chelsea was about to say something when she realized that the gentleman standing before her was her deceased father.

She fainted straight away.

11

A thousand miles away, it was a typical day in Florida. Sixteen Haitians clinging desperately for days to a homemade raft made out of 2-liter plastic soda bottles were intercepted by the U.S. Coast Guard, held in a jail in South Miami, and repatriated back to their home country. By contrast, six Cubans who were able to set foot on U.S. soil were allowed to legally enter the country. In Key Largo, about thirty people snorkeled around a statue of Jesus Christ located twenty feet underwater in John Pennekamp Park. At Spook Hill in Lake Wales, an optical illusion gave the impression that cars rolled uphill. In Orlando's Peabody Hotel, a red carpet was set out for the mallard ducks which make their daily trek from the elevator through the lobby to the fountain where they spend their days. A Rolls Royce Silver Shadow was sunk to become part of an artificial reef off Palm Beach. Sixteen "pill mills" owned by the same doctor and doling out Oxy to addicts were closed down. An overnight freeze ruined Mrs. Alexander's backyard orange tree, marking the end of the last citrus fruit in Citrus County. And, in Fort Lauderdale, Laureen Dawber was thirty minutes into her radio show.

There were only two people in the cramped studio: Laureen and her engineer/producer/board operator Terry, a.k.a. Dr. Audio, who was biding his time while he looked for a job with an Adult

Contemporary station or maybe even Classic Rock. Anything would be better than what he considered to be the NeoCon and God Talk formats. He especially hated the prayer Laureen shared with him before each broadcast. Not that he thought prayer was a bad thing, but religion was personal to him and he just preferred to pray in private.

America's News Now conveniently provided Laureen with a list of talking points that they received each day from a Conservative think tank based in Texas called Right Thinking America. The right wing conservatives pretty much tied up talk radio nationally, a one-sided barrage on the American people, many of whom took it in as Gospel. Laureen was aware of the guidance "provided" for her but actually paid little attention. She had her own agenda.

The way she saw it, the country was in decay. Not a literal decay as in infrastructure but a moral decay. She saw what she perceived as a lessening of traditional values. She certainly saw change in America and, to her way of thinking, that change wasn't good. Government spending was out of control. Climate change was discussed as something mankind caused rather than the will of God and the natural ebb and flow of our planet. Schools weren't educating children correctly and taught things like evolution and critical thinking. People were taking advantage of the system by collecting welfare and food stamps. It was all too much for her and in every one of her radio shows she warned of the impending doom she felt was imminent. Further proof of the downfall of America was what seemed to be a general acceptance of homosexuality. A

188

number of states had already passed laws recognizing same sex marriages.

"Whose business is it what goes on in someone's bedroom?" asked the next caller.

"It's all of our business when what is going on is an abomination under God's law," Laureen fired back at him.

"I thought God loves everyone."

"God does love everyone. But he loves Christians more."

"Then he loves gay people too?"

"God shows his love by not destroying sinners immediately. And gay people can right their wrongs by accepting the Lord as their savior. They don't have to act on their impulses. Gayness can be prayed away. It can be transformed by other means as well, such as therapy."

"What about all these young teen suicides? There's been a rash of them in our middle and high schools."

"I think that's been more of a mental health issue than a gay issue."

"I don't agree. Many of them were receiving counseling."

"Not the right kind, obviously. They chose the lives they lived."

"They claimed they were being ostracized by bullies."

"Maybe they were just being punished by God for their sinful ways," Laureen's judgment was immediate and final. "The Devil can knock on your front door but there's nothing forcing you to let him in."

*   *   *

"So that's it? I'm dead?" Chelsea asked when she opened her eyes to see her father kneeling beside her wheelchair. "I thought I would have lost the chair. That's disappointing. But it's lovely to see you, Dad."

"You're not dead, sweetheart," Cyrus said gently.

"Don't be silly," she replied. "I hear bells."

"I believe that's the front door."

"I'll get it," Lucratelli offered.

He jumped up and opened the door to find the delivery man from Pepperoni Boys.

"What's that? Pizza?" Lucratelli asked the man.

"No, new city manhole cover," the man retorted. "We're celebrating the Feast of San Genarro early this year. You should see the fire hydrants."

"Funny."

"Medium pepper and onion. Sixteen fifty."

"For a pizza? The last time I bought a pizza it was a lot cheaper."

Lucratelli didn't tell him that was in 1942.

"Yeah, well, change happens," said the delivery guy.

"Unless you're dealing with a vending machine," Lucratelli said, waiting for a laugh that didn't come. "Sixteen fifty. Jeez. I hope there's a bar of gold in the box."

"Yeah, two. With every pie."

190

"Hold on," Lucratelli looked around and spotted the twenty dollar bill that Chelsea had obviously pulled out for her pizza order. He scooped it up and presented it to the pizza guy who handed the box to Lucratelli and turned to leave.

"Whoa there, champ. What about the change?" The last time Lucratelli tipped anyone was also in 1942. The delivery guy dug in his pocket, counted out three fifty and handed it to Lucratelli who gave the guy a dollar.

The delivery guy stared at the single dollar bill in amazement. "Yeah, thanks, sport. Now I'll be able to put my kids through school."

Lucratelli just swung the door closed.

"Imagine that. I never got a buck tip for anything my entire life. Anybody hungry?"

Chelsea and Cyrus were huddled together talking. Berry stared out the window.

"Okay. More for me." Lucratelli opened the box and dug in.

Berry was convinced that some angry angel, a Smile Patrol squad, or someone else would be sent to Earth immediately to retrieve the three of them. Since they had no money, Chelsea's place would have to be their base of operations. If anyone came looking, it certainly wouldn't be difficult to find them anyway. This was God stuff. The people who held the higher positions in Heaven would know where they were. He actually was surprised they hadn't come after them already, but as long as he had the opportunity, he was moving forward. With their base of operations determined, Berry left the apartment to initiate step one of his plan.

Lucratelli, having finished off a few slices of the pizza, looked at Chelsea and Cyrus and suddenly felt like a third wheel.

"You know, I haven't been here in a long time. I kind of miss some of the old places, know what I mean? I think I'll go check up on the old neighborhood."

With both Berry and Lucratelli gone, Cyrus and Chelsea welcomed their precious time alone.

"It's good to see you, Dad."

"Lovely to see you, too, my dear."

"So, is there really a Heaven?" Chelsea asked.

"Yes, Heaven certainly exists and it is a truly wondrous place. Hell exists as well. But neither is the way you imagine them," he said with a laugh. "Well, in some regards, yes, but not entirely."

She looked at him, grateful to see him again and spend time togeher. How many of us have lost loved ones and have longed for the ability to see them one last time? To be able to have just one more heartfelt talk? To compensate for a relationship that may have been left incomplete, unresolved. Chelsea felt blessed to be afforded this opportunity.

It might be said that anyone who is happy all of the time is either demented or fooling themselves. Happiness is elusive, not a constant state of being. We should all recognize the signs and celebrate and cherish those things, people, places, and special moments that do indeed fill our hearts with happiness. For Cyrus and Chelsea, this was one of those moments. They sat in her living room drinking tea and talking for the first time since her father had passed on years ago. That this was a special moment was not lost on either of them. And she had so many questions.

*   *   *

Lucratelli thought better of asking Chelsea for some money before he left the apartment. For one thing, having just met the person who might be the woman of his dreams, he didn't want to come off as a mooch. For another, he was fiercely independent. He had always relied on his own wits to get by.

Lucratelli was determined to make some fast cash. He prowled back alleys and dumpsters looking for items he could sell quickly on the street. This netted him some quick cash but not having had to deal with money since he died in the 1940s, he was surprised to learn how much prices had gone up. The pizza should have been a clue. Before enlisting in the service, he was able to go to a movie, buy popcorn or candy, a soda, and even stop off at a deli for a hot dog all for a quarter. Those days were apparently no longer.

No stranger to pool halls, he was thrilled to find they still existed. Stepping inside The Corner Pocket Billiards Emporium, he noticed immediately this wasn't like the seedy places he had frequented where you could kill time, make contacts, come up with a deal, enjoy a cold beer or eight, and maybe make a few bucks. The Corner Pocket was an upscale billiards parlor catering to an upwardly mobile clientele. Usually crowded in the evenings, it was

193

fairly empty this late morning, but there were a couple tables being played by individuals just wasting time, practicing shots.

Lucratelli made a big show of choosing a cue stick and then racked up the balls. He avoided chit chat with anyone and just studied the table and made shots. After each one, he would comment to himself, loudly.

He knew he was attracting attention by resorting to an old reliable trick. Slowly and deliberately he set up the number one ball against the bumper alongside the number three. On top of both, he placed the eight ball so that the three balls formed a pyramid.

Now he was attracting even more attention. A couple players drew closer to see what he was doing. Lucratelli looked up at them, nodded, and went back to studying the table, muttering to himself.

"What's that all about, slick?" one of them asked.

"Well, champ," Lucratelli replied, "I'm planning on hitting the top ball—the eight—with the cue ball without ever touching the other two balls holding the eight ball up. It's a tough shot."

"Impossible shot, I'd say," the other one remarked.

"Oh no, not impossible. I do it all the time. But circumstances have to be right."

"What circumstances would that be?" the one he called 'champ' asked.

"The right incentive," Lucratelli told them smiling.

The two observers laughed and one of them, Stu, who looked like a college freshman, told Champ they were being hustled. He suggested they just go.

"He's right, you know," Lucratelli admitted, smiling broadly. He continued to study the small triangle of balls situated against the bumper. He paced, regarding the setup from different angles.

"I still say it's impossible," Champ insisted.

"Not at all. But it'll cost you to find that out," Lucratelli smiled even broader.

"See? What did I tell you?" Stu was exasperated. "Let's get out of here before you're sorry."

But Champ was intrigued. "Ten bucks says you can't do it."

"Oh, I can do it but it'll cost you twenty," Lucratelli said.

"See what I mean?" Stu whined. "Let's go. You're getting hustled."

"Yeah, he's right. You should go," Lucratelli suggested. "Why spend twenty bucks to learn something new? Besides, this shot is so easy it really isn't worth the money."

"Come on," Stu insisted.

"Doesn't look so easy," Champ kind of mumbled to no one in particular. "Okay, you're on. Twenty bucks."

"Asshole," Stu said, but he stuck around to watch.

The bet was on. Lucratelli stepped to the other side of the table, looked up and smiled at Champ who had laid the cash on the table. Lucratelli then bucked his hip out so that it rocked the table. The motion caused the three balls in the pyramid to separate and roll a few inches from each other, the upper eight ball falling and rolling safely away from the others. He casually took aim and hit the eight

195

ball with the cue ball without touching the other balls just as he claimed he could.

Champ and Stu were silent for a moment and then both laughed out loud. They could have reacted badly, even violently, but Lucratelli's sheer chutzpah and personality—as well as learning a nifty trick they could use sometime themselves—resulted in them all shaking hands and parting on good terms. They'd been had, but they had asked for it and enjoyed the show. It was the third time Lucratelli pulled the trick off that morning and, pocketing the cash, he left feeling flush and satisfied.

*   *   *

When he was alive, Berry was probably the top direct marketing television producer in the country. He kept his operation lean and mean but he certainly wasn't able to do it alone. He had one assistant, an amiable woman named Ivonne who ran the office, overseeing the work of a number of college interns who worked for school credits instead of a paycheck. His video production crew was made up of freelancers. They, too, were the best in the business. Unlike other producers, Berry paid them a fair day rate for a fair day's work. And he fed them well. That was important. Instead of ordering in pizza or sandwiches, Berry always had a catering company provide quality meals. If the shoots ran long, they were paid overtime. He always used the same studio, the same set designer, the same shooters, the same voice-over talent, the same editor. They were loyal, giving Berry preference if his shoot dates conflicted with another booking. And he was loyal in return, bringing them all back project after project.

There were also call centers. It had been a challenge finding the right companies that could go almost instantly from a half dozen operators taking product orders to fifty or a hundred depending on the influx of calls. A hot product spot could generate hundreds of orders immediately after a commercial aired and the call center had to have the ability to roll the calls over from center to center, adding enough operators to handle the business quickly and efficiently. Those operators also had to be knowledgeable enough to read the materials provided for them to answer any question the customers might have about the product or the ordering process.

There was a fulfillment house where the products were warehoused, packaged, and shipped. Berry also employed a number of media buyers. There were many unscrupulous marketers who collected large sums of money from their clients on the promise of buying large blocks of commercial time in major markets and then bought a smattering of inexpensive TV ads on very small market stations. They then went back to their clients and told them that their air tests didn't work out and that the product was a dud, assuming they had bought any air time at all. It was a common scam in the business, but Berry wouldn't have any of it. His media buyers bought the best markets for fair prices at stations that were worthwhile. Air lists were provided to clients and all buys were evaluated. Large sums of money were spent on air time to ensure sales.

It was a system that worked, a well-oiled machine that pumped millions of dollars into Berry's pocket and the pockets of his clients. But this time, with *Maxwell's Guide to Heaven and Hell*, things would be different. Berry wouldn't make a cent.

*   *   *

Excerpt from *Maxwell's Guide to Heaven and Hell*, page 80:

The product Heaven produces is our Essence, the spark that gives us life in the first place. This is not manufactured, it is collected. Essence is donated by residents of both Heaven and Hell.

It is the main business of Heaven to collect Essence and to create new life. If the process is stopped, we are all lost.

"How's Mom?" Chelsea asked.

Cyrus took a moment to answer that question, thinking back on the circumstances that led to his wife's ultimate fate.

"I'm sad to say that she is…no longer," he said quietly, seeing tears well up in his daughter's eyes. "Let me explain. Within us all is our Essence. It is different than the common misconception that there is a soul. Essence is the basis of life and the business of Heaven is collecting this Essence. Although we all believed that donations of Essence were voluntary, some time ago it was discovered that the more people gave, the more they wanted to give. Donations were, in fact, addictive and every time someone gave some of their essence they also gave up a small part of themselves. There are people in Heaven who are more transparent

198

than others. They are the ones who have given up so much of their essence that it begins to show. They are fully aware and fully there, but they are not whole.

"And while there are some people in Heaven and Hell who have no purpose or drive to go on and thus choose to donate so much essence that they cease to exist, that was not the case with your mother. She was vibrant and full of spirit. She took an active part in the community. She considered herself a good citizen and, as such, made donations frequently. After a while, she couldn't help herself and she donated more and more of herself until there wasn't anything left."

"Couldn't anything be done?" Chelsea was taken aback.

"Originally, donations were required. Kind of the price for an afterlife. When it was discovered they were addictive there was a furor in Heaven and eventually management adjusted their expectations, responded to the will of the people, and decided donations were no longer mandatory. By then it was too late for your mother and many, many others. They just faded away gradually until they were gone."

Chelsea cried. Cyrus hated to be the bearer of such news and cried himself. They held each other for a few moments.

"How could God have let this happen?" Chelsea wondered aloud.

"I couldn't tell you what the Lord's intentions are. There are millions of occurrences that seemingly have no logical explanation. Why do people get sick? Why do bad things happen to good people? They say everything happens for a reason, but that's not true at all. God sets things in motion. Everything else is up to chance. Millions and millions of minute interactions that affect us all, both living and dead. Choices. Coincidences. We're not automatons. We have free choice and we deal with the consequences of our choices. The key, I think, is to be engaged, to get in the game. To live your life and not just coast through it. I see living as a rehearsal for the afterlife. If we can achieve some semblance of balance when living, we may be able to handle an eternity of existence. It's very complicated, life and death, and all part of a grander scheme of things that only God is aware of. We just go with the flow. Make the best of it.

"But I don't want to depress you or scare you. Heaven is a wondrous place where you can do anything, be anyone you want to be. So is life itself, but we often learn that lesson too late."

"Does God hear our prayers?" It was a question that often weighed heavily on her.

"Yes, He hears them. Whether He chooses to do something about them is another story. Most people's prayers are selfish, asking for things for themselves. Others are less so, directed more towards helping others. God would prefer that we find our own way in life and in Heaven. He doesn't micromanage. He gives us a lot of leeway. We're thinking rational beings, something we should be grateful for, I suppose.

"People think they know God. They have built religions designed to provide answers, to provide guidance. To provide them with a way of living their lives. But the truth is humans know relatively little about God and the workings of the universe. People are generally mistaken. It's like someone who only has awareness of a bicycle trying to describe an internal combustion engine. Impossible. Too complicated for them with the information they are privy to."

"Does it hurt?" she asked.

"Does what hurt?"

"Dying."

"For the most part, no. Take the two men who brought me here. The older one, Berry, died in his sleep. He didn't feel a thing. That brash young man—"

"The cute one?"

"Oh dear. Yes, Lucratelli. He died during World War Two. He felt the pain of his wounds momentarily, but then passed on without trauma. The transition to Heaven is much easier than anyone would imagine. Living is, unfortunately, often more painful than dying."

Cyrus reached into his pocket and withdrew a copy of *Maxwell's Guide to Heaven and Hell*.

"Here. Read this. It will answer many of your questions. It is the reason the three of us are here. Well, the reason those two are here. They want the world to have real answers to the questions they have. To provide some hope for them and for you."

Chelsea looked the book over, wiped away a tear, and smiled once more at her father.

"Thanks, Dad."

"Someday you'll meet God," Cyrus told her. "You'll be able to walk up to Him, say hello, and ask these questions yourself."

"You mean roll up to him," Chelsea said, nodding toward her wheelchair parked next to the couch.

"No, walk up to Him. Once you get to Heaven, you'll no longer require the chair."

*   *   *

It was a long par-four. The stream running across the fairway at about two hundred fifty yards from the tee made it an iffy drive. On the other side of the water was a stand of trees that came into play with any shot right of the center of the fairway. An approach shot to the green from the left side would be ideal.

The Devil was handed his three-wood.

"I'm hitting pretty well today. What do you think of my driving the water?"

O'Malley the caddie chuckled.

"What? You don't think so?" the Devil asked.

"No disrespect, sir, but if I thought so, I would have handed you the driver in the first place. And what would it buy you? You'd still have to hit a pretty tasty approach to get it up and down."

Lucifer regarded the man for a second and then set up on the tee. There was no sense in arguing. Risk and reward, that's what the game was all about, but you had to know when the risks were worth it.

He took a couple practice swings, remembering to take dead aim. What's the sense of a practice swing if you didn't really mean it? He stepped back, took another look, and then set back up. It was a little ritual he had gotten used to hundreds of years ago when he first started playing the game.

The swing seemed effortless. His ball started out low and center then hooked a little. It landed about ten yards short of the water just left of center. He was left about a hundred fifty yards from the flag stick; an easy nine-iron would do it. If he could put the next one close, he had a chance to putt his way to a birdie.

"Nicely done, sir," O'Malley said, honest appreciation for Lucifer's shot evident in his voice.

"Thank you." The Devil handed the three-wood back to the caddy and the two of them started walking towards the green.

"Are you expecting company, sir?" O'Malley asked.

A golf cart was racing silently across an adjacent fairway towards the two of them. It didn't take more than a couple seconds before the two men in the cart approached the Devil and O'Malley, slowing down to keep pace with them as they walked toward Lucifer's ball.

"Nice shot," one of them said.

"Michael. Gabriel," the Devil said, acknowledging the two of them. "I don't see any bags on your cart. I guess you weren't planning on a round with us." The two administrators were archangels and familiar to the Devil. They all had a shared history as part of the executive branch of Heavenly Affairs.

"Let's not be coy, Lucifer," Gabriel said. "We've met with the Smile Patrol. Bree Daniels is very concerned about this book situation. You know why we're here. The question is: Why are *you* still here? Shouldn't you be on Earth keeping tabs on those loose cannons you aided and abetted?"

"I did nothing of the kind."

"You certainly know what they are up to," countered Michael. "They will be unleashing something very potent and potentially dangerous by making *The Guide* available to the living."

"That they will," Lucifer agreed.

"And?"

"And what?"

"What are you going to do about it?" Michael asked.

"I don't intend to do anything about it. Just as I've been instructed."

"By who?"

"The Boss."

"You've spoken to Him?"

"Frequently. You know how He likes to have things shaken up. This should certainly do it."

"That's what we're afraid of."

*　　　　　　　*　　　　　　　*

"I heard you were dead," Joey Giordano said.

"Must have been wishful thinking," Berry remarked.

TV Branding Associates had been Berry's biggest competitor. They did their job well, but he'd never had much respect for the way Giordano ran the company or did business period. But when Berry died and his company folded, they were the next best thing. Berry knew they were big enough to handle the challenge he knew would be their most successful product ever.

"Why would you want to promote a book?"' Giordano asked.

"It's a unique book."

"I'll bet. What's the price point?"

"Nineteen ninety-five."

"The incentive is they get another book with the order for additional shipping and handling?"

"And you pocket the extra shipping and handling fees," Berry added. He knew how it all worked.

"Extra profit built in. I like that," Joey smiled.

"I thought you might."

"And what's our cost per unit?"

"Cost per book is zero. Zip."

"Yeah, right."

"I'm serious," Berry told him.

"And you're willing to bring it to me? Why? Why don't you just put it out yourself?"

"I'm retired."

"So you provide the product and we do everything else?"

"At one hundred per cent of the profits outside of what you pay for fulfillment. I get no royalties, maintain no rights. It's all yours."

"They say anything that appears too good to be true is just that: too good to be true."

"I've heard that. Or you could be looking a gift horse in the mouth. Up to you."

By the end of the meeting, they had a deal. Giordano didn't care what he sold as long as it was profitable. All he had to do was produce and air the TV commercials. Hiring students and interns, he was able to get a crew for next to nothing, certainly not even close to the going rate. And air time costs could be piggybacked with other client spots. Two minute commercials were passé. They were costly and it was difficult to buy two minute slots nationally. Giordano would produce a one minute direct response spot and another thirty second ad. It was a rush job and the first test airings would be in two weeks.

"So, Berry," Giordano asked, "why this particular book?"

"Read it, you'll find out," Berry suggested.

"I don't think so. Whimsical book, eccentric author. I've got it. Save me the time and explain it to me."

"It could change lives."

Giordano laughed. "Yeah, every piece of crap I've ever sold was a life changer. Berry, you're a piece of work. You really think you can change the world, don't you?"

"What's the point of it all if you can't?" Berry asked.

"Making a busload of money, you stupid schmuck."

12

The first television ad for *Maxwell's Guide to Heaven and Hell* ran on a cable superstation at 2:03 a.m. during an airing of *The Magic Christian*. The movie's title caught the attention of Josephine McCormick of Morganville, New Jersey. Though she was disappointed to see that the film was not religious in nature but about how the richest man in the world exploited people's sense of greed, she watched and, thirty-five seconds into the commercial spot, dialed the number she saw at the bottom of her TV screen. Somewhat addicted to home shopping, Josephine had in the last week ordered a set of wall hooks to hang pictures in her den (guaranteed not to leave any marks on the wall when removed), a hand vacuum for her car (which didn't seem to remove any of the hair shed by Parker, her golden retriever), a kitchen slicer that rather than chopping, dicing, and julienning left everything the consistency of oatmeal, a blanket with sleeves (in a deep maroon color that faded to pink in its first washing), a self-cleaning cat litter box (that her cat refused to use), and a blue cardigan (that fit surprisingly well). She had promised herself that she would curtail her purchases but *Maxwell's Guide to Heaven and Hell* intrigued her.

Dermond Slater answered her call. A former manager of a data processing company, he, like many others, lost his job when the economy turned and he hadn't found anything else in his field. With a wife and three children to support, Dermond took the telemarketing job, relieved that it was inbound calls only. At least he wasn't making cold calls trying to sell timeshares or solicit donations for some political campaign. The job didn't cover all of his expenses, but it was better than unemployment.

He was one of six operators at this particular call center and took orders for a number of products for various clients. Josephine's call was his first—anyone's first—for *Maxwell's Guide*.

"*Maxwell's Guide to Heaven and Hell*," he said after punching in to the call. "Thanks for calling. Can I help you?"

"Yes, I'd like to order that book about Heaven."

"*Maxwell's Guide to Heaven and Hell*. Yes, I can help you with that. The book is nineteen ninety-five plus four ninety-five shipping and handling."

Josephine started feeling the rush she got whenever she ordered.

"Okay, I get a second book for the same price, right?" she asked.

"Yes, ma'am. All you need to do is pay the extra shipping and handling charge. That would be another four ninety-five."

Under normal circumstances, the product price points were so low that the extra shipping charges were pure profit. But with Berry literally giving the books away, Joey Giordano could pocket even more. Even with the call center's cut and a fee to the fulfillment center it was a huge win.

Josephine felt chatty as she always did when ordering. It was her most enjoyable hobby. "I'm thinking of buying a couple more to give to my children," she told Dermond.

"I can help you with that," he said as he saw the other operators in the room answering their calls. The orders were coming in fast, with his call center automatically rolling over to other call centers around the country and even to outsourced call centers in India to accommodate the many orders. In all, there were three hundred forty-seven orders immediately after the first commercial ran and even more calls trickling in after the fact.

And there were still two hundred fifty more spots, all part of the first air time buy scheduled to run over the next ten days.

*　　　　　　　　*　　　　　　　　*

"Did you know that when you call people 'doc' you sound like Bugs Bunny?" Chelsea asked Lucratelli as he wheeled her through Washington Square Park. It was a beautiful day and the park was filled with street performers: jugglers, mimes, and people playing instruments. There was even a distinguished looking elderly man who walked about reciting Shakespeare.

"No, Bugs Bunny sounds like me."

"You should try 'dude' or something more up-to-date."

"Not really me. I don't think it's likely I'm gonna change this late in the game."

"Come on. You're talking like an old man or something. What are you? Like twenty-two?" she asked.

"Thanks. Actually I was born over eighty years ago. But I never got past my twenties before my untimely demise."

"Did it hurt? Dying, I mean?"

Lucratelli thought for a moment. "No, not really."

"That's what my Dad said. That dying wasn't that big a deal."

"I wouldn't exactly say that. I suppose it did hurt for an instant. I remember thinking, 'That's it? That's all I get? What about all the stuff I didn't get to do?' But I guess everyone has that feeling. Unfinished business, you know?"

"Like what?"

He wheeled her next to a park bench and sat down to join her.

"Like getting older for one thing."

"Yes, I can understand. Growing older, not necessarily growing up. Sometimes I think we don't really ever grow up. We just learn how to act better in public. What else do you miss?"

"Sharing life's experiences with someone you care about. Children. Grandchildren. I don't know. It's hard to talk about."

"Don't be embarrassed."

"I'm not. Not with you."

They both listened to a guitar player picking some bluegrass tune. Despite the music, Chelsea felt saddened and wanted to lighten the mood.

"What's Clark Gable up to?" she asked.

"Cavorting with Carole Lombard, the lucky stiff. Big difference in their ages now but they're still very much in love."

"Errol Flynn?"

"Probably drinking with Bogart and Barrymore. You know all those guys, huh?"

"I love old movies," Chelsea admitted. "I think they were better than the ones out today. I love the clothes, the cars, even the way they talk." She tried her best 1940s gun moll voice, "So I says to the yegg, you must be cracked or something. And he says to me, 'Say, listen sister, he's no good for you. Just a big lug.' "

"You sound like a dame who dresses smart and cracks wise."

They both laughed, followed by another pause in the conversation. Once again, Chelsea was the first to speak.

"I've often thought that the winds should be different colors. You could watch them move across the sky and see how they blend."

"If we were in Heaven right now, I could make that happen for you," Lucratelli told her. "Maybe someday I'll be able to do that."

"It must be wonderful there. Doing anything you like, living forever…"

"Sure, once you're dead. But even then, some people don't last forever."

Chelsea thought of her mom which brought the sadness back. Another silence. And once again, she was the one to speak. "I plan to live forever."

"Really? How do you expect to accomplish that?" Lucratelli asked.

"Twinkies. They have so many preservatives. What's their shelf life? A few hundred years? I'll start a Twinkies-only diet and will last for centuries."

"Good luck with that. I just read the factory's closing up. You'll probably outlive Twinkies."

"Are things much different here now that you're back?"

"Sure, but that's to be expected. Most of the people I knew are gone. Got old or passed away. Some of the old places are gone. Makes me a little nostalgic. But, what the hell, nostalgia ain't what it once was."

"Funny," Chelsea laughed. "What else?"

"Everyone moves quicker. Seems like everybody's in a hurry. Like they have no time for anything or anyone. Cars are different. Clothes are different. Technology's rampant. Superman's still around, but even he's different. It's all different, but in a way, it's all the same. People get up, go to work, make a living, look for a glimpse of happiness somewhere."

"If they're lucky."

"If they're smart. It's all there. They just have to know where to look. And *how* to look."

"My Dad told me I won't need my wheelchair in Heaven."

"True."

"That makes me very happy. I'm kind of looking forward to that."

"Understandable."

"Everything sounds so wonderful about Heaven. Maybe I can hurry things along."

"How so?" he asked.

"Oh, I don't know, wheel myself out into traffic or something."

Lucratelli pondered the idea of having Chelsea with him in Heaven for eternity. It was certainly appealing.

"They don't take too kindly to suicides," he told her. "God put this whole thing in motion. His Great Experiment is to see what humans do with their lives. What we become. How we progress. People who kill themselves demonstrate an inability or unwillingness to go on. Their Essence is tainted and therefore unusable in creating new life. I wouldn't want that for you. You wouldn't want that. Life is unique. It's precious. Value it while you are able to."

"Well, I'm not the most patient person in the world," she admitted.

"Me either. I'm surprised my tombstone doesn't read 'Can we move this along?' "

They both fell into another long pause.

"Do you wonder about things?"

"What things?" Lucratelli asked.

"I don't know...*things*. Do animals think?"

"Sure they do."

"About what?"

"Depends on the animal, I guess."

"Dog?"

"That's easy. Food."

"Cats?"

"Nobody knows what a cat's thinking. They're complex. But don't call them cute and cuddly. They hate that."

Another silence.

"I'd like to travel more," Chelsea said. "You?"

"I've traveled. I was in North Africa, Italy, Holland, France, Belgium."

"During the war?"

"Yeah. I call it my walking tour of Europe."

"War must be horrible."

"For the dead *and* the living. It never determines who is right, just who is left."

"Sad but true."

Once more, silence. But not an awkward pause; they were comfortable just being in each other's company.

"I like islands," she told him.

"The only island I've been to is Long Island."

"You're on an island now. Manhattan."

"Oh, right. See? I'm more traveled than I thought."

"I'd like to go to some islands in the tropics. The Bahamas, Aruba, St Croix."

"Must be nice."

"Palm trees, trade winds, beaches…"

"Rum drinks."

"I wonder if the Lesser Antilles have an inferiority complex because of their name?" she asked him.

It took a second but then Lucratelli laughed heartily. She loved his laugh. And his smile. Both were infectious.

"What's your name?" she asked. "I mean your first name."

"I don't remember."

"You just don't want to tell me. Is it that embarrassing?"

"No, it's just gone. Extinct."

"Was it endangered to begin with?" she asked.

"What do you mean?"

"Like those names parents used to name their kids but don't anymore. Names like Mortimer, Irving, Penelope, Millard. You know, endangered names."

"Gertrude," he offered.

"Yeah."

"Reginald."

"You've got it."

They both laughed and then just looked at each other.

"Want to get a bite to eat?"

"We don't have to. Isn't money a problem?"

"Not anymore," Lucratelli smiled that smile of his.

"Oh, how come, big shot?"

"I gave some guys some pool lessons they won't forget."

"Yeah, you are kind of unforgettable," she said.

Lucratelli, overcoming his reluctance, leaned in to kiss her but stopped at the last moment. Chelsea hoped he would indeed kiss her. She was taken aback when he hesitated.

"Chelsea, can I kiss you?" he asked softly.

"Do you really think you need to ask permission, you big lug?" she said in her forties voice. "Besides, I've never kissed a dead guy before."

      *   *   *

Josephine McCormick, the first customer to call and order *Maxwell's Guide to Heaven and Hell*, was also the first person to receive a copy. She had paid an extra charge to express ship her copies of the book and she had them the very next day.

After signing for the delivery, she rushed to her living room and opened the package. Inside were four copies, one for herself and three for her children, all grown and married now.

Life had not been easy for Josephine since her husband Earl had been killed. There were financial problems, difficulty making life decisions—Earl had been the one who decided everything of importance in their life together. And there was the sheer loneliness.

After being laid off from his job as a baby photographer, Earl worked in field services for a real estate company, going out to see the foreclosed properties the company listed. He took photographs and did inspections. Not structural inspections but walk-throughs to make sure the properties hadn't been vandalized, burned down, or flooded and that the utilities were functioning. It was a pretty easy gig that paid a decent wage and offered benefits, but with a list of almost two hundred fifty properties he had to see every two weeks, it kept him busy.

Each day he'd return home around four o'clock in the afternoon and spend another few hours on the computer e-mailing his reports and uploading the photographs.

One afternoon he didn't return home.

It had been early afternoon when Earl pulled up in front of a small single family house on a quiet suburban street. There was a report from a real estate agent that the key in the lockbox at this address was missing. Earl checked his notes and saw that the needed key had a 35241 code. It was a common key code and he had a bunch of those keys in the small tackle box he kept in his trunk. He retrieved the key, walked up to the front door, opened the lock box, and saw that the original key was indeed missing. He used his replacement key to open the front door and went inside to grab some pictures. He walked around the house taking two pictures in each room and when he finished the two shots in the master bedroom, he turned around to a gun in his face.

Two teenagers were standing in the bedroom's doorway. One of them, the shorter of the two, held the semi-automatic pistol aimed right between Earl's eyes.

"Get on the ground," he told Earl.

Earl's life didn't flash before his eyes. He thought, instead, of Hollywood movies. Clint Eastwood. John Wayne. What would they do in a situation like this? They'd have turned this around in seconds. But that was Hollywood. Earl was smart. He got down on the ground as instructed.

The teen pressed the gun against the back of Earl's head as his accomplice went through Earl's pockets taking the wallet from his back pocket, his car keys from the other back pocket, and whatever money was in Earl's front pocket. They also took his camera.

"Crawl in the closet," Earl was told.

He was reluctant to do so but complied, thinking that if he was cooperative, he might just survive this ordeal. On hands and knees, he made his way to the closet in the bedroom.

"You stay here and count to one hundred. You understand?"

Earl nodded and the door was closed. He started counting. By the time he reached twenty he could hear his car being started outside. At forty-five, he heard footsteps outside the closet door and figured that at least one of them came back to check on him. He didn't hear anything else for another ten count and thought they had left. The door opened. Earl had just time enough to look up into the eyes of his captor when he was shot. The youth then turned and ran out to the car. The two of them sped off as Earl dragged himself out of the room towards the living room and the property's front door. No one knew where he was. There was no telling how long he might lie there before someone found him. With great difficulty, he made it halfway out the door where he finally collapsed, exhausted. He bled to death.

The police never found the two youths. One of them, the one with the gun, was shot in a drug deal two weeks later. The other was arrested for breaking and entering when he was caught trying to burglarize a liquor store. Earl's car was returned to Josephine about four weeks after the murder with two thousand miles added to the odometer and six thousand dollars' worth of damage. It must have been some joyride.

A year after Earl's death, Josephine couldn't bring herself to go through Earl's belongings. His clothes hung in the closet. His tools were scattered around the garage. She spent her days watching television and ordering products that appeared on direct response commercials.

She unwrapped the package and held one of the small books in her hands. She knew Earl wouldn't have approved of her purchases, even this one. She thought back to their days together with sadness and longing. She missed him terribly. His laugh. His strength. His warmth. She thought of Earl as she opened the book somewhere near the middle to scan a page. She began reading on page 427:

Reunite with family and friends! Do you miss a loved one who has passed away? Our Heavenly Reunion Service is at your disposal Monday through Friday from 9 a.m. to 5 p.m.

Call, post messages, click on a link, or just stop in. We can have you back in their arms again in no time.

Holidays excluded.

Josephine felt an overwhelming sense of relief knowing that all of her sadness and all of her lonely suffering was finite. That someday, hopefully soon, she would be united with Earl and all would be well again. Well, outside of her being dead when that happens, of course.

*   *   *

Rob Boudreau spent hours leafing through his copy of *The Guide*. Originally a very successful owner of a number of car dealerships in southern Connecticut, Boudreau went on to grow a number of successful and varied businesses and currently owned a major league baseball team. He never wanted for a thing. He had a number of luxurious homes: one in Greenfield Hill in Connecticut's Fairfield County, another along the shore in Branford, a palatial apartment in New York City, a beach house in Malibu, and a ski chalet in Aspen. His collection of expensive and rare automobiles was housed in a warehouse in Greenwich. His two hundred twenty foot, four-story yacht was being redecorated in Fort Lauderdale. He owned priceless pieces of art and more jewelry than he knew what to do with.

His parents passed away when he was a child. Never married, he had no children. Outside of a few friends and business associates, he was basically alone in the world. And now he had been diagnosed with a late stage of lung cancer.

Accepting that he had limited time left, Boudreau made putting his life in order a top priority. He made arrangements for his own funeral. He sold business holdings that wouldn't flourish after he was gone. There were bids for his houses and possessions. The only question now it seemed was what to do with all his money. That was his most recent thought as he turned another page in *Maxwell's Guide*:

Excerpt from *Maxwell's Guide to Heaven and Hell*, page 863:

It's said that you can't take it with you. Actually you can, but it will just collect dust.

Everything is free in Heaven and money has no value. Sharing and goodwill are more valuable than any material gain.

Boudreau went to his desk, grabbed a few things, and left for his bank where he made a rather large withdrawal, thanked the teller, and, walking outside, handed anyone and everyone he saw at least one crisp, new one hundred dollar bill.

*   *   *   * *

Excerpt from *Maxwell's Guide to Heaven and Hell*, page 17:

God may not be omnipotent, but His limitations are beyond our knowledge.

Pastor Billy Creekside had a totally different reaction than many other readers of *The Guide*.

"Blasphemy!" he declared to the twenty-three people who made up his congregation known as Creekside's Crusaders. It was a small group, mainly relatives, but they were active, often receiving national attention for Creekside's fervent blend of theology, hate, and intolerance. They all had computers and knew how to use them to their best advantage, constantly posting and commenting on web sites, blogs, and in social media.

Their targets were many and varied. They protested at U.S. Armed Forces bases for the government's abolishment of "don't ask, don't tell" and for allowing gays to openly serve. They objected to anyone supporting the Boy Scouts, claiming they were a left-wing group promoting homosexuality and pedophilia. They even initiated a campaign to clothe naked pets in public. Television stations, cable networks, and advertisers were systematically barraged with threats of boycotts for anything that the group considered distasteful. They held rallies for right-wing conservative candidates who wanted to do away with Social Security, Medicare, or Medicaid despite the fact that many of them were themselves being helped by these very programs.

But nothing had ever fired them up as intensely as *Maxwell's Guide to Heaven and Hell*.

*   *   *

In a few short weeks thousands of copies of *The Guide* were ordered and delivered, yet so far it was still under the national media's radar. Outside of a few reviews in local papers, letters to the editor espousing a few readers' views, and some word of mouth recommendations, there was virtually no exposure on a national scale. But that was changing rapidly.

Berry was in his prime, spending most of his time riding herd on the call centers and fulfillment houses and ensuring that orders were taken and going out efficiently. He also supervised all TV, radio, and print advertising. There were additional shorter commercials produced that ran only thirty seconds as opposed to the original one minute spot.

Chelsea also kept busy, promoting the book through creative social networking posts and events as well as internet marketing. All of her work should have been handled by a fully staffed agency but Chelsea worked alone, spending the majority of her waking hours on the project, usually with Lucratelli by her side checking her array of reminders since her short term memory wasn't what it was before her surgery.

All the work was paying off: sales grew steadily while spurring a variety of reactions from anyone who read the book, knew someone who read the book, heard of the book, or knew someone who had heard of the book.

13

"Lucratelli and I are just a couple of mooks. You'll have to do it," Berry told Cyrus.

The older man contemplated that for a moment.

"I have to agree," Cyrus told him.

"Then you'll do it?"

"No, I agree you're mooks. Whatever they are."

"Thanks a lot, but I'm afraid it's up to you," Berry said. "Out of the three of us, you are the most educated. The most erudite. More cultured. And, you're older. People will listen to you. And you're a Brit."

"What does that have to do with anything?"

"You all sound so much smarter than we do."

Someone would have to face the media. Reactions to the book were starting to gain attention…fast.

* * *

At the Dawn of Mankind, people communicated simply by shouting across the cave:

"Mugli, what have you got to eat?"

"Mastodon steaks. You?"

"Nuts and berries. Want to share?"

"I don't think so."

"Get out of the cave then."

"Alright, come on over."

Later, when Man formed communities, it was a matter of just walking next door:

"Hello? Are you home?"

"Why are you yelling? Why don't you just knock on the door?"

"Is that a new thing? Listen, they've decided that the old woman down the road is a witch and they're going to burn her at the stake. Wanna go?"

"No, I'm working on something. I'm tired of my shoes confusing the hell out of me so I'm inventing the left shoe and the right shoe."

"How would you tell them apart?"

"That's what I'm working on."

Eventually other forms of communication were devised, taking different forms in different geographic areas. African villages communicated through the use of drums:

"New dance?"

"No. Lion run amok."

Native Americans utilized smoke signals.

"What are they saying?"

"Near as I can tell: Buffalo gals, won't you come out tonight."

Even later, riders on horseback carried mail from one part of the country to another:

"What'd ya get, Clem?"

"A letter from my wife."

"Good news?"

"My daughter's getting married. She was only twelve when I left St Louis…"

"Time sure flies in the West, don't it, pard?"

The railroad sped up the process while ocean voyages brought overseas messages:

"There was a war?"

"Between who?"

"Beats me."

"Who won?"

"It says we did."

V-Mail during World War Two allowed loved ones to keep in touch:

"What's that?"

"A 'Dear John' letter from my wife. But, my name's not John."

Then telegraph, phone lines, and transatlantic cables all made communications immediate. Radio, television, and satellites were able to bring entertainment and commercials to every home in the world linking cultures across geographical divides so that every person everywhere knew Ralph Kramden drove a bus and Ed Norton worked in the sewers.

Computers and the internet over dial-up lines weren't fast enough so they came up with cable, fiber, and broadband allowing anybody access to the whole archive of Mankind's history, literature, art, and wisdom.

"What's that you're watching online?"

"Football and porn. Could this day get any better?"

And once *Maxwell's Guide to Heaven and Hell* was made available, the cry was loud and far-reaching.

         *   *   *

Conservative talk radio launched an offensive against *The Guide* claiming it was yet one more example of liberals waging a war on religion. America's News Now and other right-wing cable networks and news sources joined radio's assault by spending endless hours of air time with news alerts and special reports linking the book to various left-wing, communist, and atheist conspiracies.

The Vatican was strangely mum. Besieged over allegations of child abuse, their official stand on contraception, and outrage over their non-support of gay rights, they had their own problems. Besides, they thought that *Maxwell's Guide* may possibly be added to the Catholic Church's canon of religious artifacts. Or not. The Cardinals, a very conservative bunch historically and politically, tended to individually condemn the book. Nuns, the more liberal members of the Church, were more accepting. At any rate, the Vatican promised that sooner or later there would be an official policy statement from the pope. Or the next pope.

Baptists, Evangelicals, and other religious groups reacted strongly, tending to condemn and vilify *The Guide* because they felt that it was being viewed as a new Bible and a danger to the Bible they had grown up with and were used to.

Their opposition was loud and forceful. They mobilized and attempted to launch boycotts of any and all TV stations, networks, and magazines that attempted to sell *The Guide*.

As for the general public, there were those who thought the book was simply disrespectful and sacrilegious.

There was a smattering of small cults in different parts of the country and the world that accepted the small book as Truth and that someone indeed had shared their knowledge of the afterlife with them. Other readers looked at it strictly as a work of fiction by some crazy, creative, quirky writer looking to make a buck.

The fact remained that the book was getting attention which spurred sales and a media feeding frenzy. All the notice warranted someone getting out there and talking about the book. So Chelsea, whose company was the main contact for any public relations for *The Guide*, responded positively to a request for someone to do a TV interview. It was scheduled for the next morning.

"You *have* to do it," Berry urged.

"Utterly preposterous," Cyrus spewed. "There isn't the slightest chance that I, having passed away some time ago and having been forced against my will back here, would expose myself to that type of scrutiny and possible ridicule. Who knows what the repercussions might be?"

"But you are the book's editor. You know it intimately. There's no one that would be more suitable," Berry insisted.

"Perhaps Chelsea would consent to do the interview herself," Cyrus suggested. "I could fill her in on any pertinent information.

She's nice-looking, extremely intelligent, and personable. She's also very discreet so we needn't worry about our own exposure. She'd be perfect, I'm sure. If someone has to do it at all."

"That's a possibility," Berry admitted. "Let's ask her." He called out her name but neither Chelsea nor Lucratelli was anywhere in the spacious apartment.

On the refrigerator was a note stating that she and Lucratelli were taking the "Zoey Express" and that they'd be back later that night with plenty of time to make the interview.

*   *   *

Lucratelli had helped Chelsea to her feet and held her tightly around her waist as he clutched Zoey gently to their chests. He felt the familiar vibration that he originally thought was purring but now recognized as a sign of imminent transport. There was a faint odor of cinnamon. An instant later the three of them were standing in an apple grove. The fragrant air was intoxicating. The sky was the bluest of blues and a gentle breeze stirred the leaves.

He smiled at Chelsea and slowly released her, leaning her carefully back against one of the trees. He then stooped to put the small calico cat down at his feet. Zoey scampered off, perhaps to chase critters, perhaps to check in somewhere. There was no way of knowing what cats did in their spare time.

"It's beautiful," Chelsea gasped.

"It's Heaven," Lucratelli smiled once again, that smile that never failed to light her up. He held his hands out.

229

At first Chelsea didn't know what he wanted. When it hit her, she looked expectantly at him then glanced down at her feet. She took one tentative step with her right foot, another hesitant step with her left, moving slowly away from the tree. Biting her lip with excitement, she took yet another step forward. With each motion, Lucratelli moved slowly backwards, silently encouraging.

"I can't believe it," she uttered.

She walked closer and closer to Lucratelli, then was close enough to touch him. She put her arms around him, hugged him, then turned and walked around the closest tree. She stopped and smiled at him. Then she walked around the other way. She walked faster, faster, then broke out into a hearty laugh and ran off deeper into the orchard. Lucratelli could see her darting between the trees. She wove in and out and around them, then spun around and ran, literally ran, back towards him. She stopped short just in front of him, looked up, looked at her feet again, then jumped up and grabbed hold of an overhanging branch. She swung there, laughing, and then landed with a thud. She fell silent, looked up at Lucratelli, made an adorably funny face, then broke out in laughter once more. She then ran to him and hugged him tightly.

"Thank you. Thank you so much. You won't get in any trouble for this, will you?"

"No more than usual. So, what would you like to do?"

"What *can* we do?"

"You're in Heaven. Anything you like."

*   *   *

"I'm calling for every person of faith to support us in our boycott of any TV station or network that sells air time to the heathens who have foisted this volume of filth and lies," spewed Pastor Billy Creekside, who had called in to Laureen Dawber's radio show. "We will go wherever we are needed—malls, bookstores, libraries—to see that more Americans are not exposed to this poisonous volume."

"I've heard that you're also mobilizing people politically as well," Laureen noted.

"Yes. We are urging everyone to call their representatives. Call or e-mail your senator, your congressman. Insist on legislation to abolish this type of thing once and for all. There is no place in America for this kind of so-called literature. The Bible is God's word. This book? The ranting and ravings of some godless heathen who wants to upset the whole apple cart. And the government, by doing nothing, is part and parcel to it. The government hates religion and believers. They are waging a war on our beliefs, our values. On the American way of life. And I know God is on our side in this."

"I always say God is riding shotgun."

"I know what you mean. God has our backs on this."

"There are those who say this is a free speech issue."

"I know we, as Americans, are guaranteed the right to free speech. But this is an affront to every God-fearing person out there. Free speech? That applies to us as well. Contact your representatives. And I suggest you don't just call their offices. Occupy them! Go to their local office near your town or city and tell them to their faces that you won't stand for this sort of thing. And if they won't help, they won't get the votes come next election. We'll get them out of there so fast they'll have whiplash and we'll replace them with reverent, respectful people who feel the same way we do."

"And they're out there," Laureen added.

"Yes, they are. Enough like-minded people to get the job done. We are at a crossroads in this country. Standing at the edge of a precipice. We need to stand up together with the strength of God behind us and take this country back. I'm tired of these Northeastern liberals, these college professors and secular Humanists espousing what they think they know about God and country, the environment, and the aims of our Founding Fathers. If we don't do something—the *right* thing—now, our country will be changed and lost forever."

"You see this book, this guide, as dangerous?" Laureen asked.

"I see it as an affront to our faith and our beliefs, to our very way of life, and we need to unite and take a stand," stated Pastor Creekside.

"What was it specifically when you first read the book that angered you?"

"Well, I didn't actually read it. But I don't have to. I know what's in there."

*   *   *

"Maybe I should look up some relatives," Chelsea suggested.

"Listen," Lucratelli told her, "I don't know what is going to happen. They could come get me here for jumping back to Earth. They could come after me when I return back there."

"You're a Heavenly criminal, I guess."

"I prefer outlaw. There's a difference."

"And the difference would be?"

"Criminals commit crimes. Outlaws buck the system."

"Six of one, half dozen—"

"No matter. What's important is that you and I have a very limited time here. Your dad's back at your place. Your mom, well, she's gone. You know that. You'll have plenty of time to get reacquainted with grandparents, aunts, uncles, and cousins, whatever. I mean, once you come here permanently, you'll be able to look up any long-lost family you want to. I think, for now, you should just enjoy yourself."

She was certainly enjoying this alternate reality. Even the simple act of walking was a treat for Chelsea. She and Lucratelli strolled together hand in hand to a transport stop where they hopped on a shuttle, Chelsea literally jumping on board like a little kid. They were whisked almost instantly to a mountainous area where it lightly snowed even though the temperature was warm enough to be comfortable in their light clothing. They spent a few minutes being fitted with ski equipment then went back outside where Chelsea fell right over. Laughing, she looked up at Lucratelli.

"I have no idea what I'm doing."

"I'll show you," he said, smiling that smile that she loved.

The weather, of course, was perfect and so were the conditions. Fresh white powder. They spent a little time on the bunny slope where Lucratelli showed her the fundamentals, teaching her to snowplow, to turn, how to use her body to help direct herself.

She was a quick learner. After a little while they moved on to a more intermediate trail, sharing the chair lift to the top and admiring the view. They then skied leisurely down the mountain.

After a few runs they returned their gear and walked out to a bicycle rack. The bikes were there for anyone's use as bicycles were all over Heaven. People took a bike when they wanted one and then left it wherever their journey ended, ready for the next person.

They pedaled away from the ski area and found themselves out in the countryside riding along rural roads where the trees formed archways over them. It was a multi-colored canopy of postcard perfection. Wildlife scampered by to the duo's wonder and delight.

After a while, famished, they entered a little town.

"Look at all the restaurants," Chelsea said.

"And I'm sure they are all amazingly good," Lucratelli told her. "That's a thing about Heaven: The food is great."

They stopped at a place called the Taj Mahal for some tandoori. Every bite was a revelation. Chelsea had never tasted anything so good.

After lunch, they left the bicycles at a convenient rack and boarded yet another shuttle that had them at the seashore in seconds. They found a store, The Olde Curio Shoppe, filled with maritime odds and ends such as ship's wheels, lanterns, lobster traps, and beach items like blankets, towels, umbrellas, and lounge chairs.

Lucratelli found masks, fins, and one snorkel. Borrowing them from the kindly proprietor, they walked to the nearby beach. It was perfect. Ringed by ice-capped mountains, they had a secluded, white sands beach all to themselves.

"Here," said Lucratelli. "This is for you," handing her the snorkel.

"What about yours?" she asked.

"No problem."

They both eased themselves into the warm water. Lucratelli didn't need the snorkel. Being dead already, he essentially dove, drowned, and recovered immediately. This was repeated during the length of their frolic in the ocean which was fascinating to Chelsea but old hat to Lucratelli.

Making their way back to town they held hands as they window-shopped along the main street. Chelsea was amazed at the variety of people she saw along the way. There were Vikings, natives of various countries, obscure tribes, and typical suburbanites, every color and culture and variety of human that ever lived. Languages were plentiful but everyone was able to understand each other without difficulty.

They entered a small coffee shop and sat down at a table by the window, ordering lattes. Chelsea coughed.

"Are you okay?" Lucratelli asked her.

"I'm fine, just not used to so many people smoking cigarettes. Is that common here?"

"Smokers everywhere sometimes," Lucratelli answered. "I guess since they're already dead they figure they have nothing to lose."

They went skating—not rollerblading—on real roller skates, the kind with four wheels, two in front and two in back.

They visited a planetarium that didn't have a projector, but had observation platforms that afforded them ringside seats at some of the universe's most wondrous sights.

They hiked lush woods with lichen like velvet, singing birds, and buzzing and chirping insects. They settled down on the side of a hill looking out over the vista. From a distance Chelsea could make out a patch of color, what looked like a cloud of almost transparent pink. It moved along with the wind, on the wind; it seemed to *be* the wind. From another direction, a similar cloud appeared that was violet, then another a pale yellow. They soared and floated and touched and collided and blended creating a stunning vision of pastels, an airborne color palette ever changing. The colors of the wind.

"How did you arrange—"

"Not important," he said. And it wasn't. The fact was he remembered her wish from the park about the winds being different colors and he set things in motion to make this moment possible.

For Chelsea it was all wondrous and perfect. Heaven was filled with magical surprises. Being able to walk, run, bike, and even ski and skate brought tears to her eyes.

It was the most incredible day she had ever had in her entire lifetime. And it was all due to this crazy man who talked like John Garfield and had a smile that could just knock you out.

Eventually darkness insinuated itself and they made their way back to town. They found John Lennon in a small bistro strumming a guitar along with Robert Johnson, singing about the crossroads. Lucratelli asked if she wanted to dance but she declined. She was appreciative of being mobile again, but wanted to save that first dance for the wedding she hoped would one day be hers.

*   *   *

"You need to get down there. This time we're serious."

Archangels Michael and Gabriel were again hounding the Devil to return to Earth and put some spin control on the events unfolding there. He had just finished an early round of golf and was enjoying lunch and a cold drink.

"What can I order for you two?" he asked.

"Nothing, we're good," replied Michael. "Listen those three numbskulls have gone public with *The Guide* and we think you should—"

They were interrupted by a string of obscenities from the eighteenth fairway.

"Don't mind that," said Satan, "it's just Mark Twain."

"I thought he didn't play golf. He said golf was a 'good walk ruined'."

"In his lifetime, yes. But since he's been here he's become fanatical about it. Plus, it's a game where he can drink and smoke while he plays. Suits him fine now."

"Anyway," Michael continued, "suppose these yahoos have run amok down on Earth. The book is being widely read and distributed—"

"—and taken to heart and actually believed to be authentic," Gabriel added.

"Yes, then there could be serious repercussions here," said Michael.

"How so?"

"Maybe people will change their behavior. Fewer violent crimes. Fewer wars. Less stress-related disease. People could find more innovative ways to intentionally die."

"And that would be a bad thing?" Lucifer asked.

"Donations of Essence are down as it is. Even with growing populations, it's getting hard to keep up. Production is off. If the living alter their belief systems and—"

"Evolve?" the Devil interjected.

"—it could mean serious changes here. Essence is our stock in trade. If we can't create more and more life, the whole experiment The Boss has been working on for millions of years will be for naught."

Another round of expletives spewed forth from Twain who blew his approach shot. Landing left of the green, his ball was buried near the back edge of a sand trap and looked like a fried egg. It was a terrible lie.

"So what are you going to do?" asked Michael.

"I think I'll go help Mr. Clemens there with his sand wedge before he spikes it back over the green."

*   *   *

Excerpt from *Maxwell's Guide to Heaven and Hell*, page 528:

We can't stress this point enough: you can be anything you want, go anywhere you like, do anything you please.

Just be sure that it is really what you want.

Much like *The Guide* itself, Cyrus Maxwell was an open book. If someone wanted an answer about life, Heaven, or Hell all they had to do was think of the question, open the book, and it would be there for them. Much the same with Cyrus. Duplicity did not exist for him or in him. Asked a straight question, you'd get a straight answer. No problem.

Until he was interviewed on national television.

Chelsea had set up an interview on Ric Arno's show on the America's News Now network. She had originally planned to do the interview herself but her foray with Lucratelli to Heaven was so overwhelming that time ran away from her. Plus, with her short-term memory problem, it easily slipped her mind, and not being home, she couldn't check her constant supply of Post-it reminders. Besides, once she and Lucratelli woke up at his place early that morning, Zoey was nowhere to be found. Always looking after her wards diligently, the small calico would turn up eventually, but at that time she was M.I.A.

At the network's headquarters in New York, Berry and Cyrus, already in the studio, decided to press on with Cyrus doing the interview instead of Chelsea.

"I'm here with Cyrus Maxwell, author of *Maxwell's Guide to Heaven and Hell*, a book which has garnered a lot of attention lately and is causing a lion's share of controversy," Arno said, directly to the camera. He then turned to Cyrus. "What inspired you to write this book?"

"I'm not the author, merely the editor," Cyrus answered. "The book is a compilation of subject material submitted by many people. Thousands, in fact."

"And the subject material is what, exactly?"

"It is a guide to existing in Heaven. Or in Hell, for that matter."

"Advice?"

"Sometimes. Often it is merely a reference for what to do or where to go. Like any guidebook."

"Very imaginative."

"No, very factual."

"What would you know about Heaven or Hell?" Arno asked.

"As much as anyone else, I suppose. It's where I live."

"You live in Heaven?"

"Yes."

"So you're…"

"Dead? Yes. I died years ago and have been working on the book for some time now."

There was a noticeable murmur inside the studio. Arno was psyched. This was going to be good.

"How did you get here?" he asked.

"In a taxi."

"No, I mean from Heaven."

"Oh. A cat."

"I beg your pardon?"

"A cat. A small calico that looks after my daughter. Her name is Chelsea."

"The cat's name is Chelsea?"

"No, Chelsea is my daughter. The cat's name is Zoey. We hitched a ride."

"We?"

"My associates and I."

"Also dead?"

"Of course."

"I see," said Arno, but he really didn't.

"What prompted you to return to Earth?"

"It was not a matter of choice. You might say I was abducted."

"By these associates?"

"Yes."

"What was their motivation for bringing you here?"

241

"To the studio?"

"No, back to Earth."

"They wanted to release the book. To let the world know the truth. To change things."

"Some people are touting the book as a kind of new Bible. Do you see it that way?"

"I can't relate to that," Cyrus said after some thought. "The Bible, both the Old Testament and New Testament, I find to be irrelevant. They are simple stories. Historical in some sense. There are some factual places, people, and occurrences, but what you read in your religious books here on Earth is mostly fabricated. Chronicles of their times: parables, fables, and morality tales. But not really relevant at all. Like religions."

"I don't understand."

"I didn't think you would. That's why I was brought here. Talking to the living about God or Heaven is like talking to a baby about computers. There is no real common ground. No real knowledge or understanding of the true nature of anything. Everyone here on Earth has beliefs that are based on hearsay rather than experience. Religions are inventions of Mankind. So are the main books pertaining to those religions. Yet entire histories, cultures, even countries, have been founded or guided by those beliefs. Humans think they have it all scoped out but they are so totally mistaken. And the clergy and politicians are the worst offenders."

"So you are an atheist?"

"Not at all. Atheists are gravely mistaken."

"Agnostic?"

"Stop trying to categorize me. Agnostics think there may or may not be a God. Well, at least they're open-minded. Unlike Evangelicals who think God talks directly to them. Believe me; God has no desire to talk to any of those people at all. It's like atheists think God is dead, agnostics think God's on vacation, and evangelists think God sends them postcards from wherever He is. All of them are misguided."

"Do you yourself believe God exists?" Arno inquired.

"Absolutely. I've met God on numerous occasions," Cyrus admitted.

"Really? What does God look like?"

"Whatever you want Him or Her to look like. To some, God is a man. To others, a woman. The Lord can be young or old or an animal or, as in your Bible, a burning bush. Perception is in the eye of the beholder."

"Does God answer prayers?"

"Rarely. Most prayers are selfish, aren't they? Or perhaps they are requests for things beyond our own control. But God likes to see how things pan out on their own. Oh, maybe a little tweak here and there. But what fun would it be for Him to control everything in the universe? There's more wonder in observing, not directing."

"Is that why bad things happen to good people?"

"That's another thing humans do: they assign reasons for everything. There are no reasons for tragic events. No reasons for anything actually. People who say something happened for a reason are wrong. Things just happen randomly. Sometimes there are coincidences. People drive themselves crazy trying to find reason in everything when there isn't any."

Arno had never conducted an interview like this before. Convinced that Cyrus was totally out of his mind, Arno knew this segment would go viral. People would be talking and arguing about this for a long time.

"What is Heaven like?" he asked.

"Very much like here but without money. Finances are not a motivation. Everyone is productive in their own way. There are no wars. No crime. No catastrophes, generally."

"Sounds great," Arno said. "We're in New York where there's something negative happening all the time. Heaven, in comparison, sounds like paradise."

"Yes, it's where the word comes from actually," Cyrus noted. "Then, of course, there's Hell. A bit different there, I must say."

"How is that?"

"There's absolutely nothing going on there. Hell is for those who are not at all motivated."

"Motivated to be…good?"

"Motivated to participate as a responsible member of Heavenly society."

"And if they are not responsible, they're punished? I assume they'll burn in Hell for eternity?"

"Burn? No. Not at all. More likely they'd get a sunburn. That's the only danger in Hell. They're generally just bored and lying on the beach. There's nothing much at all to do in Hell. It's like staying on a very bad vacation where there are no attractions or activities for a very, very long time. Eternity."

"What about the criminals, the evil people? They are punished, right?"

"Well, they've had problems…with their upbringing, their education, their outlook. The way they relate to others and society. They are re-educated. Their problems are dealt with—cured, if you will—so that they may or may not contribute to the general good and well-being."

"What's the purpose of that?"

"To participate in the business of Heaven."

"Business?"

"Yes. The business of Heaven is to create life. That is done by donations of one's Essence. Life is created and evolves."

"Like a soul?"

"No. Like your Essence."

"So why are we here?"

"To do this interview."

"No, I mean, why are we here on Earth? Why do we exist?"

"Perhaps as a rehearsal for living through eternity. One must crawl and walk before running. We exist on an earthly, human plane to test the waters. Eternity is a very, very long time. So we acquire the skills here on Earth first. We are part of a vast experiment.

People think the opposable thumb was a big deal, but actually, the main surprise was ideas. Humans have had some very creative ideas. Love and interpersonal relationships. Loyalty. Creativity. Art. Music. Books. All a delight to God that these *animals* He created, meaning us, have come so far. Events were set in motion to see where we'd wind up. We may or may not be the only experiment of its kind in the universe. I have no way of knowing that. Only God knows."

"Kind of depressing, isn't it?"

"No, not at all," Cyrus said, surprised. "In fact, the opposite. Knowing that we can progress, get better, and improve? Who knows what we'll be capable of in the future? It gives one a sense of optimism that there is so much out there we can aspire to.

"When is the last time you personally spoke with God?"

"It's been a while since any of us have heard from Him or seen Him."

"Could He have given up on us?"

"I doubt that. He may be busy elsewhere. Perhaps another experiment. Who knows? He hasn't taken an active part in things lately. He doesn't micromanage. He just waits to see how things pan out, I suppose."

"How do you know?"

"He left a note. It said, 'That's lunch…one hour.' We haven't seen Him since."

14

The interview was a short segment on ANN, but it was virtually the only story that was talked about that day. Before the segment was even finished the switchboards at the network lit up like a department store's holiday window. The network brass gloated that they had secured the interview. This would be a ratings bonanza the likes of which they'd never seen before.

Ric Arno's contract was just about up and he was immediately on the phone with his agent and manager to plan their strategy for a new agreement with a substantial pay increase and a partial ownership deal.

Within minutes the online universe was abuzz with reactions to Cyrus' appearance. Links to the video were posted. Hash tags popped up like #DeadManTalking, #BackFromTheDead, #HeavenIsReal, #GodExists, and #HeavensPundit. Related topics started trending worldwide. An Occupy Heaven movement would start within days.

The video of the Cyrus interview went viral within an hour. Within twenty-four hours the clips would have millions of hits and would be the most seen videos in history with more viewings than Justin Bieber, Gangnam Style, or Lady Gaga combined.

In a short time there would be press releases and statements distributed by religious leaders calling for a complete rebuttal of what Cyrus had said. They would see his appearance as an all-out attack on every religion. There would be protests held in churches and synagogues and mosques. Members of the clergy would warn their congregations not to read the book and admonish those who did.

Within days the Russians would ban *Maxwell's Guide* which in turn would cause the more liberal members of the United States Congress to condemn the Russians' oppressive condemnation of any person's right to read or believe anything they cared to believe. Some governments would take preventative steps to discourage protests, an attempt to quell any unrest and avoid any potentially violent confrontations. A small country in the Middle East would put a bounty on Cyrus Maxwell's head.

Conservative talk show hosts on radio and TV would extol their followers to rise up against the heathen attack on the Church and religion. Crowds would gather outside the studios and headquarters of any TV station or cable network that ran ads for the book or stories on their newscasts.

There would also be a group of people who would see the whole thing as a very clever, hilarious marketing ploy.

In the bigger picture, *Maxwell's Guide to Heaven and Hell* would have a global, long-lasting impact. Church attendance would eventually fall off when people realized that the old rules didn't apply. They didn't have to follow the rites and rituals deemed necessary by their various religions to get to Heaven. It would be guaranteed.

The people who thought Cyrus was truthful would have their belief in God reaffirmed. They would realize there is a God and a Heaven and that there is even a Hell but you'd never be condemned to burn forever. The release of the book would change the way the world looked at its history, its religions, its leaders, and its own morals and behavior.

All that would happen as a result of Cyrus' appearance, but at that moment he and Berry were faced with the reaction right there in the building. As soon as the segment ended, studio and network personnel flocked around Cyrus, inundating him with offers and questions. Polite as he was, Cyrus tried to answer them all but it was getting crazy. Berry stepped in to usher the older man out and away. It took them what seemed like an eternity to extricate themselves.

They stepped out onto the street and the New York rush of people and vehicles was actually a relief after the tumult in the studio and hallways.

Cyrus straightened his clothing and fixed his tie, glad that he had remembered his umbrella.

"That went rather well," he remarked, flushed from all the attention.

"Yeah. We'll see. Either they will all go out and buy the book immediately or hang you for blasphemy," Berry replied.

A less-than-perfect result of his appearance on TV had never even occurred to Cyrus. He suddenly realized that the interview might have some sort of repercussions or consequences.

"Oh dear," he said.

          *   *   *

Excerpt from *Maxwell's Guide to Heaven and Hell*, page 752:

Never let anyone decide what is best for you. Don't let other people determine what you may or may not want.

Politicians and the clergy are the worst offenders.

Pastor Billy Creekside was incensed. He looked out over his congregation of relatives and friends, all twenty-three of them, and told them they were going to pile into the church's bus and head straight to New York City. All of them.

"This Cyrus Maxwell character? He may be the editor of this foul, blasphemous volume but we know who the author really is— the Devil himself! Without the moral guidelines of the Bible, people will revert to the sins of Sodom and Gomorrah!"

Spittle was accumulating on the podium as he vented.

"We will travel to New York, our modern-day Sodom. We will find these books wherever they are, collect them, and burn them along the way. And every one of you is required to take part in this…this…Crusade!"

The crowd, such as it was, cheered, looking forward to a road trip.

One of the parishioners stood and was recognized. "Our sister Beatrice is expecting and about to pop. I'm not sure going on a trip of this sort would be prudent at this time."

"She is excused from participating and we wish her all the best during her blessed event," Creekside replied.

Another member rose and stated that his store was being renovated and a new inventory of truck tires would be arriving.

"You can stay behind and tend to business," Creekside told him. "In fact, I don't care if I have to go by myself. How's the bus?"

Their church vehicle was parked outside, a half-rusted hulk of an old school bus that had been painted over. "First Church of the Almighty" was hand painted on the sides.

Another parishioner rose. "I overhauled the engine just a few weeks ago. She's good to go. As long as we keep feedin' her water when the she overheats and keep an eye on the oil level, we should be okay."

"Good," Creekside said. "We will find this Cyrus Maxwell and anyone else connected with him and put a stop to this affront to good people everywhere. I have spoken with God and He will be there with us guiding our way. Stand with me. Stand for what's right. We will stem the darkness enfolding our world and bring it all back to the light as God strengthens us and smiles upon us in our endeavor to serve Him. God is riding shotgun! We shall prevail!"

Creekside slammed his hand down on the podium and left his congregation. He passed through a doorway and entered into his office. He opened a desk drawer and pulled out a Bible, opening it. The tome was hollowed out. Inside was a loaded 9mm Glock semiautomatic pistol.

*   *   *

They stayed at Lucratelli's place. They made love slowly and affectionately. Chelsea slept well, but Lucratelli didn't. After searching Berry's place and exploding Lucratelli's still, he knew that Smile Patrol operatives might be lurking about watching and waiting for his return. He might even expect a visit from Bree herself. At the very least, some dog, cat, bird, or insect might be observing him. It put him on edge. He knew they could locate him easily if they really wanted to…this was, after all, Heaven. People had many ways of knowing things here. The fact that they didn't disturb him and Chelsea made him even more suspicious.

They shared a lovely breakfast of coffee and omelets in a little restaurant in town, but their high spirits were shaded by a nagging realization that they had to go back. Berry and Chelsea's dad had been left alone to deal with the situation in New York and Chelsea, being alive, didn't belong in Heaven yet.

Somehow they had to find Zoey. There was no telling where the little cat might be. With people and families spread out all over Heaven and Earth she could be anywhere.

"Do we really have to go back so soon?" Chelsea asked as they were leaving the restaurant.

"Right now," a voice answered from a nearby car parked right in front of the doorway. They both leaned over to see who it might be. Chelsea didn't recognize the man behind the wheel but Lucratelli knew that smiling face immediately.

It was the Devil.

*   *   *

Only eleven people boarded the dilapidated bus on Pastor Billy Creekside's crusade to save America from itself. Some of his parishioners had pressing responsibilities that couldn't be postponed, but the ten people who accompanied the Pastor were die-hard followers.

It was good that none of them were in any particular rush to get to New York since the bus was fairly dilapidated and short hops would have to do. They made numerous stops along the way to meet with true, like-minded believers and to court the media. Outside of Valdosta, Georgia, as he did in many cities on their route north, Creekside held a press conference. He invited believers to amass books, records, magazines—anything that the faithful found offensive. The intention was that the items would be burned in a massive bonfire that would be sure to make the evening newscasts.

About forty people gathered around Creekside for a prayer meeting. Behind him was a pile of items that the locals had collected. There were CDs and records, everything from rock and pop to metal, punk, and emo. Strangely, there were old albums of artists from the forties as well including the Andrews Sisters and

Cab Callaway. There were non-fiction and fiction titles, books that ran the gamut from Twain to Shakespeare to Germaine Greer. There were magazines, comic books, photos, even bric-a-brac, old furniture, and four copies of *Maxwell's Guide to Heaven and Hell.*

"These things you have brought here are indicative of the way this country and the people in it have lost their way. America no longer has a moral compass," Creekside bellowed. "Crass commercialism and sex have become first and foremost in our culture. People of the church are ridiculed as if a belief in God the Almighty is humorous and beneath the American people somehow. I assure you this is *not* the case with true believers. We know the course and set sail for the land of the righteous and the virtuous.

"I thank you all for allowing me to join you today. We are but a small yet fervent congregation. We, like you, struggle daily. That's why I implore you, one and all, to reach into your hearts and into your pockets and wallets as well. We have the strength to go on but don't always have the resources. Our journey is a noble one, blessed by God Himself. He approves of our purpose. He told me himself. Help support us and the Lord with a generous donation and know that by doing so God will smile kindly upon you.

"We move northward from here to more communities that are seeking the same things, appreciating the same values as we do. If we cannot look to our brothers and sisters for assistance we will be forced to abandon this glorious endeavor. We're not asking for much, whatever you feel is right. Whatever God tells you to contribute. Follow His guidance and reach deep, knowing that we are all doing the Lord's work and bending to His will."

As the pastor spoke, a volunteer poured kerosene onto the pile. At the end of the makeshift sermon, the items were torched. The crowd cheered and watched the fire spread so that the entire collection was aflame. Then they all sat down at picnic tables and had a bar-b-que with briskets, chicken, sausages, and ribs that had been cooking in smokers for hours beforehand. It was a right fine family outing with races and booths, competitions, and performances from local country bands.

Eventually the bonfire was spent. Everything within it had turned to ashes except for the four copies of *Maxwell's Guide*, unnoticed by Creekside and his people. Filled with the satisfaction of the successful stop and delicious food, the group bid farewell and boarded the bus for the trip to Atlanta. Creekside sat up front behind the driver, smiling as he counted the fourteen hundred dollars they had collected from the worshippers outside of Valdosta.

*   *   *

The Devil's candy apple red '67 Pontiac GTO was slightly jacked up in the back and looked fast even when it was sitting still. White paint emphasized the lettering on the tires. The car's chrome glistened in the morning sunlight and the body's paint job was so deep and lustrous that Lucratelli and Chelsea could see themselves reflected on the side of the car.

"Hop in!" the Devil suggested.

"Do you know him?" Chelsea asked.

"Yeah, I know him," Lucratelli told her. He turned to Lucifer. "What's up, doc?"

"I knew you were heading to New York. I thought you might appreciate a lift."

Lucratelli was leery. Satan wasn't reprimanding him for the trio's escape back to Earth. He also didn't seem bothered by Chelsea's excursion to Heaven. It didn't seem right, but Lucratelli didn't want to look a gift horse in the mouth.

"Doll," he told Chelsea, "I'd like you to meet the Devil himself."

"Nice to make your acquaintance," she said meekly, only half-believing she was meeting Satan and getting into his Pontiac.

As they got into the car—Lucratelli in the back and Chelsea in the front—the Devil adjusted his rear view mirror and caught Lucratelli's eye. "Did you bring the Flux Capacitor?" he asked.

Lucratelli didn't get it, but Chelsea did. "Are we going back in time?" she asked innocently, thinking at this point anything was possible.

"Nah, just joshing with you," the Devil said. He turned the key in the ignition, the V-8 roaring to life. He stomped on the gas and the car lunged forward only to come to a complete stop immediately.

Lucratelli looked out the window and recognized the apartment building where Chelsea lived. In less than one second they were back in New York.

"We're here," said the Devil. "Made good time, too."

*   *   *

Laureen Dawber was also on her way to New York. America's News Now had a heavy hand in her radio show, sending her talking points and directing the way she slanted various stories to fit within the right-wing conservative viewpoint. Although she often went her own way, relying on her gut and innermost emotions, she pretty much played ball. After all, she didn't want to go back to the dismal life she'd had before, owing money everywhere and sharing a mobile home with her mother.

Nana was going to watch the boys while Laureen flew to New York for her first meeting with the network brass since they had offered her a show. She would be allowed to voice her own opinions on topical events then discuss those events with an ever-changing panel of pundits culled from the Network's paid and unpaid contributors. The show concept certainly didn't reinvent the wheel, but Laureen's strong personality, good looks, and conservative furor would please the conservative base of viewers the network had cultivated. And ratings were ratings.

She said her goodbyes to Nana and the boys and started her car. Backing out of her driveway, she just missed the small calico cat dozing in the shade near her back tire.

She took I-595 to Fort Lauderdale until the highway ended. Taking the U.S. 1 exit north, the road curved to the right and took her to the airport terminals and parking garages. Laureen parked, locked her car, made her way down two flights of stairs, crossed the street, and arrived at check-in. It was hot and humid. Typical. She was relieved that she'd have a few days of New York weather to enjoy. She walked to her gate with just a carry-on bag. She hated waiting at baggage to retrieve her belongings. Once she got to New York she'd want to get out of the airport and on her way as soon as possible.

Once on the plane, Laureen took out her phone to check messages then placed it on her lap while she rummaged around for the copy of *Maxwell's Guide* she brought to read on the trip. She'd heard a lot about the book and was curious what the uproar was about, especially after seeing a video of Ric Arno's interview with Cyrus. She couldn't wait to lace into the old codger herself—Cyrus, not Arno—though she thought Ric was a pompous relic who needed to be replaced by someone with more fire in their belly. And she couldn't think of anyone better for the job than herself.

Out of curiosity she googled Cyrus Maxwell. She scrolled down past the sponsored links that offered contact information and background checks. There wasn't much else.

There was information on a number of Cyrus Maxwells but most of them were too young or too old to be the man in question. She did find some info on a Cyrus Maxwell in the New York area who had been a professor, but he'd passed away a number of years ago. Come to think of it, the man on Arno's show had claimed to have returned from Heaven. *Interesting*, she thought, *but highly unlikely. And impossible. People do NOT return from the dead.* She searched the web images for a picture of that particular Cyrus Maxwell but the only available photos were so old that it was impossible to tell if it was the same man at all.

Well, she thought, *I'll have all the resources of the network available to me if all this works out. I'll find out just who this old bugger is.*

A flight attendant asked her to turn off her device. Laureen smiled at her and made a show of putting her phone away. That was the problem with being on radio. No one recognizes you.

*　　　　　*　　　　　*

Excerpt from *Maxwell's Guide to Heaven and Hell*, page 1052:

Celebrity is fleeting and not a true accomplishment. Remember, if you come across Alexander the Great, a former king or queen, or Elvis, they're just dead people. Exactly like you.

There are great TV talk show guests and there are those who are not so great. The guests a host wants to have on the show are the people whose unique personalities are winning enough that audiences literally love them. Barring that, you'd want someone with quirks. And Cyrus Maxwell certainly was quirky.

In the week or two since Arno's interview, Cyrus made the rounds to various other shows, always bringing his umbrella on set with him. It was quite the spectacle watching him use it to point and jab at a bishop or politician who ticked him off as they discussed their views of Heaven and Hell versus what Cyrus knew to be true.

Topical cartoons in the newspapers depicted Cyrus with his ever-present umbrella and not a day went by without a posting on the internet about his latest activities or appearances. He was featured in newspaper articles and made the cover of a number of recent magazine editions. E-books were quickly published speculating on his background and motivations. He was mentioned daily on broadcast and cable news shows and networks.

With all of the media coverage, Cyrus began to be recognized on the street, either besieged by fans begging for autographs and pictures or accosted by detractors who thought he was in league with the forces of evil.

Either way, he loved the attention.

He always dressed impeccably and was polite to a fault whether people were for him or against him. He was even a little bit impressed with himself of late. For this ANN appearance he arrived early with Berry and proceeded to the Green Room, shaking hands with and introducing himself to the other guests. He then he walked over to the snack table to survey the food.

"No mini quiches? Or Key Lime pies?" he asked of no one in particular.

"Sorry. But there're plenty of other things," said a production assistant.

"I specifically requested them as part of my contract rider."

"I'm very sorry, Mr. Maxwell. I have no knowledge of that," she replied.

"Oh dear. Well, no matter. What's done is done. Oh, and by the way, I'm expecting a couple of people to join me. Will you make sure they can find me once they arrive?"

"Who's coming?" Berry asked as the production assistant left to inform the receptionist of the impending arrival of Cyrus's guests.

"My agent, manager, a publicist, and some personal assistants," Cyrus replied.

"What?!?" Berry was mortified. "You don't have any of those people."

"No, not yet. That's what we'll be meeting about."

Berry pulled Cyrus aside to avoid being overheard by others in the room. "You are proof that a person is never too old to learn something new and stupid. Publicist? Assistants? What, to hold your umbrella for you? Are you out of your mind? What's next? Hollywood?"

"Well, I had considered—"

"Well, consider this: you're not George Clooney or Brad Pitt. You're Cyrus Maxwell and you're dead. Got it? This is not some new career. This is all strictly temporary. We're here for a relatively short time to introduce the world to *The Guide* and then we leave."

"Actually, I was thinking of sticking around for a while. There's talk of a book deal, possibly a talk show."

"Read my lips, Oprah: it's not happening. We are going back to Heaven and when we return, if they don't throw us out on our asses, I'll find something to do with myself. And you, you'll kiss your daughter goodbye and return to your cottage, walk your dog, and edit your heart out updating the book for the next few thousand years or so. That's it. This is not the start of a new life for you here on Earth. Do you understand?"

"So…you think I should I cancel the limo service?" Cyrus asked.

*　　　　　　*　　　　　　*

The meeting at network headquarters was a brainstorming session on how to introduce Laureen to a national TV audience. After a lengthy and very expensive lunch catered in the boardroom, it was decided that she would become one of the location hosts of the upcoming God-A-Thon.

It was an American Patriot Party event, but America's News Now was promoting the hell out of it with on-air promos, live coverage of the event from locations around the country, and open endorsements from their anchors. It was a brazen barrage of publicity from a network that was supposed to be objective. Although they constantly denied any bias or partisanship, everyone always knew where the network stood on any given issue. And the God-A-Thon blitz promoted the network as much as the event.

Remotes were scheduled from major cities all over the country. Mainly an Evangelical event, politicians were lining up in droves to participate as well. It was a public relations bonanza that Laureen and the network could adopt to promote her new position on the team. Laureen would host and report from a stadium in South Florida. Since the event was only days away, she would be scheduled for a whirlwind of taped promos, publicity shots, and coaching to get her through the whole thing "on message." The network was counting on her to comment on the proceedings, promote her new show, and give everything the correct spin that would resonate with their viewing audience base of evangelicals, conservatives, and religious right-wingers.

"Last year's event gave us a nice boost in ratings," Robert Maggert, the network's head honcho announced to Laureen and the roomful of executives. "It ran the gamut from baptisms to weddings. You'll fit right in," he told Laureen. "How long are you staying?" he asked.

"I'm flying back tomorrow morning," she replied.

Suddenly he was her best friend. "So soon? Well, darlin', since you made the trip up here from sunny Florida, let's put you to work right away. Arno's doing another show with that old coot from that Heaven book. Why don't you sit in on the panel?"

"I'd be glad to."

"Great. You'll love it. I think you could really tear him up."

"I'm not sure I would. Or should, actually."

The room fell silent. Maggert's demeanor changed radically, making Laureen nervous.

"Why is that?"

"Because as crazy as he might be there are now more people thinking about God. He reinforces the belief that God actually exists. That Heaven exists. I think that's good, don't you?"

Maggert stared at her for a few seconds. "The man tells us the Bible is bunk," he said slowly and deliberately. "He *said* religion is a waste of time. He must be brought down. Figuratively, of course. Understand?"

Laureen knew she was going to lose this one. And she wasn't stupid. She also knew that this gig would be the best opportunity she would probably ever have. And Maggert always got his way.

"Yes, I do."

"Good. Then welcome aboard," Maggert said, once again in best friend mode. "You'll be an asset to the network, I'm sure. We're all looking forward to your show and we're excited about it originating from Florida. Plenty of raw material down there. What do they call it? Flori-duh?"

"Yes, it is certainly unique," Laureen answered, a bit perturbed that on top of being rude previously, now he was insulting her state.

"We'll start making arrangements to carry your segments live for God-A-Thon. It'll be an unofficial rehearsal for the crew down there. What a hoot that'll be. And we should be able to rake in some ratings numbers."

"We cleaned up at last year's event. How about that Baptist minister who advocated putting all the gay people in concentration camps until they were eliminated one by one?" asked a producer. "We were able to bleed publicity out of that one for days."

264

Maggert laughed. "That didn't hold a candle to the KKK rally at the Richmond location."

*   *   *

After her excursion to Heaven, Chelsea tried to come to terms with her life in a wheelchair. She wasn't very successful. Skiing, bike riding, and swimming with Lucratelli on their brief visit made her yearn for not just a different type of existence but for death itself. Knowing that there was indeed a Heaven and seeing it firsthand, she decided something had to be done.

She thought about overdosing on pills but didn't know where she would acquire enough of them to do the job. She had considered shooting herself, but that was too messy. She'd never want anyone to find her all bloody.

Besides, Heaven didn't like suicides. Lucratelli had made that clear. So she began thinking of alternatives. Maybe rolling down some hill in her chair into traffic. It wouldn't be her fault if her chair strayed out in to a traffic lane and a bus couldn't stop in time, would it? That might do the trick. No hills nearby though; the Village is pretty flat.

Hiring a hit man was expensive and she'd never be able to find someone like that. Plus, it was way too Hollywood.

She rolled over to the sink and placed a large plastic container inside. Turning on the tap, she waited until it was filled about halfway. With some difficulty, she lifted it out, placed it on top of her legs, and rolled back to her bedroom. She stopped next to her bed, placed the container on the floor by her feet, and then took off her sneakers and socks.

"What are you doing?" Cyrus asked.

"Oh, just soaking my feet." She noticed the umbrella. "Where are you off to?"

"Another ANN interview. I'll be back later."

"Okay, Dad. See you later."

Eventually her father would return to his home in Heaven. Lucratelli would leave as well. She couldn't bear the thought of being alone in the world again, and if she couldn't enter Heaven as a suicide, she'd just...cease. No more loneliness. No more wheelchair. No more Post-It notes.

With her father gone and Berry and Lucratelli both out, Chelsea placed her feet in the water. She knew that in just a few moments her life would be over. She looked forward to ending it finally.

Life wasn't so great anyway. Kind of like a lentil loaf. She had vegetarian friends who prompted her to try one claiming it would be just like eating a meatloaf. It wasn't. She didn't mind lentils. An okay legume but certainly nothing to get excited about. But in a loaf it didn't look, smell, or taste like the meatloaf her mom used to make. She resented the fact that it was being touted as something it wasn't. She hated it when anything was touted as something it wasn't. Like turkey burgers being a substitute for hamburgers. Or tofu substituting for anything at all. Or her life. Her life was all right, but not as great as everyone seemed to think, and the life she was living was no substitute for life the way she imagined it should be or once was. Besides, everyone she cared about was dead already. Now that she knew what was on the other side, she looked forward to the change. It would be nice to wait until she passed away, but who knew when that would be? It could be decades away when she was old and not able to get around anymore. Who wanted that type of existence? And for another fifty years or so? Not her. No, sir. No way.

No more lentil loaf.

She reached over to the nightstand and took the radio. She held it in her lap and contemplated it for a moment. She thought she needed a send-off, something uplifting. A soundtrack to the enormous step she was about to undertake. She turned the radio on and started going up and down the dial. An angry punk song. Nope. A neo-disco tune. Not happening. The blues? Too sad. The 1812 Overture? Too clichéd. Reggae was too uplifting. Finally, she found a classic rock station playing John Lennon's "Across the Universe." *That'll do*, she thought. She turned the radio up louder and took a deep breath, holding the device just above the container of water at her feet, not hearing the *whoosh* behind her or detecting the faint smell of cinnamon in the room.

Zoey appeared in a flash and took immediate stock of the situation. Just as Chelsea closed her eyes and dropped the radio, the small calico leaped onto the night table, grabbed the electrical cord in her mouth, and pulled it from the socket. Zoey grew very attached to the wards she was assigned to and had a particular love for the forlorn girl in the wheelchair.

Chelsea heard the splash and expected an instant shock, maybe a flash of pain as the electricity shot through her, but it didn't happen. She stared at the radio, now submerged, lying between her feet in the container of water. She heard a soft mewl and looked to see Zoey who was now lying on the bed licking and cleaning her front paws.

There would be no suicide on this cat's watch.

15

Laureen had the rest of the afternoon off to prepare for her guest spot on Ric Arno's show, but she had other plans. She'd been corresponding with a few potential suitors on Heavenly Hub, the Christian dating site, sending e-mails and IMs, even a phone call here and there. The men were situated all over the country, but a couple of them were in New York, so she had made arrangements to meet one of them for a drink in the hotel bar. She had already raided her room's mini bar, nervous about meeting someone new. She was feeling no pain and thought that she would order coffee downstairs. After all, she had a TV show to do in a few hours. When she was finished getting ready and about to leave the room, there was a knock at the door.

"Laureen?" A male voice inquired.

"Yes. Just a second," she called out, thinking it was her date. She ran over to the door. "I thought we were meeting down—oh!"

Opening the door, she realized that this wasn't the person whose picture she had seen online. She was a little tipsy but sober enough to realize she had just opened the door to a stranger and, in this town or any other, that was not a safe or prudent thing to do.

"I didn't mean to startle you," said the man at the door.

"I was expecting someone else," she muttered, taken aback by how attractive this visitor was. Gathering her senses, she began to close the door quickly.

"Wait—I stopped by to discuss your appearance on the Ric Arno show tonight."

"Oh. I didn't see you at the meeting today."

"No, I wasn't included."

She turned her back on him and walked back into her room. "I'm sorry. A girl can't be too careful these days. You never know."

"Too true," he replied.

"You know what they say. The Devil can be at your front door, but you don't have to let him in."

"Also true."

"Well, don't just stand there, darlin'. Come on in. I guess we have a lot to discuss."

"Thank you," Satan said as he entered. "And, yes, we have plenty to discuss."

*   *   *

Like other management people in Heaven, Bree Daniels and Marvin Miller were concerned about the recent changes on Earth brought about by the release of *Maxwell's Guide to Heaven and Hell* there. It was the main topic of their conversation as the married couple shared dinner at a Chinese restaurant midway between their offices.

"We've been swamped with new arrivals. Droves of people who've had the existence of Heaven confirmed are finding convenient ways to have themselves killed."

"Droves?" Bree asked.

"Once they realized they wouldn't be admitted to Heaven if they killed themselves people started finding other ways to cross over. Like killing each other. Clubs that sprang up out of nowhere. They found a loophole. Have someone else do you in and you're home free, right? And the last one standing would be sentenced to death for murder. So they make it here as well."

"That's plain nuts."

"Sure it is, but it's indeed happening. They haven't reached epidemic proportions or anything, but the numbers are up significantly all over the world. It's really taxing the system. I've had to find jobs and housing for the flood of newcomers and every day there's a new wave of them. We've set up temporary locations just to house them until we get them situated. Even more importantly, donations of Essence are significantly lower."

"You'd think God would step in," Bree said.

"You know as well as I do that's not His way. I guess He wants to see how it all plays out like everything else. He even sent a memo to Administration. It basically said, 'Take care of it. Don't make me come over there.' It's a dilemma," Marvin added.

"It's more than just the number of arrivals and a shortage of Essence," Bree added. "Smile Patrol branches all over have been reporting changes they don't understand. Small but significant things: transports aren't running on time, there's a shortage of equipment and resources for projects, and there suddenly aren't enough Smile Patrol operatives where they're needed. We've even heard reports of rain and inclement weather where it hasn't been requested. It snowed in Hell the other day!"

"It's a definite problem when Hell is starting to freeze over," Marvin noted.

*   **

Pastor Billy Creekside's bus limped in to New York City with its contingent of eleven devotees along with the pastor himself. They piled off the bus, their legs wobbly after the long ride from their last stop in western Pennsylvania.

Taking a large wad of currency out of his pocket, Creekside handed a few bills to one of their party and instructed him to go park the bus.

"I'll go inside the hotel and get the rooms," Creekside told them. They would all, except for Creekside, be sharing accommodations. Each of them would be given a small per diem to cover their meals and expenses. The pastor would treat himself to a suite.

Most of them were just standing around taking in the sight of the tallest buildings they had ever seen.

"Don't just stand there gawking like a bunch of yahoos. You'd think you never seen a city before. I'm gonna want you all to fan out..."

They all took a few steps back.

"Not here," he said, shaking his head in wonder. "After you get your rooms, we'll meet in the lobby. Then we'll spread out across the city. Gather as many people as you can. We want to make a real show of force at the TV place. For now, go get yourselves situated. And don't get lost. Remember, the Devil is everywhere in this city."

He walked into the lobby, arranged for the rooms, and paid in cash. Stops along the way had been very lucrative.

A bellman rode up in the elevator with Creekside, opened the suite door, and pointed out the features. The rooms were luxurious and the view was breathtaking.

"Thank you very much, my friend," Creekside said, tipping the bellman generously. "And, by the way, where would a gentleman find some female company in this town if he was so inclined?"

*   *   *

Laureen stood up the guy waiting for her in the bar. When he called her room she apologized, explaining that she had to leave early for the TV studio. The handsome man currently in her room was too good to pass up.

Still tipsy, she was very flirtatious and thought she would take things to a physical level. Not unusual for the attractive blond who was used to getting her way where men were concerned. She moved close to him, offering him a drink. After he took his first sip, she kissed him. For a moment he forgot why he was there. He placed his drink down and embraced her, kissing her passionately. She turned around and backed up against him. As they made contact, she swayed back and forth, rubbing herself against him. It was a bold move, even for her.

Caught up in the moment, he placed his hands on her waist as she wiggled against him in a blatantly sexual manner. His hands slid up slowly and cupped her breasts.

"Oh! You are a devil, aren't you?" she asked.

"Not *a* devil, *the* Devil," he told her.

It took a moment for his comment to register. She suddenly stopped her slow sensual gyration. Her eyes narrowed and she suddenly realized what was going on and with whom. She contemplated the "Satan, get thee behind me" statement but, considering the way they were positioned, it seemed absurd. So did having the Devil in her hotel room.

Laureen moved away and turned to face him head-on, now defiant.

"What are you doing here?" she demanded.

"I told you, we have things to discuss."

She rushed to the nightstand, pulled open the drawer, and took out the Gideon Bible. She waved it over her head and pointed it at him like a weapon.

"With the power of this holy book I demand that you go back to Hell where you belong!"

The Devil laughed. "Are you kidding me?" he scoffed.

"What do you mean?"

"That has about as much power as a comic book."

"It's the Bible!" she shouted.

"Look, why don't you sit down and I'll explain a few things to you."

Laureen was dumbfounded. She had been waiting all her religious life for a confrontation of this sort and, now that it was taking place, she felt lost and out of control. She slumped into the easy chair next to the bed.

"I'll try to make this easy for you," the Devil gently told her. "The Bible has no relevance. It was written by men who were guessing at the meaning of things."

"It is the Word of God," she declared.

"It is a historical document. It gives us a look at what people at that time thought. It was a way for them to explain historical events. It was a statement of their beliefs. It attempted to put a spin on things that they couldn't understand. It is, very simply, literature. And all literature, good and bad, deals with the human condition. How mystifying it all is. How difficult life is. Trials and tribulations of living. Understand?"

"I've been taught that—," she murmured.

"What you have been taught is wrong."

"You're just here for my soul. Go to Hell."

"I will when I'm good and ready. As a matter of fact, I have a tee time reserved for tomorrow morning. And I'm not at all interested in your soul or anyone else's."

"God loves me," she blurted out.

"I'm sure he would if he knew you. You seem like a very nice person. Just misguided."

"Why should I believe you? Maybe you're not even the Devil. Maybe you're some lunatic who came in here to—"

"I can assure you I am who I say I am."

"How can you prove it?"

"What do you expect? Something like this?"

Suddenly they were transported elsewhere. A beautiful beach. The sun was shining. The weather was perfect. The sky was the bluest of blues.

"Welcome to Hell, Laureen."

She was quiet, just taking it all in. She had doubted that he was actually the Devil, but the instant transportation to the beach from the hotel room was proof enough that this was no ordinary person.

"There would normally be people all over this beach," the Devil told her. "Surfing, swimming, sunbathing. But it's chilly. It snowed the other day. That's highly unusual. It's a result of minute changes in the order of things. Changes that have occurred on Earth and are affecting everything here."

"This is not what I expected," she said.

The Devil laughed. "I know. You expected fire and brimstone and tortured souls. You won't find that here. It's not what we're about. People don't usually even get sunburned here."

Just as quickly, they were back in the hotel room.

"Why are you here?" she asked. "What do you want from me?"

"I need your help."

"Is this all some kind of trick? I know you're supposed to be manipulative."

"No, it's no trick. And I'm deadly serious. I sincerely need your help and I wouldn't ask you to do anything at all that you would be uncomfortable with."

"What do you want from me?"

"I need you to just be you."

"How so?"

"This TV interview you're doing tonight? Millions of people will see it. How they react to this book, this *Maxwell's Guide to Heaven and Hell*, will be crucial. It has come to my attention—our attention in the afterlife—that you've softened your position. That's too dangerous. We need people to reject the book."

"But how can a book that confirms the existence of God and Heaven be dangerous?" she asked.

"Too many people clamoring to get into Heaven. Too much strain on the system. People live their lives and then they die. That's the natural order of things. These people just dying to get in to Heaven—well, yearning—seem to have no appreciation for this fragile thing called life. The very act of *being* is essential. Life is precious. Dying is inevitable. I've told you that you don't know the truth about God and Heaven and Hell. That is correct. Religions have it all wrong. No one knows God the way they think they do. We are all, myself included, part of the Grand Scheme, God's wondrous experiment. He's just as curious as we all are as to where it all leads. But right now, it's leading to a dead end. If people don't want to experience life itself—if all they want to do is die and go to Heaven—the whole system fails. If you go soft in the interview tonight, there is the potential that millions of people will be encouraged to forsake life itself. That doesn't work for us."

"So by helping you, the Devil, I'll be doing God's work?" Laureen asked.

"Yes. Ironic, isn't it?"

*　　　　　　　*　　　　　　　*

Excerpt from *Maxwell's Guide to Heaven and Hell*, page 698:

There's no greater gift than a tomorrow.

"What's up, doc?"

Lucratelli walked in from the bedroom where he and Chelsea were napping before they all had to leave for the TV studio. He found Berry sitting in an easy chair, melancholy, staring blankly out the window.

"Not much," Berry mumbled.

"Down in the dumps?"

"I guess I always get a little out of sorts this time of day," Berry said, "I think it's a holdover from the old days when we were all cavemen. Night is coming. That must have given rise to fears of darkness, predators, and the unknown."

"Well, we're not cavemen," Lucratelli told him.

"Yeah, I know. Maybe it's a trace of race memory or something ingrained in our DNA. All those thousands of years of fear. So I always feel, I don't know, some kind of uneasiness just as it's getting dark. I call it an alien buzz. It passes."

Lucratelli stretched out on the living room couch. "I don't think that's it."

"No?"

"No. I think you're a little depressed because you've done what you set out to do. You've introduced the book to the world and now what?"

"Now I'm back where I started from. Sure, the book is out there. Hundreds of thousands have read it. It's been written about, talked about on TV and radio and at dinner tables. Did it really change anything? I don't know. And maybe that doesn't even matter. Maybe it was just getting it done. Another project I sank my teeth into and now what? What the hell will I do with myself when this project's over? I've got eons of time on my hands and no direction."

"You'll latch on to something. You're a smart guy. Something will crop up. In the meantime, enjoy yourself. Find a girl. Go fishing. Play golf. Hell, I don't know…learn to play the saxophone. There's a whole universe out there. You'll find your way."

"I guess you're right," Berry conceded.

"Sure I am. We'd better get going. I'll get Chelsea and the old man."

Cyrus was in the bathroom grooming: buttoning his vest, checking his tie, wrapping and unwrapping his ever-present umbrella. He had grown to love being the center of attention in these interviews. It was so different than being wrapped up in his own little world, editing the book, walking his dog, tending to his home. He knew that the notoriety would be short-lived but figured he may as well enjoy it while he could.

Chelsea spent much of her time contemplating her own demise, leaving little Post-it note reminders of the ways she might die without actually killing herself.

Berry was getting impatient. "Let's go. We'll take a cab uptown."

Cyrus started out of the apartment, stopped, mumbled a quick "Oh dear" to Lucratelli's chagrin, and turned back abruptly to retrieve his umbrella. Lucratelli, shaking his head, went to the bedroom where he found Chelsea contemplating an electrical socket.

"What?" she asked when she noticed he was watching. "It's an old building. Maybe even dangerous. You never know, something could short out or cause a fire."

Lucratelli quickly spun her chair around and wheeled her out of the apartment and into the hallway.

*   *   *

America's News Now ran blatant support and promos for the upcoming God-A-Thon to counter much of the Ric Arno show's content regarding Cyrus and *The Guide*. The panel taking part in the discussion was taking a strange turn, becoming overtly partisan.

Democrats leaned towards supporting Cyrus and his claims about the book. At the very least, liberals supported his right to his opinion. Republicans—conservatives all—were vehemently against any affront to the established way of thinking about God, Heaven, and religion in general. Among the clergy present, Catholics deplored any straying from Church beliefs and doctrines, Evangelicals were unanimous in their hatred for Cyrus and anything he had to say, and the rabbis encouraged everyone to continue questioning everything.

Watching from the green room, Berry told Lucratelli that he hoped Cyrus wouldn't ask either of the two rabbis any questions.

"You can't get a straight answer from those guys. They'll always answer in some roundabout way. They'll say, 'It reminds me of the story…'"

Laureen was especially brutal in her verbal assaults.

"You come here claiming to have arrived from Heaven with this so-called wondrous book with no proof at all about its origins or your veracity," she told him. "This is so typical of a lot of things that have gone wrong and gotten out of hand in this country. You've made a few appearances on TV or radio and you are, in society's opinion, now a celebrity and worthy of our attention? I don't think so. You're bilking the American public, getting rich off of gullible people who are struggling through their lives in hard economic times, and they should automatically believe you just because you are on television?

"America just *loves* celebrities, doesn't it?" she continued. "People are willing to accept any aberrant behavior, misguided opinion, or outrageous claims from anyone who is even semi-famous."

"This is not going well," Berry remarked to Chelsea and Lucratelli as they watched from the green room.

"You want to change people's religious views?" Laureen continued. "The world's religions have thrived for thousands of years for a reason: they provide solace. We know that God is everywhere, hears our prayers, and can provide salvation. You tell us God is busy, on vacation or something. That He couldn't care less about any individual. And we're supposed to feel good that you tell us there is indeed a Heaven? What kind of Heaven? A place where we're not even rewarded for faith or good will toward each other? A Hell that doesn't punish transgressions? If we can commit sins without condemnation, there's no reason to pursue a holy ideal at all, is there?"

Cyrus attempted to defend himself but Ric Arno kept cutting him off, ignoring Cyrus' explanations and directing more and more of the questions to the panel.

It didn't matter in the least that Cyrus was telling the truth. No one believed that he was motivated by something other than money, or that he wasn't profiting from the book in any way.

"Self-promotion is not knowledge," Laureen told Cyrus. "Did you actually come on here and not expect to be condemned? I have the Holy Bible to help me get through every day and thank God for that. It is His word I obey, not the word of some liar who is foisting this charade on our audience. You are leading people down a dangerous road, my friend. A road that leads nowhere for them except toward hopelessness and despair while you benefit from the promotion and sales that your lies generate. You are the lowest of the low."

The brass at America's News Now were elated that Laureen followed their directive. Laureen was just surprised that she was cooperating with the Devil.

*   *   *

When the show was over, Berry couldn't think of any reason why they should remain there one second longer. He quickly ushered a shaken Cyrus out of the studio and the four of them, Berry, Chelsea, Lucratelli, and Cyrus, made their way out to the street which was teeming with observers, fans, activists, and hangers-on.

Pastor Billy Creekside and his followers had been very successful in gathering a small group of extremely vocal protestors outside the station's entrance. Watching the proceedings on a giant screen the network had positioned against the building, they were incensed.

When Cyrus, his daughter, and friends appeared, the small Creekside crowd rushed them, yelling obscenities. Lucratelli pushed his way past them to hail a cab. As the yellow vehicle pulled to a stop, Lucratelli turned back to wheel Chelsea to the curb and bumped into a man moving along with him. Lucratelli felt a hard object jammed against his ribs. His instincts took over.

Creekside reached inside his sport coat and drew the Glock pistol. Lucratelli wasn't concerned about Cyrus, Berry, or himself. They were already dead. Of course, it wouldn't do to have the crowd watch one of them get shot and then be immediately resurrected. He was thinking more about someone innocent and unprotected. He reached for the gun just as Creekside pulled the trigger, the loud report stunning the crowd. Lucratelli went down and Creekside continued forward. He spied Cyrus.

"I am God's warrior doing God's will. You will burn in Hell, sinner!" He raised the pistol once more to fire at Cyrus. The crowd thinned out around him, forming a semi-circle around Creekside, Chelsea, Berry, and Cyrus.

Lucratelli stood slowly and placed his hand over the wound which was closing and healing almost instantly. He ran towards Creekside but was unable to grab the pastor's arm before he fired again. The bullet missed Cyrus and struck Chelsea in the chest.

She felt the heavy thud before the noise of the shot even registered. Berry, Cyrus, and Lucratelli quickly closed in around her. An America's News Now security guard who had witnessed the shooting leveled his own gun at Creekside and ordered him to freeze. Creekside raised his hands high and looked to the Heavens above as two NYPD patrolmen threw him to the ground and wrested the pistol from his hand.

Chelsea's own hand was held by Cyrus.

"Daddy," she said softly.

"Shhh…don't try to talk," he told her, tears welling up.

"As much as I've wanted to die and follow you to Heaven, I'm scared. Daddy, I'm scared of dying."

"I love you," he said, looking down at her fatal wound. "It will be easy. You'll take your last breath on this Earth and exhale in Heaven."

"I love you, Daddy." She looked over at Lucratelli. "I love you, too. Can we go skiing again?"

"Anything you want, doll. See you on the other side."

"Order me a cappuccino." It was the last thing she said as a living human being. She inhaled deeply and was gone.

"I'll have one waiting for you," Lucratelli whispered.

A squad car arrived, its siren blaring. Soon after, an ambulance screeched to a halt and its driver jumped from the cab, running to the back door and reaching for a stretcher. He rolled it toward the small group, unfolded it, and moved the straps aside.

"Want to give me a hand here?" he asked. Cyrus, Lucratelli, and Berry looked at the familiar face. "Or would you rather wait to be taken downtown to answer questions and fill out reports?" asked the Devil.

They moved Chelsea's body onto the stretcher and placed it in the ambulance. Cyrus and Lucratelli got in the back. Berry rode shotgun.

The ambulance shot forward and, in less than one second, stopped. It was already a world away from the scene outside the network building.

They were once again in Heaven.

"We're here," said the Devil. "Not my Pontiac, but we still made good time."

16

In the world of twenty-four hour, seven days a week cable and network news networks, internet, and blogs, even the most important stories lose their momentum after a few days. Political machinations and scandals are discussed for a day or two and then forgotten as a new topic arises. Oil spills and environmental disasters like nuclear plant meltdowns cause a good deal of stress but then fade into the media background noise in a relatively short span of time. Terrorist plots are exposed and foiled then forgotten by the general public in a very short period of time. And in spite of all that happens in their world or around them, people go about their lives until another major story garners attention. The only people permanently affected are those who suffer the consequences of the occurrences on a personal level. Individuals, friends, families, and sometimes whole communities might be affected drastically and even tragically, but they are still a very small fraction of the population.

People are often more interested in the trials and tribulations of the most shallow among us rather than concerned with anything of real significance. A star's drug addiction or rapid divorce gets an inordinate amount of attention. A single mom who has fourteen children and turns to porn for a living intrigues the world for what is essentially a moment or two. A politician sending lewd photographs to an admirer might get a cable show. A hooker causes the downfall of a business magnate and releases an exercise video. A Ponzi schemer dupes hundreds of people out of millions of dollars. Criminals, by virtue of their criminal acts, become instant celebrities. And celebrity seems to be the most coveted prize of all. It's not right, but it will probably never change.

The plus side is that the attention paid to these people and events is temporary. A couple days. A week. A couple weeks. Then the national or global eye is attracted to something or someone else.

It's the way of the world.

The furor over *Maxwell's Guide to Heaven and Hell* was over fairly quickly. Sales eventually slacked off. The controversy was over. There were still a few people and a few sects or cults that took the book to heart, believing that what we think we know is wrong and that there's an underlying truth to things that we are not privy to because of misinformation, stubbornness, or both.

Marvin and Bree discussed this at length as they sat on their back porch.

"I'm glad to see things here are back to normal," Bree said.

"Well, at least it isn't snowing in Hell any longer," Marvin agreed. "And it only rains here when it benefits the farmers or when someone specifically orders it. Essence donations are back where they should be, too."

"I'll put Lucratelli back to work at the Smile Patrol. I'm glad to see that there weren't any real repercussions for those knuckleheads. I even looked the other way as he started to resurrect his moonshine still."

"Well, at least there was no permanent harm done."

"To the still?"

"To the world."

"We hope."

*   *   *

Cyrus Maxwell sat on his porch absentmindedly petting his dog Chloe. Back on Earth, people looked at his disappearance from public life as inconsequential if they thought about it at all. Perhaps his fifteen minutes of fame expired. Perhaps he was reclusive, like a J.D. Salinger. In the general scheme of things, it didn't matter. New news occupied people's thoughts and emotions.

As Cyrus fell back into his daily routines in Heaven, he enjoyed the company of family in the town of Maxwell, sharing evenings with relatives, and relaxing with Chloe. His ability to spend time with his daughter and her husband added an extra element of richness to his existence.

He was content. On a rare occasion he'd reminisce about the time he had celebrity status, but not often. He continued his work on the book, not concerned with the reaction to it on Earth any longer. It was what it was. It was always intended for the residents in Heaven who found it entertaining and informative.

And it remained so.

*   *   *

Laureen Dawber's celebrity status was another matter. Three ENG TV crews followed her around everywhere she went. She still had her radio show as well as her own national TV show on ANN, anchoring their flagship cablecast at 9 p.m. Monday through Friday. Starting with her appearance at God-A-Thon, additional TV crews shot every aspect of her life for a new reality show called, appropriately enough, *The Laureen Life*. She was the darling of the right-wing. Conservatives now supported her for a run for a congressional seat in her district in South Florida. She would go on to win that seat and make news herself by claiming that every Democratic member of Congress was a Communist, a Zionist, a Socialist, a Muslim, or a homosexual.

She had come a long way from owing back taxes and living in a trailer park.

Her finances were secure, and her future looked bright. Nana had her own home but stayed very much involved with Laureen and the grandchildren. Laureen's deal with the Devil had allowed her to follow her heart and serve God.

And she wouldn't have had it any other way.

*   *   *

Whoosh!

Zoey took stock of the area. Fort Lauderdale. Her favorite place. Warm weather all year long. Geckos, amoles, chameleons, and iguanas to chase and play with, not too much traffic in the neighborhoods, and generally friendly dogs.

The small calico had someone new to look in on: a former teacher who had fallen, broken her hip and, although recovered, still had constant pain and limited mobility. She was collecting disability because she couldn't return to work. And she was frustrated with her life.

Zoey would be a welcome addition to her life, providing affection and companionship.

Besides chasing lizards, providing comfort was Zoey's favorite thing to do.

*　　　　　　*　　　　　　*

The second hole was a par-five. The narrow fairway opened out to a slight dogleg left. Water on both sides. It wasn't an overly long par-five and the green could be reached in two.

The Devil's drive went straight up the center. Berry's drifted right a little but he was still in the short grass.

"So, how are the newlyweds?" the Devil asked as they walked towards their respective balls.

Chelsea and Lucratelli had a marriage made in Heaven. Literally. Cyrus gave the bride away. Berry served as Best Man. Chelsea realized her dream of dancing at her wedding, taking turns on the dance floor with Lucratelli, her father, and anyone who asked her to dance.

"From what I hear, they're fine. Maybe tired," Berry told him.

291

"I'll bet!"

"No, not that. Chelsea was so used to the wheelchair that she wanted a really active honeymoon. They had plans that sounded like an Olympic training regimen: skiing, running, hiking, bicycling, swimming, rock climbing, diving, and participating in any sport or pastime that might be fun and active."

"Can't blame her, I guess."

"No, I suppose you can't."

"Lucratelli will come back exhausted," said Satan.

"Probably will."

Berry was away. The caddy handed him his five-wood.

"This club loves me."

"We'll see."

Berry's shot was straight at the green, landing a little short but rolling up to the fringe. It just eased out on to the putting surface, coming to rest about twenty feet from the flag.

"Nicely done," the Devil said as he addressed his second shot. His ball started low then gained a little height, landing on the left side of the green and rolling forward, right into one of the sand traps protecting the green.

"Rats. Oh, well, I get a chance to practice my sand shot." He handed his four-iron to his caddy and they all continued on. "I suppose Lucratelli will go back to work on the Smile Patrol?"

"It's been offered to him. I heard he's planning on it. He's also working on rebuilding his still," Berry said.

"I'll have to drop off some fixings to give that moonshine of his some kick."

"I'm sure he'll appreciate that. He's something else. Chelsea's going to have her hands full with him."

"Yeah. Like the way he dresses and talks. Only about seventy years behind the times."

"She'll get him caught up, I'm sure."

"And you? What are your plans?" the Devil asked.

"I don't know. When I was younger and alive, I thought I wanted a career. Turns out I just wanted a paycheck. Then things changed and I started to actually care. I don't know what I'll do. Forever's a long time."

"Well, you're welcome out here any time you feel like playing."

"I appreciate that, and I'll take you up on it so often you'll get sick at the sight of me."

"Doubt that."

"It didn't all pan out the way I thought it would. I thought I had a chance to change lives, to change the world," Berry admitted.

"Well, maybe you did change lives. A few anyway. Hell, you gave it a shot."

"Yeah, I guess so. I have a clear conscience about everything. I guess that counts for something."

"I've generally found that a clear conscience usually indicates a fuzzy mind."

"That could well be," Berry laughed.

"So, what now?"

"I've been giving some thought to doing some producing. Music. With all the musicians here, a person could put some amazing concerts or records together. Elvis, Marvin Gaye, Beethoven, Buddy Holly, Mozart. I could organize some very impressive stuff. Combinations of artists no one's ever seen before. Or maybe even movies. Bogart with Marilyn? Gable and Lombard? Hitchcock directing. It would be interesting to see how they'd go over. Either here or back on—"

"Don't even think about another road trip. And if you are, I don't want to know anything about it," the Devil said.

He then hit his sand shot high, the ball dropping down, hitting the stick, and coming to rest on the green about two feet from the hole.

"Well, they keep releasing what they call 'unreleased material' from artists like Jimi Hendrix," Berry said. "Why not a new album with legendary performers that people would think was recorded prior to their deaths?"

"Spare me," the Devil laughed.

Berry set up for his eagle putt knowing he didn't have to decide immediately.

He had an eternity to think about it.

Excerpt from *Maxwell's Guide to Heaven and Hell*, page 119:

There is an old saying that in spite of the length of a golf course, the game of golf is really played within a six inch area: the space between one's ears. That is a fact; it's a mental thing.

By the same token, a book's impact—this guide or any book—can be measured in that same space of one's mind. Good or bad, books affect each person differently and in ways highly personal and relative to a number of variables such as your state of mind, your memories, and your experiences.

As a result, for some people a book is simply a diversion. For others, the same book sparks something within...something that causes the person's thoughts to soar, sending them on a journey of discovery and wonder that may change their lives forever.

How ironic that the journey merely begins when the book concludes with those familiar words...

The End.

Alan Taffel is a TV writer/producer/director, the winner of an Emmy and multiple CableAce awards, a guitarist who will never play like Eric Clapton, and an avid golfer who has never hit a hole-in-one or shot a game under par. Alan lives with his wife Caryn in South Florida.

www.ingramcontent.com/pod-product-compliance
Lightning Source LLC
Chambersburg PA
CBHW021323250626
47155CB00002B/595